Praise for *A Doomful of Sugar*

"A likable protagonist and a sweet-as-maple-syrup setting are just part of the appeal. *A Doomful of Sugar* is more than a mystery, it's an engaging tale about family and the twisted paths that lead us home."

—Julie Mulhern, *USA Today* bestselling author of the Country Club Murders

"Filled with food, family, and murder, first in series *A Doomful of Sugar* by Catherine Bruns is a Vermont-set winner."

—Lynn Cahoon, *New York Times* bestselling author of *Secrets in the Stacks*, a Survivors' Book Club mystery

"*A Doomful of Sugar* is a delightfully decadent maple-infused mystery to die for! Bruns pens a smart multilayered puzzler in this first in a series that is sure to become a reader favorite!"

—Jenn McKinlay, *New York Times* bestselling author

T0014938

Also by Catherine Bruns

SYRUP
TO NO
GOOD

A Maple Syrup Mystery

CATHERINE
BRUNS

Poisoned Pen
PRESS

Published by Poisoned Pen Press, an imprint of Sourcebooks
P.O. Box 4410, Naperville, Illinois 60567-4410
(630) 961-3900
sourcebooks.com

Printed and bound in the U.S.A.
LSC 10 9 8 7 6 5 4 3 2

For Frank, with love

CHAPTER ONE

THE SOUND OF EXCITED LAUGHTER was all around as I went back and forth between tables in the café, offering up extra syrup for pancakes. The syrup was a beautiful sight to behold as it slowly dripped down the crispy edges of the cakes and onto the plate below, causing my mouth to water.

My father, who had been one of the best maple syrup makers in the entire state of Vermont, always said that you could tell good syrup by its density. "The thicker, the better, *habibi*," he'd told me. *Habibi* meant "my love" in Arabic.

"Okay, everyone!" I called. "Let's get this show on the road. Who's ready to eat some delicious pancakes?"

A chorus of cheers went up from the tables.

"Ready!" I called. "On your mark, get set, go!"

The kids and adults all picked up their forks in unison and began digging into the fluffy cakes that my mother had prepared for our annual pancake-eating contest. I set the jug of syrup down in the center of the table with a satisfied thud as a memory of my father crossed my mind. Dad had always looked forward to hosting the pancake contests at his farm. The maple syrup farm had thrived under his ownership and hopefully mine too. I smiled to myself. If he were here, Dad would have inserted himself onto the wooden bench between the kids and told them silly jokes until everyone's sides ached with laughter.

A sharp pain pierced my heart. It had been six months since my father's murder and not a day went by that I didn't think of him. Victor Khoury had purchased Sappy Endings twenty-five years ago. He'd had big dreams for the 300-acre farm, which contained approximately five thousand maple trees, and lived to see many of them become a reality. A wonderful businessman, husband, father, and friend, Dad's life had been taken in his office one evening last fall. Although his killer was in jail and justice had been served, the result was anything but sweet. Sadly, it would never bring him back, and I missed him with every fiber of my being.

My best friend, Heather Turcot, was making her way around the tables, giving words of encouragement to both the kids and adults alike as she refilled glasses of milk. Her blue eyes were shining with delight as she laughed at something one of the contestants said. It was good to see her looking happy for a change. Heather's life had been a rollercoaster of unending stress lately. Her wedding to fiancé Tyler Murray was only two weeks away, and what she'd originally thought would be an enjoyable event to plan had been nothing short of a throbbing migraine instead.

My gaze shifted to the other tables in the Sappy Hour Café. Employee Noah Rivers was studying his wristwatch intently. "One minute left, or the first person to clean their plate wins!" he called out.

He happened to look up at that moment and our gazes met. A pleasant chill worked its way up my spine as I stared into ice blue eyes that always managed to take my breath away. His perfect, chiseled features looked as if they'd been carved out of stone, and his lashes were so thick and long that any woman would have gladly killed for them.

It seemed silly to call Noah an employee, but it was a bit awkward to refer to him as my boyfriend in our work environment. We'd started off on the wrong foot when I came home to take over the farm last November. Our romance was progressing slowly, but as the old saying went, good things came to those who waited. Noah and I weren't rushing things, especially since we both bore scars from previous relationships. After five years, there were still times that I smarted over my broken engagement. As for Noah, his suffering was much more pronounced and painful than mine. His wife, Ashley, had died at the hands of a drunk driver a little over a year ago. He and his six-year-old daughter, Emma, were still adjusting to life without her.

Noah startled me out of my thoughts by letting out a loud whoop. He raised the right arm of a teenaged boy and gestured with the other hand to his plate. The only thing left on it was a small puddle of our amber maple syrup. "We have a winner!" he yelled.

Applause broke out in the café as I presented the young

man with his prizes. In addition to a gold medal strung on a red ribbon, I'd gifted him two large pieces of maple candy and a gift certificate for the café.

"Come on, everyone," Noah called. "It's time to head over to the sugar shack for a maple syrup boiling demonstration!"

The crowd moved out of the café, talking gaily among themselves. Instead of following, Noah strode over in my direction and rewarded me with a smile. His dark silky hair was slightly tousled, and the urge to run my fingers through it was tempting. Noah was more than just a handsome face though. One of the things that I liked about him—and there were many—was how unaware he was of his good looks. He was an excellent worker, and I honestly didn't know what the farm would do without him. Noah knew everything about collecting sap and the boiling process, plus he made candles for the farm that turned a nice profit, especially around the holidays. He was originally from the South and had served with the Marines after graduating from high school. When he returned from duty, Noah had gone to work on a maple farm in Upstate New York. After the tragedy with his wife, he'd wanted a new start and eventually found his way to Sugar Ridge, Vermont. It was impossible not to admire his determination and strength.

Noah nodded to Heather, who pretended to be occupied with cleaning the tables, then addressed me. "Any chance you're free to go to the movies with Emma and me tonight?"

"I'd love to," I said honestly, "but with Heather's shower

tomorrow, there's a lot of last-minute things to take care of. Could I have a rain check?"

"Of course." He smiled, but I caught a flash of disappointment in his eyes. There was nothing I would have liked more than to be with him and his daughter tonight. In the past few months, I'd come to love Emma as my own child.

"Why don't you come by tomorrow night after the shower, and I'll make you dinner," he offered. "Em can help."

My cheeks warmed as I stared at his perfect features. "Sure. That sounds like fun."

Noah's gaze shifted to my lips, and he started to lean in closer. At the last second, he glanced around the room, then took a step back when he noticed Heather staring. He winked at me and took off for the sugar shack, where his adoring public waited.

It was the second and last day of our Open House Weekend. Over seven hundred people had passed through our front door since Friday morning. We'd had a full slate of activities planned for yesterday and today. The boiling demonstration that Noah was conducting would be followed by a maple candy–making demonstration, which was something I had recently learned to do myself. After that, people would be free to browse our gift shop and the sugar bush outside until closing time.

Selma Khoury, my mother, was behind the counter of the café, where she'd been baking all day. At the moment, she was busy whisking another tray of muffins into the oven. As a courtesy, we'd offered free coffee and maple muffins to the public and had gone through a huge quantity of them. The café smelled divine, with a hint of pancakes still lingering in the air, accompanied by the warm, intoxicating buttery-maple scent of the muffins, which could drive anyone to distraction. She was too preoccupied to pay any attention to what we were doing, and that was fine with me.

When my father first started the farm, adding the café was a no-brainer. People loved maple lattes, warm or iced, at any time of the year. Dad's will had surprised everyone when he stated that his wish was for me to take over the farm. I never thought I would be able to succeed. After a while I'd finally realized that this was where I belonged, and my confidence continued to grow every day.

Heather helped me gather up paper plates from the table. "That was fun! Leila, I can't believe it's the first time I've ever been to a Sappy Endings Open House Weekend."

I tossed the paper plates into a nearby trash can. "I'm so glad you could come. It's a good thing we had to reschedule it, right?" Open House Weekend was a tradition in Vermont during the spring at maple syrup farms, but a late season snowstorm had forced us to cancel our event two weekends earlier and reschedule. On the original day, Heather, who worked as a hairdresser, had been out of town styling hairdos for an entire bridal party. I was grateful for her assistance today.

She glanced at me worriedly. "I feel so guilty about this, Leila."

"Guilty about what?" I joked. "Helping me pass out pancakes?"

Heather smiled. "No. But I'm ruining your social life. You should be snuggling up with Noah tonight instead of doing last-minute things for my shower. Plus tapping season is finally over and I know you're exhausted."

I waved a hand dismissively in the air. "Oh, please. It's not a big deal. This is part of my duty as maid of honor. You'd do the same for me. Besides, I want to make sure your shower goes perfectly tomorrow."

"And that's another thing for me to feel guilty about," Heather continued. "You only get Sundays off and I'm monopolizing this one."

"Would you stop? After today, we're going to start closing at two o'clock on Saturdays for the summer. It will almost feel like another day off. As for your shower, I've had fun arranging it."

Heather shot me a dubious look. "Come on, Lei. I know you hate that sort of thing."

My friend wasn't totally wrong. Heather and I were opposites when it came to looks and hobbies. She was blond and blue-eyed while I was dark-haired with an olive skin tone. People had often wondered how we ever became friends in the first place. For more than twenty years though, we'd stuck together like maple syrup and pancakes.

Heather was a girly girl who loved clothes shopping, experimenting with different hairstyles, and browsing for antiques. I hated all of those things and would rather spend my days burying my nose in a good book or working on the farm. Fortunately, planning Heather's shower hadn't been nearly as time-consuming as the wedding was for her. I'd decided to hold it at Sugar Ridge's local country club. Close to sixty women had responded to say that they would attend. More than two hundred people were expected for the wedding, but several relatives from across the country were only flying in for the big day.

My biggest problem was that I still hadn't bought Heather a present. I always waited until the last minute to take care of those important details. Fortunately, there was a china and silver store in the center of town that had the place setting she'd registered for, and they were open until seven o'clock tonight. Thankfully they offered gift wrapping as I was terrible at anything creative.

I slung an arm around Heather's shoulders. "Okay, maybe it's not my kind of thing, but you're my best friend, and that's all that matters. Just think! Two weeks from today you'll be married. And to a doctor," I added. Heather was proud of the fact that her fiancé was a pediatrician.

To my surprise and horror, she burst into tears.

"What's wrong?" The strain showed on her face, and for a moment, I wondered if Heather might be having second thoughts about her marriage. No, that was impossible. She'd been madly in love with Tyler for years. Heather also loved the idea of being a doctor's wife, even though she occasionally grumbled about the long hours he worked.

Heather sat down on one of the wooden benches and stared up at me with a forlorn expression. "Oh, Lei. I'm so scared about tomorrow."

"What's there to be scared about?" I asked in confusion. "We're going to have lunch, cake, and you'll open presents. Lots and lots of presents to help furnish your new home."

Heather blew her nose into a tissue. "But I'm meeting some of Tyler's relatives for the first time, and I'm worried what they'll think."

"Oh, please," I scoffed. "They're all going to love you." How could they not? Heather was one of those people with a sunny disposition who was an absolute joy to be around. Her natural beauty radiated from the inside.

She wrung her hands together. "Okay, maybe I'm worrying for nothing. Tyler says they're all nice. I mean, they can't be as bad as my uncle Grant's new wife." She winced. "Jeez, I don't know why I call her *new*. They've been married for five years, but I've only met her once."

"Grant is your dad's brother, right? I don't remember ever meeting him."

Heather nodded. "He's not really interested in family events. Grant is ten years older than Dad, and they've never been close. I feel terrible for saying this, but I don't like him very much. And ever since he married Monica, Dad says he's become even more distant." She leaned in closer, as if afraid someone would overhear. "It absolutely kills my father that he took her name."

My mouth fell open. "Are you kidding me? He's Grant Butterfield instead of Turcot?"

"Monica insisted upon it." Heather rolled her eyes. "And she holds the purse strings, so if Uncle Grant wants anything, he has to tip his hat and ask nicely."

I realized that some men did take their wife's name in this day and age, but I didn't know any personally, and this surprised me. "He lives in New York, right?"

"Yes, he's only an hour away but is always too busy to come for a visit. Mom and Dad didn't want to invite them to the wedding, but we had no choice." Her face turned the color of a ripe tomato. "Dad says they're always up to no good."

"Gee, I can't wait to meet them," I said sarcastically.

Heather puckered her lips as if she'd eaten a lemon. "My uncle has always acted like he was more important than everyone else, and what's even worse is that Dad lets him get away with it. He's a regular doormat around him." She sighed. "And Uncle Grant thinks he's better than Dad because he married a rich woman. You know how hard my parents work. They've been saving for my wedding for a long time."

I did know. Heather's father, Garrett, had worked for General Electric for over thirty years and mostly on his feet. Her mother, Olivia, had been a receptionist at the local elementary school for almost as long. She'd started there while Heather and I were in school and liked the fact that she could be home for Heather after school and during summer vacations.

"I'm worried about spending any amount of time with Monica," Heather confessed. "Dad said she feels Vermont is a backward state. She's from Long Island, so she thinks living in a rural area automatically makes us a bunch of hicks."

"Don't worry; we've run into her kind before," I said. "We can handle her."

Heather continued. "I've never met her son, but he's also coming to the wedding. Dad's not a fan of him either."

"Whoa. Hold on a second," I said. "When did she and Grant have a baby?"

Heather laughed. "Devon is from Monica's previous marriage. He's around our age. Monica's first husband died when Devon was only five."

"How sad." I thought of Emma, who had lost her mother at the same age.

"It is sad," Heather agreed, "but Monica spoiled him so much that Uncle Grant told Dad it's pathetic. Devon's never even held a full-time job."

My mouth dropped open. "You're kidding. How does he live?"

Heather cocked an eyebrow. "How do you think? Monica gives him an allowance. And I'm not talking about the five bucks a week that you and I got when we were kids."

"Actually, I got ten," I teased.

"Show-off." Her mouth quivered into a smile. "At least you helped out at the farm and everything. Devon gets a hundred times that amount for doing nothing."

I let out a low whistle. "Wow. Must be nice."

She sighed. "I'm already bracing myself for the country girl jokes."

"Don't let it bother you. You'll see Monica tomorrow and at the wedding, then maybe only once a year after that for either a wedding or funeral."

"I'm worried that she'll be looking down her nose at me the entire time," Heather confided.

"Don't waste your time worrying about her."

Heather swallowed nervously. "I wish I didn't have to worry about what she thinks, but Dad borrowed money from them for the wedding. It's just a short-term loan, but I feel awkward about the whole thing. And I don't like the thought of my father groveling at their feet with them thinking they're better than him."

"Yeah, I've been there." My mother had taken it upon herself to arrange a marriage for me several years ago. She and my father had both been born in Lebanon, where the tradition was still popular. They'd been good friends with the Salems, who had followed them to America about five years later. Mark was a year older than me, and while loathing the idea of a ready-made husband, I'd managed to fall in love with him anyway. We had dated for over three years, and then Mark had backed out of our wedding a month before the big day.

"Lei, there's something that I should tell you." Heather glanced over at my mother, who was chatting with a customer at the café counter while pouring more muffin batter into pans. "Maybe we should go into your office."

I didn't like the sound of this. "Okay." I picked up my coffee and followed her out of the café. A walkway area separated the Sappy Hour Café from the gift shop. A few people were milling around in there, picking up bottles of syrup and maple candles, but they could take those purchases to my mother to be rung up.

The walkway area led to a long corridor. At the very end, situated near the back door, was my office, marked with a sign that simply read, PRIVATE. As this had been my father's office for many years, I'd hesitated about making changes. Perhaps the time had come to add to the current furniture, which consisted only of a wooden desk, chair, and file cabinet.

Heather opened the door and was greeted with a plaintive meow. She laughed out loud at the sight of Toast, my orange cat, lying on top of the desk. Toast had been a stray who adopted me during my first week of work at the farm. He was an indoor cat, but once in a while I brought him along to work with me. He seemed to enjoy the change of scenery.

Heather pulled a chair closer to the desk and nuzzled Toast's face with her own. He immediately began to purr like a V-8 engine. "How's my favorite kitty today?" she cooed.

"Toast is good," I said. "He was neutered the other day, and I suspect he's not happy with me. Other than that, he's fine. So what's going on? Is there something else about your aunt and uncle that you haven't told me?"

Heather paused with her hand buried in Toast's thick fur. "No. It's about Mark."

My body froze. "What about him?"

"Have you...talked to him lately?" Heather asked casually.

Something in her tone suggested that she was fishing for information. "Heather, you're my best friend. If I had talked to him, you'd be the first to know. Now, tell me what's wrong."

She bit into her lower lip. "He's in town. I wasn't sure if he'd come to see you."

"He's here? In Sugar Ridge?" My stomach twisted like a giant pretzel. "Why would he come to see me after all this time? We haven't spoken in almost five years."

She shrugged. "Hey, you never know. I figured he knew you were back home, so maybe he stopped by for a visit. Your mother must know he's here. She's friends with his parents, right? They were close before the marriage talk ever began."

"Mom's still friends with Maya, but since she's been running the café, she hasn't really seen much of anyone." My mother's maple-flavored baklava and other treats were the talk of the town. When she took over the position last December, it was supposed to have been short-term. I suspected that working at the café helped her deal with the loss of my father. Mom was tough, but even she had her limits. She was up at dawn, worked all day, then came home to take care of the house before falling into bed at nine o'clock. She never complained though.

"How long is Mark here for? Have you seen him?" I wanted to bite my tongue off as soon as said the words. The fact remained that while I'd once loved Mark, he hadn't loved me back enough to marry me. It was a deep wound that I thought had healed after all of these years, but now I was starting to wonder.

Heather's face grew stern. "Tyler saw him at On Tap last night. He told Mark that you'd been back since your father's death, and he seemed surprised. I mean, wouldn't his parents have told him that you were back in Sugar Ridge for good?"

"Not necessarily," I admitted. "His parents always thought he could do better than me."

She tossed her head. "Well, they were never very smart."

"I'm sure his being back in town has nothing to do with me," I said. "He's only home to see his mom and dad."

"Are you going to tell Noah that your ex is in town?" Heather asked.

I shrugged. "What's the point? It's not like I'm expecting Mark to stop by and chew the fat."

Heather scratched Toast's behind the ears. "I'm glad that I told you in case he happens to catch you buying Oreos at the Jolly Green Grocer."

I laughed out loud. Next to my mother's baking, Oreos were my go-to dessert. I watched as Toast lapped up the attention from Heather. He lifted his chin, closed his eyes, and deep purrs filled the room. "He's got you wrapped around his paw," I teased.

Heather looked up at me wistfully. "I think I'd rather hang out with Toast this weekend."

"You're worrying over nothing," I said. "Tomorrow is a day to celebrate you. And remember all the fabulous gifts you're going to get. I want you to have a good time and not think about Monica, okay? Let me handle her."

Heather sighed and hugged Toast against her. "Some days I think it would have been easier if we'd eloped."

"But you've always wanted a big wedding," I protested.

"Eloping isn't your style." It was more my speed. Heather and I both knew this, but she was too polite to say so. "You're going to marry the man you love. All the hard work is done, and it's time to start enjoying yourself."

CHAPTER TWO

THE MOUNTAIN RIDGE COUNTRY CLUB was one of the loveliest establishments in Sugar Ridge, and perhaps the entire state of Vermont. The white pillared building was set on over fifty acres of manicured grounds, and the sweeping green mountains served as a lovely backdrop. In addition to the main building and an eighteen-hole golf course, there were tennis courts and an in-ground swimming pool that would open in June.

My parents had been longtime members of the country club, but we rarely went there. Mom and Dad had always liked the idea of mingling with their neighbors and enjoying some downtime over dinner or a round of golf, but the truth was that there had never been much time for them to social-ize because of the farm. I'd happily taken advantage of the discount available to my family and rented out their banquet room. Even with the discount, the shower had still been quite pricey, but my best friend was worth the expense. Heather had two cousins and a friend from college who were also in the bridal party and, to my relief, they'd offered to chip in as well.

The formal banquet room combined both elegance and charm. Sunshine streamed through the floor-to-ceiling windows. Exposed wooden beams in the cathedral ceiling gave warmth to the versatile room. Crystal and blue willow china adorned the lacy tablecloths, while crystal chandeliers glistened from above. There was a bar in the adjoining room if guests wanted beverages other than the coffee, tea, or soda that was complimentary with the lunch.

I stopped to check the place-card setting table by the double doors. Ninety-eight. Phew. It was a bit of relief that over twenty people hadn't been able to attend. The sad part was that Heather's parents were paying an astronomical bill for the wedding, with more people attending from the groom's side than the bride's. At last count, over two hundred people had accepted.

Someone was calling my name, and I turned to see my mother heading toward me. She was dressed in a turquoise-colored suit that went well with her Mediterranean complexion and short dark hair. Mom carried a silver-wrapped package with a matching bow in one hand and a cake dome in the other.

"Leila, what should I do with this?" she wanted to know.

I reached out and grabbed the dome from her hand. "I'll put it next to the bridal cake." The smell of maple syrup and vanilla wafted through the air, making my stomach rumble. Mom's maple Bundt cake tasted amazing, but then again, anything she made was always perfect. She had cooking and baking skills I could never hope to duplicate, even if I'd wanted to. My only interest in baking was eating the final product.

A sinfully sweet cinnamon glaze was drizzled over the top and sides of the cake, and my mother had decorated it with candied pecans. I regretted my choice to skip breakfast this morning because now all I could think about was a slice of the moist, sweet cake. "This smells amazing."

My mother's features broke into a delighted grin. "I hope Heather likes it. It's too bad that you didn't trust me enough to make the shower cake for her."

Not again. I groaned inwardly. "Mom, you've been so busy that I thought it would be easier to have the club make it. Besides, it's already included in the price."

Mom walked over to the dessert table and gave a loud sniff as she examined the aforementioned cake. It was on top of a four-tiered rustic cupcake stand, iced in white with pink flowers decorating the edges. *Congratulations Heather* had been written in the center. The three lower tiers contained vanilla-and chocolate-filled cupcakes that were also iced in white and pink frosting.

Mom turned up her nose at the cake, then glanced at a platter of chocolate chip cookies provided by the resort. "I'll bet they made everything from a box mix. No one takes pride in baking from scratch anymore."

With a sigh, I counted to ten in my head. It was obvious my mother's feelings had been hurt. I'd tried to do the right thing but had failed, once again.

When I left Vermont almost five years ago, Mom and I had not been on good terms, thanks to my broken engagement. My return home last November had started off rocky as we'd tried to adjust to life without my father and coexist under one roof, all while not strangling each other. After Dad's killer had been sent to prison, we'd started getting along better than I'd dared to hope for. I had no intention of rocking the boat again.

Selma Khoury was an amazing woman, stronger than steel, and I was proud to call her my mother. We would never see eye to eye on many things, but I'd learn to accept that. Mom's greatest wish was for both of her children to be married and her front porch covered with grandchildren. She often mentioned how she wanted to spoil them before being too old to enjoy them.

My mother was multitalented, kept a lovely home, and had made three meals a day for her family for over three decades. Besides the treats baked at the Sappy Hour Café, she thrived at cooking traditional Lebanese dishes. Mom was also a talented seamstress and had altered Heather's bridal gown by hand when the boutique she'd bought it from made a mistake with the length.

My mother turned away from the dessert table and her hawklike glance scanned my outfit. Her lips pursed tightly together. I didn't care for dresses, but because of the formality of the occasion, today I was wearing a black skirt and black and white blouse. They were both comfortable and lightweight, but I figured my mother would have something negative to say about my choice.

As usual, she didn't disappoint. "Leila, you wear too much black. And why didn't you wear a dress or lighter color? This isn't a funeral."

"Because I wanted something that was comfortable to wear, and black goes with everything. Besides, you know that I don't own many dresses." Only three, in fact.

A murmur of voices from the coatroom alerted us to the arrival of new guests. My mother seemed to be in no hurry and reached for my hand. "Leila, I need to talk to you about something."

Uh, oh, here it comes. "Mom, I already know that Mark is in town. Let's not make a big deal about it, okay?"

Her dark eyes widened. "Mark is in town? When did this happen? Have you seen him?"

I wanted to smack my head against the wall. Me and my big mouth. "Isn't that what you wanted to talk to me about?"

She shook her head. "I wanted to speak to you about your plan to move out. Now, I know that we have our differences, dear, but I was hoping you'd decide to stay home through the summer."

"I don't know, Mom. It would be nice to have my own space, and—"

It was too late. Mom had already redirected her focus onto the subject of Mark. "Where did you see him? Did Ziter and Maya have you over to their house? How long is he in town for?"

My patience was starting to wear thin. "I haven't seen Mark or his parents. Tyler ran into him and mentioned it to Heather. Excuse me, but I should go and greet the guests."

But my mother had no intention of letting me out of her grasp. She clung to my arm the same way she'd been clinging to the hope that Mark and I would reconnect after all these years. "Let's invite him over for dinner this week," she said eagerly. "I'll make meat pies and tabbouleh. He loves my cooking."

"Good Lord, no!" My tone was sharper than I'd intended, and a couple of women who had entered the banquet room stared over at us curiously. I lowered my voice. "Mom, he isn't here to see me. And I'd rather not see him. We have nothing left to say to each other."

My mother's mouth set in a stubborn, thin line. "You never told me why he suddenly decided that he didn't want to get married. I don't believe it was cold feet."

You always believe what you want to believe. "He wasn't the right man for me. It's all in the past. Besides, you know that I'm dating someone else and am very—"

"There you are!" Heather's voice rang out as she hurried in from the coatroom. She wrapped her arms around me and my mother. "Mrs. Khoury, your daughter should be a wedding planner. Everything looks gorgeous, doesn't it?"

"Yes, and you look lovely, dear." My mother smiled fondly at her. She then glanced over at me with a look that seemed to say, *This might have been your shower if you'd tried a little harder.*

Heather did look lovely. She wore a white wraparound dress that showed off her curvy figure. Her long hair had been curled and cascaded around her shoulders and her face, which was flushed with excitement. She bussed my mother on the cheek. "I'm so glad you're here."

"Hello, Selma. Leila," Olivia Turcot, Heather's mother, greeted us both with a warm smile. "Leila, what a pretty blouse."

I shot my mother a smug look. "Thank you, Mrs. Turcot." I grabbed the white orchid corsage from a nearby table and pinned it on Heather's dress. "There! Now, you're officially ready to meet your guests."

Heather remained by my side as the guests came into the room. I instructed people where to leave their presents and find their place cards after they greeted Heather with hugs and kisses. All of the place cards had been claimed, except for four. Monica's was among them.

Tyler's mother, Janice Murray, whom I'd met before, greeted both my mother and me. She was an attractive woman with dark curly hair like her son's.

Janice took Heather's hand between her own. "My goodness, it's hard to believe that the big day is almost here." She turned in my direction. "Leila, it's so nice to see you and your mother again. How are things at the farm? I heard that Open House Weekend was very successful."

I handed her a glass of punch. "It was. I think everyone enjoyed themselves."

"I wish we could have made it," Janice said regretfully. "Hopefully we'll get up there this summer. Will things slow down now that tapping season is over?"

My mother and I exchanged a knowing smile. "Things

never completely slow down at the farm, Mrs. Murray. There are always a million things to do."

"She's just like her father." Mom beamed. "He would have said the same thing."

"Livy, honey!" A sharp, booming voice vibrated through the room. Everyone stopped what they were doing to see who it belonged to.

I caught a look of irritation on Olivia's delicate face before it quickly vanished. She forced a smile to her lips. "Monica, how lovely to see you." She bussed the woman's cheek. "Monica, you remember Heather, right?"

Heather stepped forward and held out her hand. "Hello, Aunt Monica. It's lovely to see you." She gestured at me. "This is my best friend, Leila Khoury, and her mother, Selma. They run the local maple syrup farm in Sugar Ridge."

Monica's sharp eyes moved quickly around our circle. She smiled and nodded to each person in turn but seemed to be appraising everyone, as if we were jewels. A sparkling diamond choker was drawn tight against her thick neck, while the tennis bracelet on her right wrist contained large diamonds and emeralds that constantly caught the light from the chandelier above.

Heather's aunt was in her early fifties with short, cropped auburn hair, piercing blue eyes, and a porcelain complexion that made me wonder if she ever saw the sun. She was thick-waisted and wore a beige dress that bore the mark of an expensive designer. Her stilettos were the same color.

"Oh, my, she gets cuter every time I see her." Monica

gushed and handed Heather a small package wrapped
in gold paper. "I hope that you two will be very happy
together, but let me give you a bit of advice, honey. If you
want the marriage to last, don't have kids. They only end
up breaking your heart."

An uncomfortable silence filled through the room.
Heather looked like she wanted to disappear, while Olivia
pursed her lips together in distaste, as if afraid a retort
would slip out. My mother and I both smiled politely but
said nothing.

After a slight pause, I removed the package from
Heather's hands and placed it on the gift table. I'd been
in Aunt Monica's presence for less than five minutes but
already didn't like the woman. Her mouth apparently had
no filter, and there was something phony about her manner
that immediately put me on guard.

Monica helped herself to a glass of punch and downed
the entire drink in one gulp. She smacked her lips. "You
don't know how I needed that. The roads out here are so
dusty and dry. But I guess that's what happens when you
live in the wilderness."

Heather glanced around in a panic, as if hoping no one
else had heard the rude comment.

"How's business at your jewelry store, Monica?" Olivia
asked politely.

Monica helped herself to another glass of punch.
"Fabulous, just fabulous. We have some lovely diamond
pendants and combs at Treasure Chest that my friend
Belinda designed earlier this year. You simply must come

in and see them, hon. Remember, relatives get a twenty percent discount on any purchase."

"That's very generous of you," Heather commented.

Monica stared at the waitstaff who were placing individual salad bowls by each place setting. "Please tell me that we're eating soon because I'm simply starved! Livy, honey, I had hoped there would be a nice variety of hors d'oeuvres to tide us over."

Mystified, we all watched as Monica walked over to the dessert table and removed a vanilla cupcake from one of the tiers. "This should tide me over for now." Without another word, she sat down at her assigned table and began peeling the paper away from the cake.

"Monica." Olivia finally found her voice. "Those are for dessert. They're not hors d'oeuvres."

"Oh, pooh." Monica dipped her pinky finger into the buttercream frosting and lifted it to her mouth. "No one's going to miss one little cupcake. Next time have some cheese and crackers out, for goodness' sake!"

I bit into my lower lip to temper my reply. Heather's concerns had been valid. Anyone who had to associate with Monica for an entire afternoon would need the patience of Mother Theresa. Her loud voice immediately attracted the attention of other guests who had just arrived. Heather and her mother went to greet them, but I noticed my friend's gaze shifted back toward Monica every few seconds, as if worried what the woman might do next. A few women were already whispering among themselves and staring in Monica's direction.

My mother pulled me aside. "When is lunch scheduled to be served?" she whispered.

I nodded toward the two male servers who were placing baskets of rolls on each table. "Any minute now."

"Thank goodness," Mom murmured. "I can't believe that aunt of Heather's. How rude can a person possibly be?"

"She takes the cake." I watched as Monica swallowed the rest of the cupcake in one gulp, and then stopped a server and asked him to bring her coffee.

Mom shook her head. "I do hope that she behaves herself for the rest of the afternoon. If she keeps it up, this crowd might lynch her."

"It's definitely a possibility," I admitted.

CHAPTER THREE

THANKFULLY, THE LUNCHEON PORTION OF the shower passed without any more embarrassing outbursts from Monica. Everyone seemed to enjoy the food, and several people complimented the meal, which consisted of salad, roasted chicken, a twice-baked potato, broccoli, and dinner rolls. The room was filled with the sound of laughter and silverware clinking.

Since I hadn't eaten earlier, I devoured my plate in record time and reached for a second dinner roll, which I spread with a thick coat of butter. Heather sat to my left, absently picking away at her plate.

"Come on, girl, you've got to eat," I urged her.

She shook her head. "I'm too nervous. I have this terrible feeling something bad is going to happen."

"You always did think that you were psychic," Angie, Heather's friend from college, teased. "Stop worrying.

Nothing's going to happen. Look around. Everyone's having a great time."

Heather took a sip of her iced tea but said nothing. I followed her worried gaze to Monica's table. Because of her position as Heather's aunt, she'd been seated at the table closest to ours, along with Olivia and my mother. I shot my mother an apologetic look, but she pretended not to notice. She was by far the best choice to sit next to the unfiltered Monica. My mother could put Emily Post to shame with her polished, dignified manners.

"Relax," I said. "She's sitting with both of our mothers. They'll keep her under control. Besides, the only thing that's left is to open presents and eat cake."

Heather groaned. "Those presents are going to take forever to open. And everyone will be watching me the whole time. It's so unnerving. She's bound to say something negative."

I sighed. "Will you at least try to look like you're enjoying yourself?"

She rewarded me with a grateful smile. "It probably sounds like I don't appreciate this, but believe me, I do. I've dreamed of my wedding for so long. Now that it's almost here, I'm so scared that something's going to ruin it."

Or someone. I watched as Monica rose and hurried across the room with her cell phone pressed to her ear. With any luck, she'd remain out of the banquet room until all the presents had been opened and the cake had been served.

I pushed back my chair. "I'm going to grab a glass of

wine before we open the presents. Do you want anything from the bar?"

Heather shook her head. "No thanks. I'm sticking with nonalcoholic drinks today. I'm too afraid of getting tipsy and doing something to embarrass myself."

"Stop worrying, okay?" I went into the adjoining room where the bar was located. A gas fireplace greeted me on one side and a long narrow mahogany bar on the other. The room was empty, except for a woman mixing drinks behind the counter. She appeared to be a few years older than me and was busy pouring rum into a blender and humming to herself. Her name tag read *Amber*. She looked up and smiled pleasantly. "Yes, miss. What can I get for you?"

"A glass of chardonnay, please." I didn't drink often but could always ride home with Heather if necessary and grab my car later. Besides, I needed to squelch my own nerves. All of Heather's wedding preparations and Mark's return were suddenly digging up memories from my own bridal shower. I remembered with a pang how my mother and I had scurried around to return the gifts afterward, with sincere notes of apologies attached. It had been the most humiliating experience of my life.

Amber set a glass of wine in front of me. With a smile, I paid for my drink and took a long sip. When I turned my head, I noticed Monica standing on the outside patio with her phone next to her ear. Her voice traveled through the glass door at the speed of a rocket, making me cringe.

"She's a keeper, huh?"

Surprised, I turned around as Amber gestured toward Monica. "I told her to go outside and finish her shouting match. I was afraid that everyone in the banquet room would hear."

"Wow, she's really ticked off at someone," I murmured.

"Yeah, I'd hate to be them," Amber agreed. "She said that they'd be sorry for disobeying her command. Maybe she's got some type of corporal punishment planned."

I blinked once—no, twice. "It must be one of her employees."

Amber snorted. "Well, if I worked for her, I'd take the nearest bridge."

I edged closer to the door, curious about the woman and what made her tick. Why did she act so entitled? Had she always been this way? I didn't understand how some people thought that they were better than everyone else and deserved preferential treatment.

Monica's voice became increasingly loud and went through me like a knife. "This has gone far enough," she shouted. "I'm not going to stand for it anymore, do you hear me?"

In a sudden fit of anger, Monica yanked the door open. A rush of chilly air greeted me as she flounced inside and, not paying attention, almost ran right into me. She grunted a "Sorry," then headed straight for the bar. She fanned herself with a cocktail napkin, obviously overheated from her shouting match. "Is my strawberry daiquiri ready yet, honey?"

Amber topped the waiting glass with a dollop of

whipped cream and added a straw, then pushed it toward her. "Enjoy."

Monica took a sip of her drink and stared thoughtfully into the fireplace. An expression of longing softened her features and surprised me, but not as much as her next comment. "It's nice of you to throw this lovely shower for Heather, hon."

"She's my best friend. I was happy to do it."

"Everyone wants something for nothing these days," Monica mumbled as she stirred her drink.

I wasn't sure if she was talking about Heather or someone else. "I'm sorry?"

Monica stared at me as if she'd forgotten who I was. "Never mind. It's a long story." She took another sip of her drink. "Let me tell you something, honey. Learn to trust no one in this world. You're much better off, plus you won't get hurt. The only reason people are nice to me is because I have more money than God."

"Oh, I'm sure that's not true."

She gave me a wistful smile. "Yes, it is. The world is full of backstabbers, my dear. Believe me, I've learned the hard way."

Before I had a chance to respond, Monica picked up her drink and left the room. With a smile, I nodded toward Amber, who'd overheard our conversation, and then followed Monica back into the banquet room. I hadn't realized there was a sensitive side to the woman with no filter. The remark she'd made left me feeling a bit sorry for her.

Heather was standing by the punch bowl, smiling and

talking to one of her guests. She glanced over at Monica, then her eyes shifted back to me. I caught an expression of concern cross her face. She said something to the woman and swiftly moved to my side.

"Everything okay?" she whispered.

"The time has come," I teased dramatically and handed her the cake knife. As the old saying went, silence was golden. With any luck, I'd only see Monica one more time in my life—on Heather's wedding day.

I put my wineglass down on the cake table and clapped my hands together. "Everyone, may I have your attention, please?" I hated to make speeches, but as maid of honor and the host today, it was necessary. Everyone stopped talking and looked over at us expectantly.

"Thank you all for coming to honor our lovely bride-to-be. Heather has been a huge part of my life since we were six years old, and I couldn't imagine it without her. I hope that she and Tyler have a long, loving marriage and happy life together."

The room broke into applause as we hugged, and Heather reached for a nearby napkin to dab at her eyes. Armed with the knife, she made the first cut in the cake. After she had placed the piece on a china plate, the server took the rest of the cake away to slice it up and serve the guests while we got ready to open gifts.

Heather's bridesmaids and I moved a couple of chairs next to the gift table. Heather sat down in one that had been draped with a *Bride-to-Be* sign as I lowered myself into the chair next to it. I would record the gifts while the bridesmaids handed them to Heather to open and display for the guests.

The guests had their cell phones poised for pictures while they waited patiently to receive their dessert, except for Monica. She rose and hurried over to the dessert table, as if afraid that someone might beat her to it. On the way, she almost knocked Heather's grandmother over. Monica didn't hesitate to help herself to the maple cake, a handful of cookies, and the solo piece of bridal cake that Heather had sliced.

A murmur ran around the room, and some of the women even clucked their tongues in apparent disapproval. Olivia downed the rest of her wine in a hurry. My mother raised one lone eyebrow menacingly in my direction. It was a talent that she'd perfected when I was a small child, and I had become good at deciphering the meaning. This one seemed to be saying, *Doesn't that woman know she's supposed to wait until the servers come around?*

Poor Heather looked horrified, so we tried to distract her. Angie passed her a square box wrapped in rose-colored paper. Heather removed the card and read out loud, "This is from my godmother, Anna."

She hastily unwrapped the paper to reveal a Mikasa place setting, while everyone in the room oohed and aahed appropriately. After a warm thank-you to her godmother, who was sitting at the same table as my mother, Heather passed the box on to me. I made sure that it was closed properly, then gave it to Heather's cousin, who placed it on a nearby empty table. I quickly jotted two words down on Anna's card: *Place setting*.

Heather's next gift was from one of the girls she worked with in the hair salon. It was a black and white lace nightie, so sheer that it made her face turn as red as a tomato. Several of the guests whooped good-naturedly. Still blushing, Heather passed it on to her cousin, while Monica spoke loudly enough for the entire state of Vermont to hear.

"Oh, my goodness! I hope you can fit into that, honey!"

The room was so quiet that you could have heard a place card drop on the floor. Olivia shot Monica a dirty look, as did many of the other guests, but she seemed not to notice. Sweet Lord. If that woman made one more disparaging remark about Heather, or anyone else, I might say something that I was bound to regret.

An hour later, there were only a handful of presents left to be opened. Two huge stacks of boxes rested against the wall and on a table. Tyler was coming by with a friend later to transport the items to their new house. Among some of the gifts that Heather had received were silverware, crystal, towels, and every kitchen appliance under the sun that I could think of.

Angie brought her a small oval-shaped box, about the size of a coffee cup. Heather's face was flushed from the activity, and a small bead of sweat trickled down the side of her face. She thanked Angie, glanced at the card, and her complexion paled. Heather stared nervously over at my mother's table. "This is from Aunt Monica Butterfield."

I held my breath, afraid of what might be inside. Heather opened a Williams Sonoma box and removed a lovely set of pewter salt and pepper shakers. I didn't recall them being on Heather's registry, but anything from that store was expensive. Monica definitely had good taste.

Heather almost smiled in relief as she held up the shakers for all to see. "Thank you, Aunt Monica. They're lovely."

As she went to put the shakers back in the box, a small amount of salt fell out of one. I noticed that the seal on the bottom of both shakers had been broken. Heather and I exchanged horrified glances, but she merely looked up at the crowd and managed a smile. Fuming on the inside, I took the box from her. *Really? What kind of person brings a used gift to a bridal shower?*

Heather wouldn't care if someone gave her a gift that was worth less than five dollars. She only wanted people to share in her special day. The idea of the used gift made my blood boil, because Monica was easily the richest person in attendance today. My father once laughed as he told me that people who had the most money were usually the least generous. "How do you think they got all that money, *habibi*?"

Heather opened the last of the gifts and looked relieved to be done. She stood and beamed at everyone in the room. "Thank you all for thinking of Tyler and me, and for your generous gifts. But the best gift I could ever receive was to have all of you join me here today."

The women responded to her speech with a tumultuous round of clapping. This was the cue for anyone to help themselves to remaining desserts before leaving. My mother's Bundt cake was long gone, but there were still cookies and half of the shower cake remaining. Heather had already asked the servers for boxes in case guests wanted to take some with them. She didn't want any leftovers coming home with her. "I have a wedding gown to fit into," she'd reminded me.

The guests mulled around for a few more minutes over coffee and punch, chatting gaily among themselves, and then started to depart. Several of them stopped to hug Heather and her mother, and a few even told me what a lovely shower it had been and that I'd done a great job arranging everything.

Monica was one of the last guests to leave. She approached Heather with three bridal favor boxes clutched in her left hand. The favors were small boxes of maple candy that Noah and I had created, with Heather's name and the date of the shower on the outside.

She gave Olivia and Heather both air-kisses. "Lovely to see you, Livy. Do drop by Treasure Chest sometime and have that cheap husband of yours find something nice for you to wear at the wedding."

Olivia's smiled was strained. "Have a safe trip home, Monica."

"Thank you for coming," Heather added politely, while I struggled to keep silent.

Monica's gaze roamed over the stack of gifts against the wall. "It looks like you got some great loot, honey. Enjoy it. That's the best part of getting married."

Heather chuckled, but I could tell that the comment bothered her. She waved politely at Monica, who cut in front of an elderly woman with a cane on the way out the door. Once she had left, Olivia let out a long breath that sounded as if she'd been holding it forever.

"Thank goodness that's over." Olivia stared sympathetically at her daughter and me. "I'm sorry, girls. We do our best to tolerate Monica, and thankfully we don't see her often. But she's a tough act to take."

"She certainly is." I clenched my fists at my sides.

My mother frowned at my gesture. "Leila, that's so unladylike."

"I didn't want to invite her," Olivia admitted, "but there was no other choice."

An uncomfortable silence followed. Heather raised her eyebrows at me, and I understood the gesture. If she hadn't told me about the loan earlier, I too would have been curious as to why Monica was here. A bridal shower was supposed to be for well-loved friends and close relatives. Monica didn't fit into either one of those categories.

Mom nudged me in the side. Maybe she was afraid I was going to say something else, but I knew better. There was no need to add to the discomfort of the situation. My mother probably wondered herself why Monica had been invited, but she was too polite to ask.

"Maybe we'll get lucky, and she won't come to the wedding," Olivia said hopefully.

My mother picked up her purse and the empty cake dome, and gave Heather a kiss on the cheek. "Congratulations, dear. I need to get going. Toast has been alone all day, and I do worry about him."

I suppressed a smile. It was adorable how my mother had formed such a loving bond with our cat. He was the first pet for both of us. My father had severe allergies, so having a cat hadn't been possible while he was alive. When I found an apartment, Mom and I would need to talk about shared custody of Toast.

"Leila, are you coming home or going elsewhere?" Mom asked.

What she really wanted to know was if I was going to Noah's. My mother liked him, but in her mind, Noah would never measure up to Mark.

"I'm supposed to go over to Noah's tonight." Though the thought of a quick nap at home first was appealing. Adrenaline had been flowing through my veins all day, leaving me exhausted.

She nodded. "Well, if you change your mind, there's a pan of grape leaves that I made last night. See you at home, dear."

My mother's smile was more brittle than a pencil, and I suspected that she was thinking about Mark. I said a silent prayer that she wouldn't call his mother and invite the family over for dinner this week. How I wished I'd never brought his name up.

Heather glanced at her phone. "Tyler just texted me. He and a couple of his friends were watching a baseball game and lost track of time." She rolled her eyes. "Men. He'll be here shortly with the truck. Will you stay with me, Lei?"

Her expression was so wistful that I couldn't bring myself to say no. "Of course. I could use a cup of coffee, anyway."

Tyler's mom gathered up her things, while Olivia did the same. Both women gave Heather a warm hug, and

Olivia embraced me as well. "Are you sure you don't need us to do anything, Leila?"

I shook my head. "Thanks, but the staff will take care of cleanup. All Heather and I need to do is wait for Tyler and his buddies to load the gifts into his truck."

"Do you need a hand with the food?" Heather asked her mother. She was taking an extra meal home to Heather's father, along with a plate of cookies.

"No, thank you, dear. We're parked right out front." Olivia gave us both a finger wave, and the two women departed.

"Whew." Heather lowered herself into a chair and pulled another one over so that she could rest her feet on it. "Why am I so tired? I didn't do anything except eat and open gifts. I can't imagine how worn out you must be."

I sat down next to her and glanced at my phone to see if there were any new messages. "You're tired because it was a stressful event. With any luck, you'll only see her one more time this year."

"Tell me about it. I can't believe how rude Monica was to everyone. And the sad part is she acted like she did nothing wrong." Heather frowned. "That was mean what she said about my negligee."

I hated to see my best friend so upset on what should have been a happy occasion for her. "She's probably unhappy with her own life and enjoys putting other people down."

"What exactly does she have to be unhappy about?" Heather asked. "Yes, it was sad that her first husband died, but according to Dad, she's always lived a life of luxury and never had to lift a finger. Then she inherited Treasure

Chest when her father died ten years ago. That place is a gold mine. Yes, pun intended. The only other relative she has is a brother down south, but he's estranged from her."

"Big surprise there," I remarked.

"Can you imagine parents picking one child over another to leave everything to?" She put a hand to her mouth. "Oh, wow. That was a stupid thing to say. I'm sorry, Lei."

I laughed. "No worries. Simon and I are past that now." When my father had died, he'd chosen to leave the farm to me instead of my younger brother. Dad and Simon had always been sparring partners, similar to my mother and me. "Simon's loving his job as head reporter at the *Maple Messenger*. He never had any interest in the family business."

Heather poured herself a cup of coffee. "From what I've heard, Treasure Chest is all that Monica thinks about."

I swallowed the last of my coffee. "Forget about Monica. You have more important things to think about. Two weeks from today, you'll be on your way to Aruba."

She closed her eyes and breathed deeply. "It can't come soon enough."

"Remember, the wedding should be about you and Tyler. It's your day. Not anyone else's."

Heather reached over and gave my hand a tight squeeze. "You're such a good friend. What would I do without you?"

"Back atcha," I said.

"Ma'am?" One of the servers waved at me. He was in the process of removing a tablecloth across the room and lifted a purse in his hand. "Does this belong to either one of you ladies?"

The purse was brown with green stripes—a classic-looking Gucci bag.

"No, it's not mine," Heather said.

"It isn't mine either." We both stood and moved across the room for a better look. "Whoever it belongs to will be back, I'm sure."

The man handed the bag to me and went on with his work. I turned to Heather. "Who do you know that owns a Gucci bag?"

She shrugged. "Maybe you should look inside for identification."

"All right." With reluctance, I reached inside the purse to remove a matching Gucci wallet. I hated looking through someone's personal property but opened it and stared down at a New York State driver's license. The photo belonged to the woman of the hour. "The purse is Monica's."

Heather winced. "Oh no. I was afraid you were going to tell me that. Now what?"

"Do you have her phone number? We'll have to call her so she can come back."

She shook her head. "Monica's probably in New York by now. Maybe Mom can come grab it. Or Dad can meet Uncle Grant somewhere and give it to him."

Heather went back to the table where we'd been sitting to call her mother, while I placed Monica's wallet back inside the purse. A small Post-it Note fluttered to the floor. I picked it up and read the words that were printed on it.

END IT NOW OR I TELL HIM EVERYTHING.

The note was unsigned. I sucked in a deep breath. Holy molasses. Monica was having an affair? From the content of the note, it sounded as if someone was blackmailing her. I studied the message closer. It had been written with a black magic marker in capital letters, most likely to convey shouting. The words were slanted, leaning to the left side of the note. On impulse, I reached into the pocket of my dress for my phone and quickly snapped a photo of it. Why, I wasn't sure, but figured I must have learned a thing or two from checking into my father's murder.

Like a child caught with her hand in the cookie jar, I glanced around the room. Convinced no one had seen me, I shoved the Post-it Note back into Monica's purse. As my fingers came in contact with the satin interior lining, the purse began to vibrate, and I almost jumped five feet into the air. I peeked inside again and noticed that the screen of her cell phone was lit up with a *Missed Call* message from a private number.

I glanced over at Heather, but she was still on her phone and not paying any attention to me. An ice-cold chill ran down my spine. I could understand leaving a party without a purse or your phone, but both? If it had been me, I would have noticed that at least one of these items was missing right away. And Monica Butterfield didn't strike me as the forgetful type. So, where was she?

I went into the next room, where Amber was wiping down the bar. She smiled as I approached. "Did everything go okay?" she asked.

"Perfect," I said. "Did you happen to see the woman

who was in here with me earlier? It looks as if she left her purse behind."

Amber paused, white cloth in her hand. "The one who was wearing all the diamonds and shouting on her phone? No, I haven't seen her since."

I thanked her and walked out to the vestibule, past the chalkboard announcing that Heather Turcot's bridal shower was at two o'clock. The only cars left out front belonged to me and Heather. I walked around the side of the building. There was a white paneled van out back, but no other vehicles.

The wind was picking up, and I'd forgotten to bring my jacket. I wrapped my arms around me for warmth as I hurried across the road. There was a white Honda CRX parked in a small lot across the street along with a black Mercedes. The rear of the Mercedes was facing me. My stomach tightened as I observed the New York State vanity plate: *DIAMOND1*.

I ignored the smattering of raindrops that had started to descend from the sky and approached the vehicle at a slow, steady pace. The side windows were tinted, so I went around to the front of the car and stared inside. My blood quickly turned to ice.

Monica's body was slumped forward with her face pressed into the steering wheel. Something was sticking out of her back, but I couldn't tell what it was.

My entire body began to shake. For a long moment, all I could do was stand there and stare, my high-heeled black boots cemented to the ground. With a trembling hand,

I reached forward to grab the door handle and yanked it open. To my shock, Monica tumbled out of the car and onto the ground. Her eyes were wide open, staring directly into mine.

CHAPTER FOUR

"DRINK THIS, SWEETIE." AMBER PLACED a glass of brandy in front of me. Heather, seated next to me, was already on her second glass. Amber tried to smile at us but failed miserably. She left the bottle when she returned to the bar.

After my discovery of Monica's body, a member of the kitchen staff who'd been putting garbage out back had heard my screams and rushed over to assist me. He'd quickly called 9-1-1 and then escorted me back inside the country club. We waited while the police conducted their investigation outdoors.

"I can't believe it." Heather's entire body was shaking, a sign that the brandy hadn't done its job. Tears streamed out of her eyes and dropped onto the table.

Tyler, who'd arrived with a friend only minutes earlier, had a protective arm around her shoulders. His expression was grim. "Did you get a hold of your mother?"

She nodded weakly. "I asked her and your mom to come back. All I said was that it was an emergency. I didn't want to tell them over the phone that—"

"Heather?"

We both stared up into the pale and bewildered faces of Mrs. Turcot and Mrs. Murray. "What happened?" Olivia asked.

"Mom—" Heather's voice faltered, and she put her face into her hands.

"It's all right, sweetheart," Tyler said. He was an attractive man with a thick head of curly dark hair, pensive hazel eyes, and shoulders that belonged on a linebacker. He turned to address his mother and Olivia. "Monica is dead."

Olivia's complexion turned an ashen gray, and she began to sway back and forth. Tyler jumped forward and helped her into a nearby chair.

"Oh my God," Janice whispered.

"What happened to her?" Olivia asked weakly.

Heather spoke up. "Leila found her inside her car a little while ago. She—she was stabbed."

Janice clutched at her throat and addressed me. "Are you all right, dear?"

I nodded mutely. No, I wasn't all right. I'd never found a dead body before. The moment that Monica fell out of the car and to the ground kept replaying in my head, like a scene from a horror movie.

Olivia reached into her purse for her phone. "I—I guess I'd better call your father. He can tell Grant."

"Grant's already on his way here," Heather said. "The police called him. He told them he's coming with Devon." She let out a pitiful wail. "Oh God. This is all my fault."

Tyler reached for her hand. "Stop saying things like that, sweetheart."

"But it's true." She sobbed. "Monica was obnoxious and rude during the shower. She said mean things. When it was all over, and she'd finally left, I kept hoping that somehow, she wouldn't end up coming to the wedding."

"Honey, you can't blame yourself," Olivia said.

"Excuse me." A male voice spoke from behind me. I turned around to see a man of about forty wearing a navy-colored suit. "Which one of you ladies is Leila Khoury?"

I slowly raised my hand, having an idea of what was coming next. "I'm Leila."

The man held out his hand. "Detective Ryan Barnes."

"You must be new," Tyler noted. "I wasn't even aware that the Sugar Ridge Police Department had a detective on staff. Their force is so small."

Detective Barnes gave him a casual nod. His black hair was slicked back on the sides and starting to turn gray at the temples, and he had warm hazel eyes that seemed sympathetic to our situation. "I just transferred here from New Hampshire a couple of months ago. But let's talk about more important things right now. Miss Khoury, I'd like to ask you some questions. In private, if possible. Can we talk at the bar?"

Heather stared miserably at me, as if this was her fault too. I managed a smile for her before following the detective into the next room. Amber had disappeared. How I longed to do the same.

Detective Barnes seated himself on one of the stools and gestured for me to join him. "All right, Miss Khoury. I heard that you were the one who found Mrs. Butterfield, is that correct?"

"Yes, sir."

He glanced down at a small pad of paper in his hand. "She was here to attend the shower for Heather Turcot. When was the last time you saw Mrs. Butterfield alive?"

"It was around four thirty." I glanced at my watch. Six thirty. The sun was already sinking fast in the sky.

The detective made a note on his pad. "What made you go to the parking lot, Miss Khoury? Did you know she'd be there?"

"No, of course not." What kind of question was that? "One of the servers found her purse. She'd left it behind. Monica's phone was inside her purse. It seemed kind of strange to me that she'd left without both."

He raised an eyebrow at me in question, and I began to babble, an annoying habit when I was nervous. "What I mean is, that she would have realized it before long, and she'd been gone for at least a half an hour by then."

Detective Barnes examined my face closely. "So you guessed she might still be outside?"

My cheeks grew warm. "I didn't know for certain, but thought it was worth it to at least look for her car."

He tapped his pencil on the bar. "And that's why you went through her purse?"

"Yes, sir. I needed to find out who it belonged to."

Detective Barnes seemed satisfied by my response. "Where is the purse?"

"Heather and I gave it to the first policeman who arrived," I said. "He said his name was Officer Downs."

He nodded. "All right. I'll check with him. What did you do when you found Mrs. Butterfield behind the wheel?"

"At first, I couldn't tell what was wrong. I saw something sticking out of her back, but I guess it didn't register with me." I gulped a breath of air, remembering. "Then, I opened the car door and spotted the knife. It had a red stone on the handle—like a ruby."

The detective pinned his gaze on me. "Go on."

"Then I started to scream. One of the employees heard me and came over to call 9-1-1."

Detective Barnes pursed his lips together. "You touched the driver's door?"

"Well, I had to." The question surprised me. "I didn't know if she was dead."

He made another note on his pad. "Miss Khoury, you may have inadvertently interfered with a crime scene. The killer might have left fingerprints on the door, and it's possible we won't be able to identify them now."

What the heck? Would he rather that I'd walked away while there was a chance that Monica might still be alive? "I'm sorry. It was all such a shock. I've never found a dead body before." One had fallen on me in the past, but there was no need to get into that now. The detective would really start wondering about me then.

Detective Barnes closed his pad and rose to his feet. "Okay, I think I have all that I need for now. If you think of anything else—"

"Actually, there is something else," I interrupted. "When I was looking through Monica's purse for identification, a Post-it Note fell out. The note said, *End it now or I tell him everything.*"

The detective looked intrigued. "Is the note still in her purse?"

"Yes, I made sure to put it back. I forgot to mention this when I talked to Officer Downs."

"That's all right," Detective Barnes said. "He's still here, so I'll ask him if the note was found. Did you see anyone threaten Mrs. Butterfield during the shower?"

"No, sir, but I did overhear her yelling at someone on the phone." I pointed toward the sliding glass door and outside patio area. "She was out there. Amber, the bartender, heard her too."

Detective Barnes nodded in approval. "Yes, I already talked to her, and she confirmed that Mrs. Butterfield had sounded upset. How did she act during the shower? Was she distracted or unhappy?"

"She—" I hesitated, not sure how to phrase my response. "She seemed happy enough." What else was there to say? That Monica had seemed to enjoy making rude comments to Heather's guests? That wasn't enough of a reason to kill someone. "I did feel kind of sorry for her at one point. She was at the bar getting a drink and told me that no one could be trusted, and people were only nice to her because she had money."

"Did she say anything else?" was his next question.

"Yes, she said that everyone was a backstabber." I cringed as I said the word. Talk about horrible irony.

A loud, arrogant male voice filtered in from the banquet room. "What's the meaning of this? I want to speak with the officer in charge. Right *now*."

Detective Barnes lifted one eyebrow, sighed, and placed his notepad inside his jacket before leaving the room. Mystified, I followed.

Two men I had never seen before were standing next to the table where Heather and Tyler were seated with their mothers. The older man looked about sixty with a stocky frame. He had silver-colored hair and a matching goatee. His companion was close to my age, with shaggy auburn hair and piercing blue eyes. The proverbial light bulb clicked on in my head. This must be Monica's husband and son.

"I'm in charge here," Detective Barnes said quietly. "How can I be of assistance?"

The older man puffed out his chest. "I'm Grant Butterfield. This is Monica's son—er, I mean our son, Devon. Has something happened to my wife? Where is she?"

Officer Barnes spoke gently. "I'm sorry to tell you this, but your wife is deceased."

"Please tell me this is some kind of sick joke." Grant's lips trembled slightly, and I found myself wondering if it was for affect.

"I'm afraid it's true," Detective Barnes continued. "Your wife was found dead inside her vehicle. Someone stabbed her."

Devon made a strangling sound low in his throat. "My mom's...gone?"

"You have my deepest sympathy." Detective Barnes turned to address the rest of us. "Everyone, I would like to request that you keep the details of Mrs. Butterfield's death to yourselves for now. It's a good idea to do this until a person of interest is located, since it could end up hindering the process."

Grant shook his head and tears came into his eyes. "No," he whispered. "This is my fault. I shouldn't have let her come alone. This entire state is full of hoodlums and hicks who will do anything to make a buck."

Furious, I opened my mouth to speak, but quickly shut it when Detective Barnes gave me a reproachful look. I didn't care for Grant's unfounded comments about my hometown but reminded myself that he'd lost his wife and was grieving. I counted to ten in my head, hoping for some self-control.

Devon put his head in his hands and began to sob noisily. "I can't believe she's gone. Why? Who would do this?"

Grant gently patted him on the shoulder and brought a hand to his eyes. "Was it a robbery? I knew she shouldn't have worn those diamonds."

Detective Barnes tugged at his tie. "Actually, Mr. Barnes, it doesn't appear that anything was stolen from your wife. I've been informed that she still had jewelry on after the— er, when she was found."

"I want to see her for myself," Grant said angrily. "Where is she?"

Olivia came over and put an arm around his shoulders. "They've taken her to the morgue, Grant. Garrett is on his way here, and we'll be happy to go with you and Devon to—see her." There was a catch in her voice. "You'll need to let them know what you want done with the—her body."

Grant wiped his eyes. "Thank you, Livy, but Devon and I will take care of it. Of course, she'll be coming back to New York with us today."

Heather was busy dabbing at her eyes with a tissue. She was very tenderhearted and cried easily. When we'd seen *The Notebook* in the movie theater as teenagers, she'd gone through a whole box of Kleenex. With the exception of her and Grant, everyone else had stoic expressions on their faces. I couldn't help noting the contrast between my father's death and Monica's. Last fall, there hadn't been a dry eye at his wake or funeral. I'd known Monica for less than twenty-four hours, but it was already evident that she was nowhere nearly as beloved as my father.

Detective Barnes spoke gently. "Mr. Butterfield, I'm afraid that your wife won't be traveling to New York today, or any other state for that matter. Her body needs to be examined by the local medical examiner. After he's given clearance, you're free to have her transported. But it won't be today."

"I wish you'd called me." Noah's voice was anxious. "I would have driven out there and brought you home."

My heart warmed at his words. "It's your one day off out of the week, and I know that you like to spend it with Emma. Besides, I didn't want you to bring her to the country club and be subjected to that awful mess." Disaster, drama, and confusion were all words that came to mind. At the age of six, poor Emma already had enough experience with death to last a lifetime.

I hadn't left the country club until seven thirty, but I'd texted Noah to let him know that I wouldn't be coming over. The first thing I'd done when I'd arrived home was strip off my clothes and change into a pair of sweatpants and an old comfortable T-shirt. The day had been exhausting and all I could think about was sleep.

Noah sighed into the phone. "I'm sorry you had to go through all that today. It should have been a day of celebration for Heather."

"Tell me about it." I stretched out on the couch as Toast jumped up on my stomach and began kneading his paws into me. "She's devastated and feels responsible."

"I'd offer to come over but Emma's asleep already, and I don't have anyone to leave her with," Noah said regretfully.

"Don't worry about it," I assured him. "I'm planning to fall into bed soon. This week has worn me out."

Noah was silent for a moment. "I know it has. Jeez, you've been working hard at the farm, and now you have to deal with a murder investigation? I don't want to see you go through all this again—like you did with your dad."

"My part in this is over," I assured him. "I answered all of the detective's questions, and he said if there's anything else, he'd call. I'll probably go to the wake out of respect, but Monica's murder has nothing to do with me anymore."

"Well, I hope so." He paused for a few seconds. "I worry about you, Leila. You mean a great deal to me."

I waited to see if Noah would elaborate, but he didn't continue. In the six months that we'd been dating, this was the closest he'd ever come to professing his feelings for me. As for myself, I'd only said the three magical words to one man during my lifetime. I thought briefly about telling Noah that Mark was in town for a visit but decided against it. This wasn't a good time to bring up the subject. Anyway, Mark wasn't here to see me.

"You mean a lot to me too," I said softly. "And I'm sorry we haven't been able to spend a lot of time together lately. Once the wedding is over, things will get back to normal."

"Sure, they will," he agreed. "Emma misses you, by the way."

"Give her a kiss for me. I'll see you in the morning."

"Will do. Night, Leila." He clicked off.

My mother poked her head in from the kitchen. "Leila, everything is ready. Come and eat, dear."

I moved Toast off me and went to the kitchen table. My mother had warmed up grape leaves and *batata harra*, which were spicy potatoes. Mom roasted them until they were crispy, then tossed them in a flavorful sauce made from cilantro, garlic, and crushed red pepper. The grape leaves were handpicked from the town, boiled and baked for hours before they were wrapped around seasoned meat and rice. Despite my huge lunch, I wasted no time digging into the delicious meal.

Mom took a seat next to me and sipped a cup of *Ahweh*. It was strong Turkish coffee that she made most days if time allowed. She insisted on roasting and grinding the beans herself. She could have bought a powdered Turkish kind at a specialty store in town, but she insisted it didn't taste the same. Mom then cooked it in a *rakweh*, which was a small aluminum pot with a long handle.

"This is a nightmare for Heather's family," she murmured. "Do you think it could affect the wedding?"

I finished chewing and swallowed before answering. "I hope not. There's still two weeks. I'm sure the wake and funeral will be held way before then."

My mother narrowed her eyes. "That's not what I meant. What if she has to cancel the wedding?"

In surprise, I set down my fork. "Why would she do that? Not to sound mean, but Monica is only her aunt by marriage."

"That doesn't make any difference," my mother insisted. "Family is family. Besides, Heather's parents are paying for the reception, so technically it's their decision if they want to cancel."

"Of course they'll go ahead with it. Do you know how much money would be lost if they cancel now?" I asked. "The deposit and the entire fee for the reception. That's at least twenty grand right there."

"We were able to get the money refunded for your reception," my mother reminded me.

Why did she have to bring that up? "Yes, because we gave them more than thirty days' notice." Barely. "All venues have different rules. Heather got a better deal because of the no-refund policy."

Mom stirred cream into her coffee. "I can't believe someone stabbed the woman, right in the parking lot. What is this world coming to?"

"Someone might have been blackmailing her." I told my mother about the note I'd found in Monica's purse.

"Oh, my goodness." Mom's jaw dropped. "Do you really think it's because she was having an affair?"

"And she was rich," I added. "That's always a good motive."

A piteous yowl sounded. Toast was rubbing his orange fur against my mother's legs. She laughed and got up from the table. "Don't worry, I didn't forget you, little one. I made you a plate."

She placed a paper plate on the floor with some of the meat from the grape leaves, and Toast quickly devoured it. Mom watched him with a pleased expression on her face. "He loves Lebanese food as much as you and Simon do." She sat back down at the table and unfolded her napkin. "Speaking of which, I haven't seen your brother in three days. It would be nice if he called once in a while."

"Mom, you know the promotion at the newspaper is keeping him super busy. Don't take it so personally." I'd have to send my younger brother a text and remind him to call our overly sensitive mother once in a while.

I placed my plate in the dishwasher and gave her a kiss

on the cheek. "Dinner was great. Do you want some help cleaning up?"

She shook her head. "No, thank you, dear. Go and get some rest. Goodness knows you had quite an ordeal today."

I didn't argue with her. The day had been exhausting, and I was having trouble keeping my eyes open. I climbed the stairs and ran a bath, which always helped me to relax. Thirty minutes later, dressed in cotton pajamas and my fluffy blue robe, I settled in bed with a book in hand and Toast at my feet. The doorbell rang and a minute later my mother called out to me.

"Leila! Could you come downstairs for a minute, please? We have company."

Was this some kind of a joke? I glanced at the clock. It was nine o'clock on a Sunday evening. For those of us who rose at six o'clock in the morning, it was far too late for visitors. That was when realization set in. What if Detective Barnes had decided to come and ask me some more questions? He could have easily found our house. I glanced at my reflection in the mirror hanging on the wall. My hair was pulled back in a ponytail and my face devoid of makeup, but I couldn't care less what I looked like. All I wanted was my bed.

"Coming, Mom." I started down the stairs, wishing that this day would hurry up and end soon. There was no way that things could get any worse.

When I stepped into the living room, my mother was nowhere in sight. A tall dark-haired man had his back to me as he studied the pictures on the fireplace's ledge. I easily recognized him from his brawny shoulders and confident posture. My heart sank into the pit of my stomach. Sensing that I was behind him, he turned around. When our eyes met, a slow smile spread across his face.

"Hi, Leila. It's been a long time."

I swallowed hard. "Yes, it has. Hello, Mark."

CHAPTER FIVE

NEXT MONTH, IT WOULD BE five years since I'd seen my former fiancé. Time had been good to Mark. He was more handsome than I remembered. His self-confidence, which had never been lacking, was apparent as he walked across the room and took my hand in his. Mark's short dark curly hair was the same as always. Hazel eyes with flecks of green and gold in them gazed intently into mine, then scanned me up and down. An amused expression came over his face. I wanted to kick myself for not changing out of pajamas.

Mark's lips parted, displaying perfect white teeth. The cleft in his chin deepened as he smiled. "You haven't changed a bit."

"Neither have you." He was dressed in blue jeans and a sweatshirt from Harvard, his alma mater. Despite the casual attire, there was an undeniable air of sophistication about him that I didn't remember from before. He leaned in and kissed me softly on the cheek before I could pull away. Memories flooded my brain. The last time I'd seen Mark, I'd thought my world was ending. Five years was a long time, and I couldn't imagine why he'd come here tonight.

How convenient that my mother had disappeared. I tried to appear calm, but on the inside I was fuming that she'd let him in without telling me first.

"How are you?" he asked.

"Wonderful."

"Sorry to come by so late. Were you in bed?"

"Days on the farm start early." It was a subtle hint, but then again, Mark had never been good at taking subtle hints.

My mother appeared from the kitchen, carrying a tray between her slim hands, and beamed at us. She reminded me of Donna Reed in her white lace apron. The only thing missing was a string of pearls around her neck.

"I thought that you and Mark might like something to nibble on while you talked." She set the tray down on the coffee table. On it were two glasses of *limonada*, the Lebanese version of lemonade, and my mother's famous *maamoul* cookies.

Mark's face lit up like a Christmas tree as he reached for a cookie. "Wow! *Maamouls*! I haven't had these in ages. Mom could never come close to you in the baking department, Selma. Then again, no one can."

My mother's face flushed with pride. Her maamoul cookies were delicious, and they were no easy feat, taking several hours to prepare. They were powdered cookies that resembled Italian wedding cookies and contained rye whiskey and dates.

"What a lovely compliment, Mark. Thank you." Mom smiled gratefully. "Now, if you'll both excuse me, I'm off to bed. Good night."

She avoided my gaze as she hurried up the stairs. My mother was nobody's fool and knew that I was not pleased with her. After she had disappeared, I decided to resign myself to the situation. I sat down in an armchair and gestured at the couch. "Sit down, if you like."

Mark sat down and reached for another cookie. "You look beautiful."

"What are you doing here?" I blurted out. I didn't mean to sound rude, but his visit had unnerved me. I'd convinced myself that I had been over my ex for a long time, but I still bore some resentment toward him.

His tone was apologetic. "I know you're probably not happy to see me, but when my mother told me you were back in town permanently, I had to stop by. I hate the way we left things between us."

"The way we *left* things?" Disbelief and bitterness filled my tone. "You dumped me at the altar, Mark."

"Not exactly." He shook his head. "The wedding wasn't for another month."

I couldn't believe this. "Close enough. You humiliated and embarrassed me. My parents lost out on money for the wedding cake and gown, and I was left with over a hundred gifts to return. So, why do you think I'd be happy to see you now?"

"I'm sorry, Leila." He reached his hand out to touch mine, and the touch was similar to an electric shock traveling through my body. I jerked my hand back, and his face flushed crimson. "You have a right to still be upset with me. It was all my fault. I've wanted to see you for a long time, but I couldn't quite work up the nerve. Nothing will ever excuse my behavior, and I know now that I made a mistake. A terrible one. That's why I'm here."

"Are you saying that you wish we'd never broken up?" After five years, he'd just arrived at this conclusion?

Mark nodded gravely. "I still love you, Leila. I've never stopped loving you."

This was too much. "Sorry, Mark. It's a little too late for that. I've moved on with my life and thought you had too."

He studied my face carefully. "Mom said that you're dating the hired hand at Sappy Endings."

My stomach tightened in anger. Mark spoke the words *hired hand* as if they were something dirty or despicable, and nothing could be further than the truth. "Noah isn't just a hired hand. He's an important part of the farm and a good man." *Far better than you.*

Mark stroked his chin in the same pensive, thoughtful manner he always had. "It wasn't my intention to insult him. And I was sorry to hear about your father. Did you get my flowers? I was in Boston on business the week of his funeral, otherwise I would have come."

"My mother told me that you had sent some." Of course, he could have made time for a phone call, but I refrained from saying so.

Mark was still watching me closely. He'd always been good at guessing my thoughts, and this time was no different. "I should have called when he died. It was a mistake not to, but I honestly didn't know if you'd want to talk to me, on top of everything else that you were going through."

I exhaled sharply. "Okay, if you're here looking for forgiveness, then fine, I forgive you. But I'll never forget."

An awkward silence filled the room. "I don't blame you," Mark said. "What I did was horrible. I realize now how badly I behaved."

I rose from my chair. "Well, it was nice seeing you, but I hope you won't mind if I cut this short. It's been a long week and I'm exhausted."

"Sure, I understand." Mark stood and touched my arm. "I know that I can never make up for what I did, but was wondering if we could go out for dinner this week and talk?"

What on earth was the point? We had nothing left to talk about. I had loved him once, but he hadn't felt the same way about me. "Why?"

"Please," Mark said. "I'd like to talk about you for once, not me. I want to know all about what you've been doing with your life for the past five years. And I want to know that you're happy."

"I am happy," I said quietly. "But I don't understand why that matters to you now."

"It does matter," he insisted. "There's a good chance that I'm moving back to the area this summer, and I'd like it if we could be friends."

This was a surprise. "I heard that you were doing well in New York City."

Mark seemed pleased by my comment. "Ah. Have you been keeping tabs on me?"

Ugh. I struggled not to roll my eyes. This was so typical of him. "No, but my mother has. She and your mother still talk, remember."

His smile faded. "Sorry. My firm is looking to open a satellite office in Bennington, and they've asked if I'm interested in switching locations. The decision is up to me if I want to relocate or not, but I'm leaning toward it." He gazed at me with a longing expression that I hadn't seen since the night he'd asked me to marry him. "I'd like to be close to Sugar Ridge again—and you."

His last two words came out so faintly that I almost didn't hear them. "I see. Well, I hope everything works out for you." There was no doubt in my mind that it would. Things had always worked out the way that Mark wanted. He'd always been popular, sophisticated, and gorgeous, and nothing like me. They said that opposites attract but maybe we had been too different. Polar opposites, in fact.

"Could we have dinner sometime this week?" he persisted. "It would mean a lot to me."

I hesitated for a moment. If I refused again, that wouldn't matter to Mark. He would continue to pester me until I gave in. Or he would call my mother and she would pester me as well. Perhaps it was better to get it over with.

"If I agree, do you promise to leave me alone after that?" I asked.

He looked wounded by my comment. "If that's what you really want, then yes. I promise."

I walked toward the front door, hoping that he would follow, and turned to face him. "I'm not the same person I was five years ago, Mark. And neither are you. If it's that important to you, we can be friends, but that doesn't change the past. Nothing will."

"You never did pull any punches, Leila." A smile ticked up at the corners of his mouth. "That's one of the things I always loved about you."

The use of the word *love* made me cringe inwardly. It had been a bad choice on his part. He reached for the doorknob, but as an afterthought, went back over to the coffee table and picked up another cookie. He gave me a sly wink. "I never could resist your mother's cooking."

To my surprise, Mark leaned down and kissed me on the cheek again. "How does Tuesday night at seven sound? I'll make a reservation at Medium Rare."

I wracked my brain, trying to remember if I had committed to anything else for the evening. "That should be fine."

"Great." Mark smiled disarmingly into my eyes. "Shall I pick you up here?"

"No. I'll probably be working late, so let's just meet at the restaurant."

Mark didn't seem happy about that but didn't press me. "Okay, see you then." As he gripped the doorknob, he said softly, "I hope that Noah knows what a lucky guy he is."

I watched as he got behind the wheel of his BMW. He gave me one final wave, started the engine, and zoomed down the street. When I closed the door and turned around, my mother was standing at the foot of the stairs. The gleam of hope in her eyes was impossible to miss.

"Well?" she asked impatiently. "Does he want to get back together?"

I couldn't believe my ears. "Mom, that's never going to happen. Plus, I already have a boyfriend, remember?"

She waved her hand dismissively in the air, as if swatting at a fly. "Oh, Leila. Noah's a nice man and a hard worker, but you're comparing apples and oranges here."

"Excuse me?"

"You were once engaged to Mark," she explained. "And he's part of our culture. Those things matter."

To my mother, it was as if the five years had never happened. I stared at her, not knowing what to say. She'd been delighted when I first started seeing Noah, but it was as if none of that mattered anymore. In her opinion, no one would ever measure up to Mark.

"This could be a new beginning for the both of you," she said eagerly. "What are you going to wear to dinner Tuesday night?"

Boy, she was really something. My mother had better ears on her than Dumbo. It was annoying but also kind of comical. "Why couldn't you tell me that he was here? I didn't want to see him—and especially in my pajamas! We have nothing left to say to each other."

She threw up her hands. "Oh, for goodness' sake. How was I supposed to tell you? You left your phone on the kitchen table."

"How about, 'Leila, Mark is downstairs?' That should have been easy enough to yell up to me."

Mom blew out a sigh. "You're just like your father. So stubborn."

"I'll take that as a compliment." Dad was never far from my thoughts. He'd once told me that things had a way of happening when you least expected them. But I'd never thought that meant having a former fiancé return after you'd finally gotten him out of your system.

"Good night, Mom. Pleasant dreams."

She let out a huff of irritation and turned on her heel before hurrying back upstairs. Well, the feeling was mutual.

No sooner had my mother disappeared from sight when my phone buzzed from the kitchen table. I hoped to heaven that it wasn't Mark. I picked it up and saw Heather's name on the screen. Grateful, I blew out a sigh of relief. "Oh, wow, I'm so glad it's you. You'll never guess what happened."

"Leila." Heather's voice was strained. "Lei, I—"

My heart stuttered in my chest. "Heather, what is it? Are you all right?"

An anguished wail burst from the phone. "No, I'm not."

I clutched the phone with both hands, thinking the worst. "What's wrong? Did something else happen?"

"Yes." Heather began to sob. "The wedding is off."

CHAPTER SIX

"HEATHER, I DON'T UNDERSTAND," I said. "If both you and Tyler still want to get married, then why is the wedding off?"

She dabbed at her bloodshot eyes with a tissue. Heather's entire face was swollen and blotchy from crying all night. She reached across my desk for another tissue, and pulled Toast close for a hug. I'd brought him to work today, thinking that Heather would need his furry support. I'd been right.

She stroked his fur lovingly. "He's such a good therapy kitty."

Toast gave a little chirp, as if agreeing with her.

I tried again. "Okay. You wouldn't tell me the whole story on the phone last night, so would you please let me know what's going on now? Maybe I can help."

Heather shook her head in dismay. "It's a disaster. There

simply can't be a big wedding with Monica's killer on the loose. Uncle Grant insists that it's inappropriate until the person is brought to justice."

"No offense, and I'm sorry that the woman is dead, but who the heck is your uncle to make such an important decision?"

She shifted uncomfortably in her seat. "My parents have already agreed with him, so the matter's closed."

"But you and Tyler are paying for part of it," I protested. "Don't they realize how much money will be lost?" There was no way that Heather's parents could afford to give their daughter her magical wedding at a later time.

"Let's change the subject," she suggested.

I examined her face closely. "Okay, what is it you're not telling me?"

A tear rolled down Heather's cheek and was lost in Toast's fur. He didn't seem to mind and continued his steady purring while she sniffed. "As far as paying for the wedding, Tyler and I are only taking care of our honeymoon and the band. His parents are paying for the rehearsal dinner, but everything else is being taken care of by my parents—and the loan from Uncle Grant and Monica."

"I see." Now we were getting somewhere. Grant had invested more money into the wedding than I'd originally thought. More than likely, it had been Monica's money, but that point was moot because of her death. I still felt like I didn't know the entire story. "Is he holding the money over your parents' heads?"

She paused and gave a slow nod.

"It's a lot of money for your parents to lose." I found myself wondering why Tyler's parents hadn't offered to foot more of the bill but didn't ask. It was none of my business. Heather's parents may have been too proud to tell them their funds were limited.

Heather blew her nose into a tissue. "I probably sound like the worst bridezilla in the world. But it's always been my dream to have a big wedding."

"Yes, I remember." I reached over to squeeze her hand. "The fairy princess tale."

She nodded and blinked back tears. "Yeah, just like Cinderella. The handsome prince, a beautiful dress, and everyone I love there to see me get married. Well, there's no point in sitting around crying about it anymore. I need to accept the fact my dream wedding is simply not going to happen."

"Don't say that," I protested. "If Monica's killer is found before the wedding date, you can still have your special day."

A small spark appeared in the corner of Heather's eyes. She stared at me, openmouthed. "Lei, will you help me?"

"Of course. What do you need?"

Heather's entire face brightened. "I need you to help me find out who killed Monica."

I almost choked on my maple latte. "Wait, what? Is this some kind of a joke?"

"I'm dead serious." She cringed. "Sorry for the bad pun. Uncle Grant told Dad the police don't have any leads. There were no fingerprints found at the scene of the crime. Well, except for yours and Monica's, of course."

Now it was my turn to wince. "Heather, I'm no detective, and neither are you."

She pointed a finger at me. "Don't sell yourself short. You're the one who found out who killed your father." Heather leaned back in her chair to devour the rest of her breakfast sandwich. My mother made exceptional ones, with scrambled eggs, sausage or smoke-cured bacon, Vermont cheddar cheese, and a spoonful of maple syrup on a homemade biscuit or English muffin. We usually sold out of them by noon. "Come to think of it, I may have helped a little too."

"You did," I agreed. "As for me, it was relentless determination on my part." And somewhat reckless determination as well.

"I understand if you don't want to be in any danger," Heather remarked, "and would never hold that against you. But I've got to try. So, since today is my day off, I'm going shopping in New York this afternoon. At Treasure Chest."

"You're kidding."

She shook her head. "This is about more than my big day, Lei. I can't stand to see my parents lose all their money. Please don't try to talk me out of it, because my mind's made up."

I'd seen that look of determination on Heather's face before. It was the same one she'd worn the day of freshman cheerleading tryouts in high school. There had only been two available spots on the team, and twenty girls auditioning. Heather had risen to the occasion and outshone everyone else that day. She was charming and sweet, but no pushover. When she wanted something, she went after it with everything she had. We were alike in that manner.

"All right." I picked up the office phone. "If it's not busy, I can leave a few minutes early. I'll just need to let Noah know. What time were you thinking of leaving?"

Heather gave a whoop of delight and roused Toast from his nap. "Yes! I knew that you would never let me down."

"What are friends for, right?"

————————

At four o'clock, I locked my office door and almost ran straight into Noah, who was on his way in to see me. He looked apologetic. "Sorry. I thought you weren't leaving for another fifteen minutes."

I held up the cat carrier with Toast inside. "I have to drop the king off at my house before I go and meet Heather. He doesn't like being left alone in the office for too long, and my mother won't be leaving for another hour."

"It's not like he's spoiled or anything." Noah laughed. "By the way, the tractor trailer just departed. Ten fifty-five-gallon drums of our delicious syrup are now on their way to Mexico."

"Wow, terrific." Canada was the top producer and exporter of maple syrup, but we occasionally got orders from other countries. It had been a great sap gathering season, one of our best ever. My father kept meticulous handwritten records for the past twenty-five years, and I'd spent quite a bit of time reviewing them. I knew he was smiling down at me from above.

Noah leaned in close. "So are you." He placed his lips over mine while I wrapped my arms around his neck, basking in the woodsy scent of his cologne. It was intoxicating and enveloped me like a warm blanket on a cold winter's night. I never wanted the kiss to end.

"Was there anything else?" I teased after we finally broke apart.

"If there was, it's gone from my head," he joked, and then snapped his fingers. "Actually, I wanted to remind you I'm taking the day off tomorrow. Em's so excited. It's the first field trip I've ever chaperoned."

"And you're as excited as she is—I can tell." He was such a wonderful father, and I was happy they would have some quality time together. Noah had only missed one day on the farm since I'd been here. "Don't worry, I remembered. The theater production of *You're a Good Man, Charlie Brown*, right?"

He nodded. "Do you want to meet up tomorrow night when we get back?"

With a pang, I remembered my dinner date with Mark. "No, I promised to meet a friend for dinner. How about Wednesday night?"

"Sure," he said noncommittally. "It's no big deal. Be careful this afternoon, okay? No more dead bodies, please."

"We'll be fine."

"I don't know." Noah looked doubtful. "Whenever you and Heather get together, trouble seems to follow."

He had a point. "Don't worry. How much trouble can we get in shopping for diamonds?"

Noah's eyes widened in surprise, and he immediately fell silent, while I cursed to myself. That had been the wrong thing to say. I didn't want Noah to think I was fishing around for an engagement ring. We had never discussed marriage, and the last thing he needed was any pressure from me.

I decided to change the subject. "Look, I'm sorry that I've been so busy lately, but I couldn't tell Heather no. I don't want her going to New York by herself. She's been so upset about the wedding."

"That's understandable." Noah thrust his hands deep into the pockets of his overalls. "Well, you two ladies enjoy yourselves."

For a split second, I almost told him about Mark. Seeing him last night, after all these years, had left me in a vulnerable state, and I needed to talk to someone about it. Poor Heather had her own problems, and there was no way I would ever tell my mother. In a blink of an eye, I was twenty-three years old again, fresh out of college and ready to devote myself to my new lawyer husband. "Noah, I—"

"Haven't you left yet?" My mother was hurrying toward us, wiping her hands on a dish towel. "Noah, I was wondering if you could give me a hand in the café for a minute. There's a bag of flour I can't lift. I tried paging you out in the sugar shack."

"No problem." Noah immediately followed her up the hallway. He acted relieved that she'd interrupted our conversation.

"Do you need me to stay as well?" I called out to my

mother. Heather was probably pacing the floor as she waited for me, but I didn't feel right about taking off and leaving Noah and my mother shorthanded. This was my farm after all, and I expected to take full responsibility.

"No, dear. Go ahead. It's only an hour. I just want to get a head start on some of my baking for tomorrow." She hurried away with Noah but glanced back at me. "You're dropping Toast at home, right?"

"Yes, he's all ready to go."

Noah looked back and waved, as if it were an afterthought. "I'll call you as soon as I get back tonight," I promised, but he didn't respond. It was possible that he hadn't heard me.

When I arrived home, I made sure Toast had food and fresh water and left him napping on the couch. Five minutes later, I pulled into Heather's driveway. She was already waiting outside and practically jumped into the car when she saw me.

"What took you so long? You're ten minutes late." She pulled the seat belt across her lap.

"Sorry. I had to drop Toast back at the house, and it took a little longer than I thought." I always felt guilty leaving the farm before closing, but I knew Noah and my mother could handle things. Like me, they had enough to do. Even when there was no syrup making or sap boiling, there were always plenty of little things to keep us occupied, like lines to be repaired in the sugar bush, syrup to be boxed up for the orders that came in every day, or candle and candy making for the gift shop.

Heather closed her eyes and leaned back in the seat. "I didn't mean to sound like a jerk, Lei. Did you have plans with Noah?"

"Yes, but it's fine," I said.

She opened her eyes and swiveled her head toward me. "Can you see him tomorrow instead?"

I gripped the steering wheel tightly. "No. I'm having dinner with Mark tomorrow night."

Heather nodded absently and pulled her compact out of her purse to check her face. "God, my eyes are still swollen. Maybe some drops would help—" With a gasp, she dropped the compact onto the floor. "What did you say?"

"I'm having dinner with Mark tomorrow night."

"*Mark?* As in Mark Salem?"

"The one and only."

"Did the earth just move?" Heather wanted to know. "Because I never thought this day would come. Why are you going out on a date with that man, after what he did to you?"

"It's not a date," I said. "He stopped by the house last night and was very insistent on us having a chance to talk. I only agreed because, well, you know Mark. He won't stop asking me until I go."

Heather's eyes became as round as dinner plates. "Okay, slow down. He came to your house last night? Why am I only hearing about this now?"

"Because I didn't have a chance to tell you earlier," I said simply. "It wasn't the right time."

Heather looked so miserable I was afraid she might start

to cry again. I reached over and squeezed her hand. "Will you stop? It's all good. I didn't see the point in bringing it up when your entire world was crashing down."

"It would have been the perfect time," she said sadly. "It would have distracted me from all of the chaos going on in my life right now. Look at how selfish I'm becoming."

"You're not being selfish. Think positive. Everything is going to work out."

Heather was silent for several seconds. "Have you told Noah the real reason why you and Mark broke up?" she asked.

I gripped the steering wheel tightly between my hands. "No. He never asked."

She mulled that over for a few seconds. "You should tell him, Lei, before your relationship gets more serious."

"I know." We both fell silent for a minute. I thought back to that awful day again, when Mark had shown up at the house unexpectedly and suggested we go for a drive. An hour later I'd returned with a broken heart and tearfully told my parents the wedding was off. My mother almost had a stroke. She was certain I'd done something to make Mark change his mind and wanted to know what it had been. The only person who knew the truth was Heather.

She shot me a sympathetic look. "Are you afraid of Noah's reaction?"

I shrugged. "Maybe a little, but Noah is not Mark." The two men couldn't be more different. Mark had always been ambitious, doubling up on courses in college so that he could graduate early and start law school a year sooner.

As a husband, father, and former Marine, Noah had seen a lot more of the world and approached everything with a calm demeanor. He was more laid back than Mark and didn't fly off the handle as easily. Maybe he had been completely different before the death of his wife, but somehow, I doubted it.

"You'll figure it out," she said confidently. "I have every faith in you."

"It works both ways," I remarked. "You're going to have your dream wedding, and I don't want to hear any more about it being canceled. I'm already planning to stuff myself with cake that day."

She laughed as I swung the car into the parking lot of a tiny strip mall around five thirty. Treasure Chest was sandwiched in between a café and bookstore. There was a line of people out the door of the café, most likely dining after work or bringing takeout home. Due to the onslaught of traffic, we were forced to park at the other end of the mall.

Heather nodded toward the crowd. "If your mother was in there doing the cooking, people would be waiting down the block."

She spoke the truth. During the winter months when we were busy gathering sap, the café was a lifeline for the farm. Syrup brought in decent money all year round, but we had a steady group of customers who depended on their breakfast sandwiches, baklava, and maple lattes every day.

"She's a big reason we're turning a profit this year." At first, I hadn't been crazy about the idea of working so closely with my mother all day, but most of the time she stayed out

of my way, and I tried to do the same. She was never supposed to be a permanent employee and had recently started
to hint how it would be nice to take on an extra part-time
helper, in case she wanted to take an occasional day off. I'd
posted an ad online earlier today and hoped we would find
someone soon.

Treasure Chest consisted of a large showroom with glass
counters that extended around the perimeter of the room
to form a rectangle. The cases contained all types of gold,
silver, and diamond jewelry that lit up the room like daz-
zling fireworks in a night sky.

"What excuse can we give for coming in?" Heather
stopped to admire a diamond tennis bracelet. "There's no
way I can afford anything here."

I removed my watch from my wrist. "I think the battery's dying. I'll ask to have a new one put in."

"Look at this, Lei." Heather pointed at a case of custom
jeweled knives and shuddered. "They make me think of
what happened to Monica."

I studied the contents. "Yeah, except the knife that killed
her wasn't like these. That one had a ruby on the handle. It
must have been fake though." I wished I'd thought to take
a picture of the weapon but hadn't exactly been thinking
clearly at the time.

"They look like antiques," Heather observed. There
were several with silver handles and a few with emeralds
decorating them.

"Quite right," someone with an English accent answered.
We looked up to a see a man in his fifties watching us

with a shrewd expression. He wore a black suit and red bow tie, and bowed politely at us. "Would you like to see one, ladies?" he asked.

"No, thank you. But they are quite extraordinary." I took a moment to study the man. He was about my height, with a balding head and handlebar mustache.

"Indeed," the man agreed. "I once worked for a knife distributor, but their quality was lacking. Their knives were the type that you see advertised on television as a buy-one-get-one-free set. These are vintage and have all been restored to their former glory."

"They're beautiful," Heather said in awe.

"I think so. In fact, I'm the one who talked the owner into purchasing them." He rubbed his hands together in satisfaction. "Now, how can I be of assistance, ladies?"

I held out my watch to him. "Can you put a new battery in this? It's been losing time every day."

The man squinted down at the face of my watch. It had been a Christmas gift to me from my parents a few years ago, and I treasured it, mostly because I knew that my father had been the one to pick it out. "Hmm. I know that I don't have the proper battery in stock, but I could order it. Would you care to leave this with me in the meantime? I'll have it cleaned for you as well."

"I guess that would be okay." I recited my name and phone number, and watched the man as he wrote them down on a slip of paper.

Heather pointed at the diamond bracelet she'd been eyeing. "I was wondering how many carats are in this bracelet. And the price," she added, as if it were an afterthought.

The man lifted one caterpillar-like eyebrow at her as he approached the case. He took a key ring from his pocket and unlocked the case, then displayed the bracelet on his arm for Heather to view. She gasped in excitement.

"Four carats," he said. "And the price is twenty thousand dollars." He pointed at another one next to it that didn't sparkle quite as brightly. "This magnificent piece is only fifteen thousand and has three carats. Quite a bargain, if I do say so myself, madam."

"They're both lovely," Heather sighed, "but a little out of my price range."

I attempted to hold back a snort. Yeah, a little out of our price ranges by about fifteen thousand dollars. "Do you have the prices all memorized?"

He tapped the side of his head. "It's all in here, madam. I know everything about this store. Far more than even the owner did. May she rest in peace, of course."

Heather smiled sweetly at him. "Are you Jason, by any chance?"

"Indeed." The man puffed out his chest. "Jason Ambrose, store manager, at your service." He reached into his breast pocket and handed each of us a business card.

Heather clasped the card and his hand between both of hers. "I'm Heather Turcot. We were passing through on the way to visit my uncle Grant—Butterfield, that is."

The glass lid of the case slipped between Jason's fingers

and fell into place with a thud. His eyes widened in suspicion. "I didn't know that Monica had a niece."

"Yes, Monica married my uncle a few years back," Heather explained. "And she always said such nice things about you."

I knew that Heather was fibbing, but marveled at how naturally she'd managed to pull it off. Lying had never come easily to my friend.

Jason's mouth twitched slightly. "Did she now?" He opened his mouth to say something else, but the phone rang, and he hurried behind the main counter to answer it. "Good evening, Treasure Chest." He listened for a moment, his nostrils flaring. "No comment." He slammed the phone back down into its cradle.

"Another reporter?" I asked.

He frowned at me. "I hardly think that is any of your business, young lady. But if you must know, yes. The phone has not stopped ringing since Monica's death. It's not like I don't have enough to do around here."

"We heard she wasn't easy to work with," I volunteered, hoping Jason would take the bait.

He put his hands on his hips. "All right, ladies, what exactly do you want? Are you here to make sure that I'm doing my job? Or perhaps you're reporting back to Grant?"

"Oh no, I'm sorry if we gave you that impression." Heather hesitated for a second. "The truth of the matter is that Monica was killed at my bridal shower."

Jason brought a hand to his mouth. "Oh. So, you're the bride-to-be who found her!"

Heather flushed and shook her head. "Actually, Leila's the one who found Monica."

Jason looked at me with new interest, and I sighed. "We were wondering if you had any idea of who might have killed her."

"The police have already been here, ladies," Jason said in an amused tone. "I'm afraid you're too late to play cop today."

He was a bit arrogant, but I found his snooty attitude entertaining. "Jason, please. This is very important. If Monica's killer isn't found, Heather will have to cancel the wedding. Her parents have spent a lot of money, and she doesn't want to see them lose it."

His face softened as he studied Heather's delicate face. "I don't know what I can tell you…" Jason sighed. "All right. The woman is dead, so I can be frank. Monica Butterfield was not my favorite person. Then again, she wasn't anyone's favorite person, including Grant's." He fixed catlike green eyes on us, as if ready to pounce. "And should either one of you dare to repeat this to anyone, I'll simply deny it was ever said."

"We won't say a word," Heather promised.

"What didn't you like about her?" I pressed.

Jason's mouth twitched. "How much time do you have? The woman was an albatross hanging around my neck. I've managed this shop for the past ten years, without a word of gratitude from Madam Butterfield. I've worked Sundays by myself, overtime, stayed late when necessary, and even sacrificed my days off when needed. But did she ever bother to say thank you? Not once, madam, not once. I have a life too, you know."

"Of course," Heather said sympathetically.

He sniffed. "As manager of Treasure Chest, I was hired with the promise that I would get to run things as I pleased. Of course, it didn't happen. Monica was always breezing in here whenever she felt like it, wanting to know why there weren't more sales and jacking up the prices when it suited her. She was rude to the customers, and her mouth had no filter. Shall I go on?"

"Not necessary," I assured him. "I met her at the shower."

Jason's face and the top of his head were a bright shade of pink. He reached into his suit pocket for a handkerchief, which he dabbed against his forehead. "Apologies, ladies. It's wrong to speak ill of the dead, I know."

"If things were so bad, why didn't you quit?" I asked.

"Because Monica told me when she retired in two years, I would be her first choice to sell the store to." Jason stared into space and a gleam came into his deep-set eyes. "Maybe now that she's gone, I'll finally get my chance."

CHAPTER SEVEN

HEATHER AND I EXCHANGE A surprised glance. Jason may not have meant anything by the remark, but it almost sounded like he was glad Monica had died. She'd been standing in his way all along, and now he was free to run Treasure Chest as he pleased. If that didn't sound like a motive to kill, I didn't know what was.

Jason must have realized what he'd implied and stared at us sheepishly. "Surely you don't think—no. That's not what I meant."

Patiently, we waited for him to go on.

In desperation, Jason wrung his hands together. "All right, I'll admit I wasn't fond of the woman, but I never would have caused her any physical harm." He paused. "I'd have to get in line anyway—behind her family and so-called friends."

"Are you saying a member of Monica's family might have killed her?" Heather's face instantly paled.

"I seem to be sticking my foot in my mouth today." Jason glanced over his shoulder at the surveillance camera mounted on the wall. "I don't mean members of *your* immediate family, my dear. I'm talking about Monica's husband and son. Grant and Devon Butterfield."

"You can't be serious," Heather sputtered.

"Did you know the two of them were talking about a divorce?" Jason asked.

Heather's mouth dropped open. "I had no idea."

Jason seemed to enjoy the part of tattletale. "Grant's been having affairs for years. And as for Devon, that son of hers is a spoiled brat who's never learned to stand on his own two feet. He's, what, twenty-six now? They had an argument about something, and Monica threatened to cut off his allowance."

"Any idea what they fought about?" I asked.

He let out a snort. "Maybe she figured it was about time the baby became a man."

"Tell us about Grant's mistress," I said.

Jason's eyes shone like emeralds. "I don't know who the unlucky woman is. She may not even be local. Monica once mentioned to me that Grant went away on trips for a business he's been trying to start up. Research, she called it."

Heather furrowed her brow. "I don't know of any business that Uncle Grant owns."

Jason clucked his tongue against the roof of his mouth. "Come, come now, darling. No offense, but your uncle doesn't have enough ambition to start his own business. Monica was lying. She didn't want the truth to get out."

"What exactly is the truth?" I asked.

He looked pleased with himself. "Only that Grant was looking for someone to warm his bed, and Monica clearly wasn't interested anymore. The love went out of their marriage as soon as they said, 'I do.' In all honesty, I'm not sure they ever loved each other. It was more of a marriage of convenience."

The phrase made me cringe inwardly, thinking about my own defunct engagement. I'd once overheard a distant relative say the same thing about Mark's and my union. The words had cut me deeply. Our relationship may have started out as arranged by our parents, but I'd quickly fallen head over heels in love with Mark, and he with me. Or so I'd thought at the time.

"Okay, let me get this straight," I said. "Grant may have murdered Monica because he wanted to be with someone else, while Devon could have killed his mother because she was cutting off his allowance?"

Jason tossed his head. "Devon couldn't stand his mother. They were barely on speaking terms when she died. Somewhere in his delusional brain, Devon thought that if he refused to talk to his mother or see her, she'd start giving him money again. Who knows? It might have worked if she wasn't murdered."

"Will Devon take over the store now?" I asked.

Jason picked up a cloth and started polishing the glass case until it shone. "I think that's highly unlikely. All he's interested in is cash for himself and keeping that ditzy girlfriend of his in diamonds."

"That would be Alexis," Heather volunteered. "My mother told me he'd been dating someone. Did Monica like her?"

Jason examined his work. Satisfied with the cleaning job, he put the cloth behind the counter. "Not at first, but she did a one-hundred-and-eighty-degree turn a few months ago. Don't ask me why. She once referred to Lexy as trailer trash, so something significant must have happened to change her mind. Personally, I have my doubts Devon will ever marry the girl. They've been dating for five years, and he still hasn't put a ring on it yet."

Heather's eyes widened. "I had no idea they'd been dating for so long. I never heard a word about it."

Even though there was no one else in the store, Jason lowered his voice. "I believe he's just using the poor girl, and she's too dumb to know the difference. Sorry if that sounds harsh, but I call them as I see them."

It was refreshing how he didn't pull any punches. I leaned across the counter eagerly. "How did Lexy feel about Monica?"

"Smudges!" Jason clucked his tongue like a chicken and picked up the cloth. "Now look what you've done. Do try to be careful, madam."

Heather and I watched as Jason tsk-tsked and removed my fingerprints.

"Sorry about that." I said. "Please tell us more about Devon's girlfriend."

Jason puckered his lips together in disapproval. "There's not much to tell. Like I said, Lexy Snyder keeps waiting for her big day. It's obvious she's over the moon for Devon, but I don't think he feels the same way. Maybe one day the young lady will wake up and realize she's wasting her time. She seems to be missing a few brain cells."

"You didn't answer my question," I said. "Did Lexy care for Monica?"

"Oh, please." Jason snickered. "Who would want that woman for a mother-in-law? Monica once said that Lexy came right out and blamed her for being the reason Devon hadn't proposed yet. Lexy insisted Monica told Devon that if he married her, she'd cut him off from the family fortune." He made a face. "Honestly, I wouldn't have put it past her." His cell phone buzzed, and he held up a hand. "Pardon me for a moment, ladies."

"Wow," Heather whispered. "We were searching for motives, and it looks like we've got plenty."

I glanced at the wall clock. "I think we've found out all we're going to for tonight. Are you ready to take off?"

"If you want to." There was a note of reluctance in Heather's voice.

"Did you have something else in mind?"

She bit into her lower lip. "No, don't worry about it."

"Come on, where do you want to go?" As soon as I'd said the words, it dawned on me. "Ah-ha. You want to stop and see Grant, don't you?"

Heather swallowed nervously. "I don't really *want* to but feel like we should at least stop and talk to him. And I'd rather not do it at Monica's wake where everyone, including my parents, can overhear."

"What the heck are we going to say?" Grant might be her uncle, but they had never been close, so it was bound to be an awkward situation. "You can't exactly come out and ask if he murdered his wife. It wouldn't go over well."

"Don't say things like that!" she exclaimed. "Can you imagine what would happen if he did do it? My parents would freak out. Tyler and I would have to run off to Vegas to get married."

She was right. Things would become far worse for her family. "Any word on the funeral arrangements yet?"

Heather pulled her phone out of her purse and studied the screen. "Funny that you should ask. Mom just texted and said Monica's body was released earlier today, and the funeral home has already transported her back to New York."

"That sounds awfully fast," I remarked.

She shrugged. "I guess the funeral director came to get Monica. Mom said my uncle knows him personally. Uncle Grant also went ahead and scheduled the wake for tomorrow night. He told my father he just wants to get it over with as soon as possible. The service is from four to eight, and the funeral is Wednesday morning." She looked at me pleadingly. "Can you come to the wake with me? Tyler won't be able to get there until around seven. What time are you meeting Mark?"

"Not until seven, but Noah's taking the day off, which means that if the farm and café are busy, I'll need to stay late." The farm had to come first, and it was rare I ever left exactly at five o'clock. Today had been an exception.

"Please?" Heather begged. "It would give you a chance to talk to everyone about Monica."

I had to laugh. "More detective work?"

"Come on, Lei," she pleaded. "With all of my relatives there, I'll have to be on my very best behavior."

"Which means no asking questions for you," I added.

She nodded. "Exactly. I have to be careful what I say around them. It will be easier for you because no one will be paying any attention to you."

"Gee, thanks," I mocked.

"Sometimes people are more likely to say things to strangers," Heather observed. "Maybe you could find out things about her. It would also give you a chance to watch Uncle Grant and Devon, and maybe check out Lexy as well." She furrowed her brow. "What was it I read once? Every murderer—"

"Is someone's best friend?" I guessed. "Agatha Christie said that."

She snapped her fingers. "No—wait, I've got it. People who commit a murder will always show up at the funeral so they don't throw any more suspicion upon themselves."

It made sense to me. The last wake I'd attended was my father's. I hadn't known it at the time, but his killer had been at both the wake and funeral. "All right. As long as the farm isn't busy and I get out on time, I'll be there."

The more I thought about it, maybe this wasn't such a bad idea after all. I could change my clothes at the farm, then drive over to the funeral home. I'd leave from there to meet Mark at Medium Rare. It would give my mother one less opportunity to grill me about dinner with my ex.

"Awesome. Thanks, Lei." The worry lines started to disappear from Heather's delicate features. "Let's stop and see

Uncle Grant. Maybe we could find a bakery on the way. I wish I'd thought to ask you to bring something from the café."

"And your uncle won't think it's weird that we traveled all this way to bring him some cookies?"

"People always bring food when someone dies," Heather explained. "Besides, we're only an hour away."

He was her uncle, after all, even if they had never been close. "Okay, fine. I was only afraid that we might raise his suspicion."

Heather lowered her eyes to the floor. "I wasn't exactly honest with you, Lei. My parents haven't been saving money for ages. They were at first, but—"

"But what?" I asked.

"My father lost his job a while back," Heather said sadly. "They didn't want me to tell anyone. Dad was so embarrassed, even though it was cutbacks and not his fault. Anyway, they had to use most of their savings for daily expenses until he found something else. Mom and Dad knew how important the wedding was to me, so they went to Monica and Uncle Grant for a loan for almost all of it."

"I wish you had said something sooner," I told her gently.

"And I wish that I'd been more practical like you. You never wanted your parents to spend so much money on your wedding."

"Everyone wants different things out of life. There's nothing wrong with that." My mother was the one who'd wanted a big affair for me, partially because she and my father had been married at the courthouse. It was one more thing we had argued about.

I shifted my purse on my shoulder. "Let's tell Jason goodbye and head on over to Grant's."

Heather looked worried. "Do you think we ought to call first? What if he's not up to accepting visitors?"

"No, let's just drive over there. If we call first, that will put him on guard."

Jason ended his call and walked back over to us. "Sorry about that, ladies. Two guesses who was on the phone."

"Grant?" I asked.

Jason's face looked as if it had been carved out of stone, and I wondered what happened. "No, that was the lovely Alexis Snyder, trying to track down her boyfriend. Devon has disappeared, which he has a habit of doing most nights. She mistakenly thought he might be here. Rumor has it that the young Mr. Butterfield is to be the new owner of Treasure Chest."

Heather sucked in some air. "Didn't you say you were to buy the place?"

"I wanted to." Jason's voice was as cool as an icicle. "Monica promised I would get first dibs when the time came, but it just goes to show you can't trust anyone. Apparently, she told Devon a few months back that she'd changed her will and was leaving the store to him. Nice, huh?"

"I'm so sorry," Heather said sympathetically.

His mouth hardened into a fine line. "Granted, the will hasn't been read yet, but why would Monica lie about it? If

Devon does decide to sell at some point, he's going to want a sum far larger than I can afford."

"That's a shame," I remarked.

He sniffed. "It may be time to consider turning in my notice and getting away from the Butterfield family. Now, if you ladies will excuse me, I'm closing up early. I'm done with talking about the Butterfields tonight."

"It was nice meeting you," Heather said, but Jason had already turned on his heel and was on his way into the back room. The man was clearly furious, and I didn't blame him.

We walked out of the store and got into the car. "Well, that was interesting."

"What do you think?" Heather asked as I started the engine.

"Honestly? I think if Jason didn't already hate Monica and her family, he certainly does now."

Heather nodded. "At least he was cooperative. And helpful."

"Maybe a little too helpful. Don't forget, he had a motive too." I didn't want to think that Jason had been responsible for Monica's death, but at this stage, anything was possible.

I pulled up Google maps on my phone. "What's the address of Grant's house?"

"Twenty-three Maiden Lane," Heather replied.

After I punched the address into my phone, we took off. Heather spotted a bakery along the way, and we quickly stopped so that she could run in and pick up a chocolate cake. While I waited, I sent off a text to Noah to tell him we were still in New York. He didn't respond.

The sky was already growing dark when we pulled onto Grant's street about ten minutes later. Grant and Monica lived in a large brick Colonial, set on a corner lot in a newer subdivision. The entire area had more of a spring feel to it than Sugar Ridge did at this time of the year. The lawns were already a lush green with flowers starting to bloom. Because we lived in a higher elevation and the temperatures were cooler, spring was still a work in progress for us.

Heather pulled into the marble-paved driveway. There were no cars to be seen, and only one small light emitting from an upstairs window. "Maybe we should have called first," she said. "It looks like no one's home."

"Oh well." I leaned back against the seat. "At least it didn't take us long to get here. Plus, we did find out a lot of information from Jason. The night wasn't a total loss."

We got out of the car and climbed the stairs to the wraparound porch. The mailbox next to the door was over-stuffed with letters, as if someone hadn't been home in a while. "Do you think he's staying here?" I asked. "Jason said that Grant and Monica were having problems. Maybe they'd already separated."

Heather shrugged and pressed her finger against the doorbell. The musical notes from the song "Diamonds Are a Girl's Best Friend" echoed through the entire house. "I should have known," she sighed.

We waited a minute before ringing the bell again, but there was still no answer. Heather and I stepped off the porch and walked back to her car. I could tell that she was disappointed. "Don't worry," I said. "We'll see him at the wake. I'll make small talk with him and see what I can find out."

As I opened the car door, I happened to glance up at the dark sky. A wisp of white smoke was floating upward through the air and disappeared. For a moment, I didn't understand what was happening. Another strand of smoke followed, and I hurried around to the side of the house.

"What's wrong?" Heather called out. "Where are you going?"

I reached the backyard and spotted smoke coming from one section of the roof. "Call 9-1-1!" I screamed. "The house is on fire!"

As Heather ran back to the car with the cake to grab her cell, I ran around the perimeter of the house, trying doors, but they were all locked. Even though no one had answered our knock, I was fearful someone might be inside, either asleep or unaware of the fire.

I was about to give up when I found an open garage window. When I climbed through it, I noticed a black Mercedes parked inside. I spotted a door that connected to the rest of the house and placed my palm over its surface. The door was cold. Holding my breath, I opened it. A vestibule lead to a large modern kitchen filled with stainless-steel appliances. I raced through it, yelling at the top of my lungs. "Hello! Mr. Butterfield? Are you in here?"

"Leila!" Heather screamed from outside. "Where are you?"

The kitchen led to a hallway that connected to a large comfortable-looking family room on the left. To the right was a closed door. Smoke billowed out from underneath it. A spiral staircase was in between the two. For a moment, I stood stock-still, trying to decide what to do next. I ran to the front door and opened it, then almost ran straight into Heather, who was standing on the front porch.

"Thank God," she cried. "I was afraid you might be trapped."

"Quick! Are there any bedrooms on the bottom floor?" I asked impatiently.

She furrowed her brow. "I—no. They're all upstairs. My mother once told me that—"

I didn't wait for her to finish. "Let me check upstairs and make sure no one's there."

"Leila!" Heather grabbed my arm. "Don't go back in there!"

I shook her off and went back in the house, taking the stairs two at a time. I checked all of the bedrooms, but they were unoccupied. As I hurried back down the stairs, a horn from an oncoming fire truck could be heard. Smoke had started to fill the area, and I instantly became light-headed. I started to cough and panicked, rushing for the front door. My foot slipped and I went down in a heap, cracking my head against the hardwood floor. Helpless, I remained lying on the floor, too stunned to move.

CHAPTER EIGHT

FORTUNATELY FOR MY SAKE, HEATHER looked inside and saw what had happened to me. She began screaming at the top of her lungs. Within seconds, two firefighters were inside as well, helping Heather to lift me off the floor. I was carried outside and seated on the back of an EMT van. An oxygen mask was placed over my face, but after a couple of minutes, I removed it. "I'm fine, thanks."

"What in God's name were you doing in there?" The firefighter, whose ID tag identified him as Phillips, wanted to know.

Heather threw her arms around my neck, practically strangling me in the process. "This is my uncle's house, sir. His name is Grant Butterfield. We stopped by to see how he was doing when Leila spotted smoke coming from the roof. She was worried he might be inside."

"We confirmed there's no one in the house." Phillips

frowned at me. "That was a brave thing you did, miss, but not terribly bright. You could have been killed. Next time, wait until help arrives, all right?"

I sincerely hoped there wouldn't be a next time. "Yes, sir."

"Are you having any problems breathing?" Phillips asked.

"No, no. I'm all right. Thank you."

Satisfied with my response, Phillips joined the rest of his crew, who were busy unraveling the hose from their truck. Heather and I stood next to each other and watched as they went to work on the blaze. Within a few minutes we heard someone yell, "It's out!"

Heather kept her arm around my shoulders, as if to support me. She gently touched the bump on my forehead. "Maybe you should go the emergency room and have that checked."

I waved a hand dismissively. "I'm all right, just a little embarrassed." And I was grateful to Heather. Things could have gone very differently if she hadn't been around. "I'm glad you had my back."

"Always, girlfriend."

A small crowd had gathered across the street, most likely neighbors observing the entire scene play out. Heather and I watched as a white Cadillac screeched to a halt in front of the driveway, blocking off the fire truck. A second later, Grant Butterfield could be seen sprinting toward the house, his face the same color as the flames. Phillips caught him before he could enter.

"Whoa! Hold on a second. Do you live here, sir?" Phillips asked.

"Of course, I live here!" Grant barked. "What is the meaning of this? What's happened to my house?"

Phillips placed a hand on his shoulder. "The fire's under control, sir. We've managed to contain it to one room at the rear." He nodded at us. "You're lucky these two young ladies happened to see the smoke."

"Indeed." A flicker of annoyance crossed Grant's face as he approached us. He pointed at Heather. "Why are *you* here? Haven't you done enough already?"

Heather's face fell. She was clearly devastated by his words. "Uh, Uncle Grant, we came to offer our condolences. And chocolate cake," she added. "We wanted to see how you were doing—"

"Monica's death wasn't Heather's fault." I was horrified that he'd tried to pin his wife's murder on my friend.

Grant pointed a sausage-like finger at me. "You two are up to something. What are you *really* doing here?"

"If it wasn't for them, your entire house could have been destroyed," Phillips said calmly.

"Oh my God!" someone screamed.

We all looked up and saw Devon rushing across the lawn toward his stepfather, a look of horror on his face. "What happened?" he asked in between gulps of air.

Grant dabbed at his wide forehead with a handkerchief. "I don't know. A fire started in the house. This doesn't make any sense. I only left here about an hour ago, and everything was fine."

Devon shifted his focus to Heather and me. "Did you both come here to see Grant—I mean, my stepfather?"

"We brought cake." Heather's cheeks turned a dusky pink, and an uncomfortable silence followed.

Devon wrinkled his nose at her and turned back to his stepfather. "Thank God you weren't inside."

Phillips gestured at me. "This young lady was brave enough to go inside and check to see if you were at home."

Grant's mouth tightened. "How did you get in?"

"The garage window was unlocked." I started to babble as I always did when nervous. "I was worried you or someone else might be asleep, so—"

The older man's eyes darkened and narrowed, sending a chill down my spine. "How fortunate that you happened to be nearby."

"What exactly are you saying?" Heather's nostrils flared. My friend didn't lose her temper often, but when she did, she was like a volcano getting ready to erupt. She took a step toward her uncle and waved a finger in his face. "Leila risked her life trying to make sure no one was inside. Including you, Uncle Grant. I know you're probably in shock, but you could at least thank her."

My face grew warm, but not from the heat of the fire. I hated to be the center of attention. "Heather, it's fine. I'm glad no one was hurt."

Grant clucked his tongue in disapproval. "Young lady, I will need to speak to your father about your lack of respect for elders. I don't know where he went wrong."

A tall fireman came over to Phillips. "We'll need to wait for the arson inspector but found this among the debris." He opened his gloved hand to reveal a pipe. "Looks like someone was smoking and either dropped it on the floor or forgot it was there."

Grant's mouth fell. "That's impossible. I don't smoke and neither does Devon."

"And I don't live here anymore," Devon added quickly. "What room did you find it in?"

"It looked like some type of study," Phillips volunteered. "There was a wooden desk and built-in bookcases. Someone left a stack of papers on the desk, and the pipe was lying in the middle of them."

"That was my mother's study." Devon sniffled and rubbed his eyes. "It's where she kept all of her paperwork related to her business. God, how I miss her."

The heated look Grant shot him was so intense that I half expected Devon's face to melt. I wasn't sure what Devon said to annoy him. Had someone been deliberately trying to destroy something in Monica's study, and did it have anything to do with Treasure Chest?

"Was there jewelry in the study?" I asked.

"Of course not," Grant said stiffly. "We have safes for them at the store, obviously."

I didn't like the condescending tone in which he spoke to me but decided to let it go. There was no proof Grant had anything to do with the fire. For all I knew, his attitude was due to his wife's death and the destruction of their home.

"And your wife?" Phillips asked. "Where is she?"

Devon shifted from one foot to another and cleared his throat. "Uh, my mother was murdered over the weekend, sir."

Phillips looked startled by the revelation. "I'm so sorry."

"Grant, I think you should come home with me tonight." Devon turned to the firefighter, as if to further explain. "My stepdad's been under a lot of stress since my mother's death."

"Of course." Phillips's expression was sympathetic. "That's perfectly understandable." He nodded at a police officer who was approaching us. "Hello, Officer Parks. This is the gentleman who owns the house, Grant Butterfield."

I noticed how Grant's ruddy complexion started to grow noticeably pale as he stretched out a hand to the police officer. "Thank you for coming, Officer."

"Sorry to hear about your house, but I'm glad no one was hurt." Officer Park's gaze shifted to Devon, then over to Heather and me. "Are these your kids?"

"No," Grant almost spat out. "That is, I mean—this is my stepson, Devon Butterfield. The blond woman is my niece, Heather."

Grant didn't bother to introduce me. Maybe it was better to fly under the radar.

"Butterfield," Officer Parks repeated and stared curiously at Grant. "I heard about what happened to your wife. I'm very sorry for your loss."

"Thank you." Grant removed a handkerchief from his pocket and wiped his eyes. "I'm still in shock over what happened. Monica was loved by so many people."

Heather nudged me in the ribs, as if afraid I might say something.

The officer made notes on his iPad. "Is there any chance this incident could be related to your wife's death?"

Grant puffed out his chest. The gesture reminded me of a rooster strutting around. "There's every chance." He shot us a death glare. "And for the record, I don't believe it's a coincidence that these two women happened to be nearby."

"What are you suggesting?" I asked in disbelief.

"Dad," Devon spoke up calmly. "We have no proof they were involved in starting the fire."

Heather's jaw dropped. "Uncle Grant, I can't believe you would even say such a thing. We were in the area, so we thought we'd stop by and see how you were doing."

"I didn't say you started it," Grant fumed. "But I know what you're up to, missy. You're acting like some kind of Nancy Drew wannabe. All you're worried about is your wedding, not my poor wife!" He began to sob into his hands.

Maybe Grant did miss Monica, but I thought his performance was a bit over the top.

Officer Parks held up a hand. "Okay, let's try to calm down, people. This is understandably a difficult situation for everyone involved. If it's a case of arson, and I'm not saying that it is yet, we'll know when the inspector gets here." He smiled cordially at Heather and me. "Ladies, can I have your phone numbers if I need to get in touch?"

We recited our numbers and waited as he typed them into his iPad. "Thanks. You're both free to leave."

But I wasn't ready to leave. I wanted to find out what was in Monica's study that someone wanted destroyed, and why Grant was trying to win an Academy Award for his performance. I hesitated for a moment, trying to think of a way to prolong our departure. Unfortunately, there didn't seem to be one.

Always the better person, Heather went to her uncle and put her arms around him. "I am very sorry about Aunt Monica. Please let us know if you need anything."

Grant gave her a cordial nod as he walked toward the house with Officer Parks. He didn't even bother to acknowledge me.

Devon called after him. "I'll walk the ladies to their car and be right back, Grant."

Once we reached the vehicle, Devon opened the driver's side door for me. "I'm really sorry about what my step-dad said to you both. He hasn't been himself since Mom's death."

"That's all right." Heather smiled. "I feel awful that she died at my bridal shower."

"Do you have any idea who would have wanted to hurt your mother?" I asked suddenly.

Devon shook his head. "Mom and I weren't on the best terms lately. I don't really know what was going on in her life. She had certain plans for me that I disagreed with."

Was he talking about Lexy? "We heard you're the new owner of Treasure Chest," I couldn't resist saying.

He looked startled by my comment. "Boy, news travels fast. I don't have any plans to become a businessman, though. There're better things to do with my life."

I was amazed by his admission and remembered what Jason had said. Devon was only a couple of years younger than me but had never even held a job. I couldn't imagine not working for a living. Monica may have been rich, but at least she'd gone into the store daily. How could a person live like that?

"Do you think you'll sell the store?" Heather wanted to know.

Devon shrugged. "Eventually. For now, there are other people to run it for me. Personally, I'm not crazy about the manager, but he's knowledgeable enough." A malicious grin spread across his face. "I'll bet he was ticked to hear I was going to inherit the place. The guy's wanted to buy the place for years. When the time comes to sell, maybe I'll just have to the double the asking price. Serves that pompous windbag right."

"Why don't you like him?" Devon's attitude about Jason bothered me.

He wrinkled his nose. "Because he looks down his nose at me. I overheard him once tell my mother that I needed to get a job, for my own sake. Then, all of a sudden, she cuts off my allowance. It must have been because of him."

"You don't know for certain," Heather pointed out.

"Oh, but I do," Devon said. "And you know what? I wouldn't be surprised if he was the one to set my mother's house on fire. He'd do something like that out of spite. If I find out it was him, he's going to be sorry."

Heather raised her eyebrows at me. We both knew Jason had nothing to do with the fire. I thought about saying as much, but then Devon would know that we'd been at Treasure Chest prior to coming here. It was best to keep silent for now. Besides, Heather didn't need any more headaches.

Devon's phone buzzed. He glanced down at his screen, and I caught a flicker of irritation cross his face. "Please excuse me, ladies. It's my girlfriend. Lexy and my mother were quite close, so I need to tell her what's going on. Thanks for stopping by."

Heather handed him the cake, and we got inside the vehicle. We watched Devon make his way across the lawn with his phone pressed against his ear.

"This is all too weird," Heather murmured as we drove away.

I glanced at the clock on the radio. It was five minutes past eight. "Honestly? The fire must be related to Monica's murder. The person who started it was looking for something in her study, but what? And who are they?"

She shrugged. "I wish we knew. Devon sure has a grudge against Jason. Doesn't it strike you as weird that Monica left the jewelry store to Devon instead of my uncle?"

"Not really," I said. "Jason told us Monica and Grant weren't getting along. If only we knew the woman that he was having an affair with. Maybe she was his motivation for getting rid of Monica."

Heather rubbed her eyes wearily. "Something tells me Monica's wake is going to be quite the spectacle. I wish we could do some more checking around tomorrow, but I know you've got to work, and I have a full day at the hair salon."

I stopped for a traffic light and sighed. "To be honest, I'd rather stay at Monica's wake and ask questions instead of meeting Mark tomorrow night."

She looked amazed by my admission. "I know how much you loved him, Lei. Maybe a part of you still does, no matter how much you care for Noah."

"I'll always care what happens to him," I admitted, "but a lot of things have changed since then. And Noah's a wonderful man."

Heather nodded. "Yes, but it's not that easy to turn feelings on and off like a faucet."

"It doesn't matter," I insisted. "I'm never going to forget what happened. I said I'd go to dinner with him, but that's all. It should pacify his ego—which, by the way, has continued to expand since we broke up."

"Yeah, Mark's always had a sizable one," Heather agreed.

"I guess I never noticed it back then."

Heather shot me a look of disbelief. "I don't think you wanted to see it, Lei. Sometimes when people are in love, they refuse to see the other person's faults. It didn't help that he was your first serious boyfriend either."

I folded my arms across my chest. There was some truth to what she said. "Okay, maybe you're right. But that was a long time ago, and I'm not the same person anymore. I won't get weak in the knees every time I see him. Besides, it doesn't matter. One dinner and then we both go our own separate ways—forever."

We drove on in silence for a few minutes until Heather spoke again. "Did you tell Noah about Mark being in town?"

"No. It's probably best not to mention it."

She glanced at me doubtfully but didn't elaborate. "Whatever you say."

It was nine o'clock when I arrived home. My mother's bedroom door was closed and her light off, so I assumed she was asleep. Tomorrow morning, over breakfast, I'd tell her what had transpired tonight. There was no need to wake her now.

I went back downstairs, found some cold *kibbi* in the fridge, and ate a couple of pieces with a glass of milk while standing at the counter. The best thing about *kibbi* was that there was never a wrong time to enjoy ground lamb.

It had been a long day, and I was both physically and mentally exhausted. Toast waited expectantly at the foot of the stairs for me. He was ready for bedtime too and followed me to my room.

When we got upstairs, I washed my face, brushed my teeth, and changed into a pair of white cotton pajamas. Toast settled by my side in bed, butting my hand with his head and looking for any extra pats while I studied my phone messages. He stared at me with adoration as I scratched him under the chin.

"You're my real love, aren't you?" I kissed him on the head, and he purred away.

Mark had texted while Heather and I were on our way home. Hi, hope you had a good day. Looking forward to seeing you tomorrow night.

A tingle ran through me, and I hated myself for it. Was I worried that I might fall for him again? No, that was ridiculous. I'd been over Mark for a long time. Noah was the only man who made my heart beat fast these days. I thought about what Heather said in the car. It's always difficult to forget your first love, no matter how badly they might have hurt you.

I started to type out a response to Mark, then thought better of it. Instead, I dialed Noah's number. I needed to hear his voice. He picked up on the third ring and sounded sleepy. "Hey."

"Shoot, I'm sorry. Did I wake you?"

He yawned and chuckled into the phone. "No big deal. I fell asleep while I was reading Emma a story. It's an occupational hazard with me. So, what's up? How was your trip to New York?"

"More eventful than I thought it would be." I told him about the visit with Jason and the fire at the Butterfield house.

Noah whistled under his breath. "Yeah, I'd say that was quite an evening." He sounded more alert and concerned. "Are you all right?"

I hesitated for a second. Despite everything that had happened tonight, all I could think about was being with him for a nice quiet evening, either watching TV at his house, playing a game of checkers with Emma, or being held in his strong arms as he kissed me. I'd sensed earlier at the farm he might be drifting away from me, but maybe that was all my imagination. "I'm fine. Like you, I'm just tired."

He was silent for a moment. "I'm sorry about leaving you shorthanded tomorrow. Maybe I could come in for a couple of hours at the end of the day—"

I was quick to interrupt. "No, that's not why I called." Noah was the heart of the farm, and he deserved a day off to spend with his daughter. "I only wish that I could give you more time off, but it's tough to spare you."

"Thanks for the compliment." We were both silent, waiting for the other one to speak. Finally, Noah spoke. "Is something else bothering you?"

"No," I lied. "I wanted to hear your voice. It seems like ages since we spent some time alone—outside of the farm, that is." I reminded myself there was no reason to tell him about my dinner with Mark tomorrow night. It was completely innocent, after all. Plus, Noah knew about my broken engagement. There was nothing between us any-more, and Mark would be returning to New York at the end of the week. Hopefully he'd stay there. "I've missed you."

"I've missed you too, Leila." His voice was soft and incredibly sexy. It seemed unfair to ask him where our rela-tionship was headed, and I sincerely hoped he hadn't taken the comment about shopping for diamonds out of context. We'd need to deal with this eventually, but not tonight.

Noah cleared his throat. "How about we plan some-thing for Friday night? Wednesday's up in the air because Em has a soccer game, and they might have to move the start time back. And tomorrow night you've got the wake and dinner with your friend."

"That's right." A wave of guilt settled over me. "What should we do Friday?"

He chuckled softly. "Emma's grandmother is picking

her up that morning, and she's spending a couple of days with her in New York."

My pulse quickened. "What about school?"

"Friday's a teacher's workshop, so school is closed. Why don't you come over here right after work?" He paused for effect. "I'm sure we can figure out something fun to do."

My face heated at his words. "Sounds good." Actually, it sounded wonderful. And that would be the perfect time to tell him about Mark and his return to town. We would get everything out on the table then.

"Good night," Noah whispered. "Sleep well."

CHAPTER NINE

THE NEXT DAY AT THE farm flew by. I spent most of it making maple syrup candy in the sugar shack. Although I had watched my father make it countless times before, Noah had been the one to teach me the process last winter. It was simple enough, but time-consuming. Because we sold so much of it, we had to make the candy a couple of times each month. I enjoyed the downtime and the quiet solitude.

We kept a small one-burner stove in the sugar shack for this sole purpose. I filled a stainless-steel pot with maple syrup and set it on the burner to heat. When it began to boil, I took a candy thermometer and inserted it into the syrup. The syrup needed to reach a temperature of 240 degrees Fahrenheit. At that temperature, most of the water had been boiled out and the candy making could proceed.

I transferred the syrup from the pot and filled two

pitchers, then slowly poured the syrup into the candy molds. Once they were full, I placed them on the steel trays and moved them to a four-shelf wire rack. Tomorrow I would remove the pieces from the trays and dip them into more syrup, which was known as crystal coating. This was done so that the candy pieces didn't turn white. Afterward, the individualized pieces were left on the trays and covered for another day or two. Then, the following morning, Noah and I would box the candy up and move them to the gift shop for sale. The entire process took between three and four days.

Some maple farms added butter to their candy, but my father had always been against it. "People want the candy so they can experience the true taste of our delicious syrup," he'd once explained to me. "There's no need to add anything. You can't beat the natural flavor!"

While I sat there filling the molds, I was comforted by my father's presence. He was always closest to me in the sugar shack or my office, since it had previously belonged to him. I thought of him every day and pictured his face, nodding his approval and beaming. The sight of me in my apron checking on the boiling syrup was certain to make him smile. Yes, he'd been right all along. My father had known, long before I did, that the farm was where I truly belonged in this world. In the past six months, it had become my second home.

Noah suggested we think about making maple sugar and butter as well, but we would need to hire someone in order for that to happen. He had too much else on his plate, and so did my mother and me. Perhaps once we found a helper for Mom in the café, it would become doable. I hated to see her looking so tired all the time. Mom wanted to be at home, tending to her house, baking goodies, and enjoying Toast's company. I didn't blame her. She was almost sixty and had worked hard her entire life. She deserved a break.

After I'd finished the first step of the candy making, it was almost noon, so I went into the café. Mom needed to meet the washing machine technician back at our house, so I waited on customers while she was gone. There was a stack of invoices and unpaid bills waiting for me in my office, plus a reservation for a tour of the sugar bush at three o'clock. We never had a dull moment around here.

Mom returned with homemade tomato hummus that I quickly spread onto one of the maple bagels she'd made earlier and inhaled within seconds. It was the only lunch I had time for, and despite my initial reservations, I was looking forward to a dinner out.

"I don't get it," I said to my mother when I locked the doors at five o'clock. "Things are supposed to be slowing down at this time of the year. All the sap has been collected. Noah just needs to finish the boiling this week, but it feels like we're busier than ever."

She beamed at me with pride. "The farm is like life, Leila. Unpredictable. The calendar may say it's spring, but our customers enjoy maple goodies now as much as they do in the fall. And they love our syrup year-round. Your father would be very proud. You've done a wonderful job, dear."

Any reference to my father still reduced me to tears, but for my mother's sake, I simply gave her a kiss on the cheek and went into my office to get changed. When I emerged ten minutes later with my backpack and purse in hand, she was still there, wiping down the café's tables. Her eyes immediately scanned my outfit, and a frown creased her face.

"Really, Leila. Black again? Can't you ever wear anything with some color to it?"

I gritted my teeth in annoyance. It had been obvious to me from day one that my mother had longed for a girly girl or a mini me. She wanted a daughter who loved to wear skirts and dresses, someone to try different hairstyles on, and bake and sew with. That would never be me. The dress I'd chosen for the wake and dinner with Mark was knee length and black with small blue flowers and short, rounded sleeves. To me, it seemed respectable for both occasions.

"Mom," I said patiently. "I'm going to Monica Butterfield's wake first. Heather asked me to meet her there. I told you about it over breakfast this morning."

My mother's jaw dropped. "No, you didn't. You told me about the fire at the Butterfield house and that you and Heather had stopped to see her uncle."

Count to ten, count to ten. "Yes, I did. I said that I was stopping by the funeral home first before meeting Mark at Medium Rare."

"That's over an hour away," she objected. "You'll be late to meet Mark."

"The funeral home is actually right over the border into New York. If traffic is good, it will only take me half an hour or so to get there."

My mother stuck her lower lip out. Her expression was similar to that of a child who'd been denied a piece of candy. "But I was positive he was meeting you at our house. I thought we could all have a nice chat before you went off to dinner."

Thank goodness Heather had asked me to go to the wake with her. "Sorry, Mom. I'm meeting him at the restaurant."

She frowned. "Why are you going to the wake? You didn't know the woman."

I hoped my poker face wouldn't fail me now. My mother could usually detect when I wasn't telling the truth. "Heather asked me to go. It's important to her."

"Leila, what are you really doing?" Mom asked suspiciously. "I hope you're not planning to get involved in that woman's murder. You could wind up getting yourself killed. Remember, it almost happened with your father's death."

She didn't have to remind me. I was well aware of the fact that both of us had come close to meeting our maker six months ago. In an attempt to make peace, I went over and gave her a peck on the cheek. "I'll be careful, I promise. Don't wait up." I reached for the front door.

"Wait!" my mother called, halting my exit. She hurried over to me. "Why don't you bring Mark back to the house after your dinner for some dessert? I have more maamoul cookies and baklava. I know he loves both of them."

I wearily rested my head against the doorjamb. "We're taking separate cars, Mom."

"What about Friday night?" she asked eagerly. "He could come to our house for dinner."

Good Lord, no. "I have plans with Noah. We've seen very little of each other outside of work lately."

"Oh," she huffed. "I see."

I whirled around to face her. "Mom, you need to realize that it's over between Mark and me. Our dinner tonight is only an attempt at friendship. He walked out on me five years ago, and I'm not going to date him again. I will never be Mrs. Mark Salem."

Saying the name out loud made me cringe. I remembered how I'd proudly written it out, over and over, after Mark had proposed. I'd wanted to see how glorious the name looked on paper. Had I really been so blind to his true colors back then?

"You don't love Noah," Mom insisted. "I know you, Leila. You're still in love with Mark. And he's such a good match for you. Why, he's not even thirty yet and will make partner soon. Think of the life and opportunities you could have with him!"

"Please don't tell me you know how I feel, Mom. Because you don't." She didn't understand a lot of things, not even the reason for our breakup, but I'd been too stubborn to tell her the truth back then. "Money isn't everything. You, of all people, should know that."

She lowered her eyes to the floor. My parents had next to nothing on their wedding day, but Simon and I had heard many times about how deeply in love they were and that finances had never mattered. "Love conquers all," she'd always told us.

My mother appeared momentarily flustered. "I'm sorry. Noah is a nice young man, and the farm needs him. He's a good father and Emma is adorable. But Mark has a great future. Noah may never even want to get married again. Have you thought about that?"

I refused to answer. She didn't need to know I had wondered the same thing.

"Leila, I think a person is lucky if they find true love once in their lifetime. Some people don't ever get that. Noah had his chance already…like I did." Her voice faltered.

My mother's words cut deeply. There was already a fair share of scars from my broken engagement that I would carry with me for the rest of my life, but she seemed intent on adding to them. I realized how brokenhearted she'd been since my father's death, but I for one firmly believed in second chances. "I don't believe that's true, Mom."

"Mark is moving to the Bennington office," she continued. "You could still work part-time at the farm a couple of days a week."

"What do you mean?" I asked in an incredulous tone. "I have no intention of leaving the farm."

She prattled on, as if she hadn't heard me. "As the wife of a star attorney, you'll spend your days socializing and doing charity work. You'll be too busy to spend time at Sappy Endings."

Nothing had changed. My mother still had my entire

life planned out. I'd thought this was behind us forever, but Mark's return had thrown a wrench into everything. "How did you even know about his move to Bennington?" She must have spoken with Mark's mother, Maya. Or maybe *conspired* was a better word.

"Maya told me." Her face flushed. "I was at the Jolly Green Grocer the other day when I ran into her. I'm going to her house later this week. She recently started a crocheting club and wants me to join."

How convenient. No doubt they would spend the entire evening talking about the dinner their children had recently shared. Maya was no different than my mother. As soon as Mark got home tonight, she would grill him like a steak.

"Don't you see?" Mom's face lit up. "You're getting another chance with him. How many people can say that?"

"Mom, I don't want another chance. I told you things were over between us."

She grabbed a hold of my arm and spoke in an urgent voice. "Leila. For goodness' sake, don't throw this opportunity away. Whatever you did five years ago, just don't do it again!"

I turned away so that she couldn't see the tears forming in my eyes. "I told you Mark was the one who ended things between us."

"But you never told me why!" Mom said in an exasperated tone. She paused for a second, then spoke more calmly. "I know you never would have cheated on Mark, so you must have done something else to upset him."

I shook my head in disbelief and whirled around to face her. "After five years, it's still the same. You always assumed that I was the one who went and ruined everything."

My mother stared at my tearstained face and brought a hand to her mouth. "Oh, Leila. That came out wrong. I didn't mean—"

"Don't wait up." I let the door slam behind me. Blinking back tears, I ran to my car, and with trembling fingers, beeped the door unlocked. Once inside, I revved the engine and tore out of the parking lot as if something were chasing me.

Something besides my past.

CHAPTER TEN

I HAD BEEN SO UPSET by the argument with my mother that I made it to the funeral home in record time. The clock on my dashboard read 5:40 p.m. when I finally secured a spot in the parking lot. I'd have almost an hour to mingle and question people.

As I exited the car, I exhaled deeply, thankful for the long drive and a chance to get my emotions under control. If I had told my mother the reason for the breakup years ago, it would have changed everything, but it hurt to know she still considered the incident my fault. She'd been furious back then, while I was so embarrassed. All I'd wanted to do was run as far away from Sugar Ridge as possible. I had jumped at the first teaching offer I received out of state and, less than a month later, been on my way to Florida. After that, my mother and I had not spoken for more than a year. Our relationship had remained frosty until I returned home last fall.

The line for Monica's wake stretched out in front of the gray one-story building and wrapped around the side of it. *Shoot.* I'd forgotten there might be a wait. Monica was a business owner and no doubt knew many people.

With no other choice, I glanced at my watch and reluctantly took my place in line. At this rate, I would still be in line at six thirty. As I stood there fidgeting, my phone pinged with a text from Heather.

Where are you?

My fingers flew over the keyboard. I've been in line for ten minutes. I didn't think there'd be such a long wait.

Her reply came back within seconds. Tell the doorman that you're Monica's niece, Heather. You can cut the line.

Well, this was awkward. I don't know.

Just meet me by the front door, she typed back.

I slid out of line and boldly made my way up the steps, after uttering the words, "Excuse me," several times. All eyes were fixed upon me, and my face began to warm as people whispered and nudged each other. Thankfully, Heather had arrived. She said something to the doorman, who held the door open for me and smiled politely.

Heather was wearing a black pantsuit with matching pumps. Her long blond hair was pulled into a neat bun at the back of her head. She looped her hand through my arm. "I'm so glad you're here."

I stopped to sign the registry behind a petite woman who also had her hair pulled back in a style similar to Heather's. The unique floral-spray pin embedded in her auburn locks immediately caught my attention. It was decorated with rubies and crystals, and even though I knew nothing about jewelry, it was exquisite and looked expensive. I found myself wondering if it might have come from Treasure Chest.

A man in a dark gray suit with a name tag that read *Gregory* stopped at the woman's side and smiled. "I'm terribly sorry about the misunderstanding, Mrs. Fuller."

"It's all right," the woman assured him. "I know that technically I'm not family, but Grant did tell me that I wouldn't have to wait. He said he'd take care of everything."

Gregory looked faintly embarrassed. "Of course. Please feel free to enter the viewing room whenever you like."

The woman signed the book with a flourish, grabbed a mourning card, and walked toward the viewing room, where another line had started to form. As I wrote my name down, I glanced at the one above mine. *Mrs. Belinda Fuller.*

I pointed at the name. "Do you know her?"

Heather shrugged. "Not personally, but when I went to use the ladies' room, I overheard her complaining to the doorman. She was very upset no one had left her name with him. I guess she didn't feel she should have to wait in line like everyone else."

"Maybe she's related to Monica. Let me see what I can find out about her, and then I'll meet up with you after I pay my respects."

"Well, I hope it won't take too long." Heather looked anxious. "I can't stand it in there much longer. Grant's been crying nonstop, and my relatives keep coming up to me and patting me on the shoulder, asking, 'Have you rescheduled the wedding yet?'"

Good lord. This was worse than I'd thought. "I'll be as quick as I can." I hurried over and took my place in line behind Belinda. There were about a dozen people standing in front of us, waiting to observe Monica and pay respects to her family. While I stood there, I craned my neck toward the receiving line. Garrett Turcot, Heather's father, was positioned awkwardly at one end, looking like he preferred to be anywhere else. Olivia was next to him, talking quietly with a priest. Grant and Devon stood next to her. An elderly woman was holding both of Grant's hands and crying along with him.

Belinda stifled a sob, startling me out of my thoughts. It seemed like a good time to try and strike up a conversation. "Are you okay?" I asked gently.

She nodded and stepped out of line to grab a tissue box from a nearby table. "Sorry. I just can't believe that she's gone."

Belinda looked to be in her late forties. Her large gray eyes watched me curiously. "Are you a friend of Devon's?"

"No. My name is Leila Khoury. My friend Heather is Grant's niece."

"Oh, I see. Well, I'm Belinda Fuller." She continued to stare until I began to wince under her gaze. Maybe she was doing some investigating of her own. "Heather—is she the one whose bridal shower Monica was at?"

Poor Heather was making quite a name for herself. "That's right."

An uncomfortable silence followed. I hoped that Belinda wouldn't ask for any further details. There had been an article in the *Maple Messenger*, our local newspaper that employed my brother, Simon, about Monica's murder. How Monica had died was not revealed, but they had mentioned how her death had occurred at a local bridal shower she'd attended.

"Are you a friend of Monica's?" I asked.

A tear rolled down Belinda's cheek as she nodded. "We've been best friends for years. We did community theater together back in college. That's how we met."

This was a surprise—not that Monica had done community theater, but that she and Belinda were close in age. Belinda looked at least ten years younger and was quite attractive, with a petite figure and striking features. "What kind of shows were you in?"

She laughed. "We did one play together, *Arsenic and Old Lace*. I was her understudy. I kept hoping that she'd get sick so I could go on for her. Isn't that terrible? We've been inseparable ever since."

"This must be an awful shock for you," I said sympathetically. "Who could have done such a thing?"

Belinda wiped at her eyes with a tissue. "I hate to say this, but Monica had a lot of enemies, starting with her employees. Well, with the exception of me, of course."

"You worked for her?" My guess about the hairpin had been right.

Belinda nodded. "I didn't work in her store, but yes. I'm a jewelry designer. When she inherited the business from her father, she asked me to come and design some new pieces."

"Did you design the hairpin you're wearing? It's gorgeous." I didn't wear much jewelry, but often used clips to hold back my shoulder length hair. The one Belinda wore would match the deep red shade of my maid of honor dress, and ruby was my birthstone. A win-win situation for me.

She flushed with pride. "Yes, I did. Thank you." Belinda reached into her purse and handed me a business card. "There's a few like this at Treasure Chest, but if you'd like a comb custom made, I'd be happy to make you one."

It seemed like an awkward time for her to try and make a sale, but as my father used to say, "Business is business." He'd once sold an entire case of maple syrup during Sunday mass. My mother had not been as jovial about it as my father.

"I'd love to have one exactly like yours for my friend's wedding, but it's less than two weeks away." Maybe I wasn't crazy about wearing a formal gown, but Noah was my date, and I wanted to look nice for him. "There might not be enough time."

"Oh, that won't be a problem. I work fast, so you could have it in a few days. Why don't you give me your number?" Belinda suggested. "I could either leave the comb at Treasure Chest for pickup or deliver it to your home."

I recited my phone number for her. "I live in Vermont. I wouldn't want you to travel that far."

"Nonsense," she said. "I travel all over the Northeast with my jewelry."

"Perfect. Can you give me a price?" I should have asked her sooner. They might be more expensive than I'd hoped.

Belinda quoted me a price, and to my relief, it was in my range. "I'll give you a call when it's done, and we'll arrange a day and place for you to pick it up."

"Perfect. Thank you."

The couple in front of Belinda moved to the kneeler, and I knew our time was limited. "I'm sorry about Monica. Do you really think it was someone she worked with?"

"I do." Belinda glanced around, as if to be sure no one could hear her response. "Jealousy is a terrible thing. There's a lot of people out there who would love to have Treasure Chest as their own." The couple moved from the kneeler and went to speak with Grant. Belinda gave me a little finger wave. "Nice to have met you."

She took her position on the kneeler, made the sign of the cross on her chest, and sniffed loudly. Did she think that Jason could have killed Monica, like Devon?

When it was my turn at the kneeler, I made the sign of the cross and bowed my head. Monica was wearing a lavender-colored dress, and her auburn hair rested against a pink satin pillow. She simply looked like she was sleeping. A string of rosary beads was clasped between her hands. I couldn't help but notice she wore no jewelry, not even a wedding ring. Who had inherited all of those priceless gems? Would Devon give any to Lexy?

After a few seconds, I rose and moved to the receiving line. Belinda was still there, hugging Devon tightly, until it was obvious the contact was embarrassing him.

Belinda moved on to talk to Grant and kissed him on both cheeks.

Devon watched me approach and smiled hesitantly. "Miss Khoury, right? It was nice of you to come."

"Please call me Leila. I'm very sorry for your loss. How are you and your stepfather holding up?"

Devon waggled his hand back and forth. "It's tough, but we're managing. Listen, I wanted to thank you again for what you did last night. If you and Heather hadn't called 9-1-1, my mother's entire house might have gone up in flames."

I found it interesting that he didn't say Grant's house. "I'm glad we were there. Did you find out if the pipe was the cause?"

Devon nodded. "Yeah, the arson inspector said someone had lit the pipe. It belonged to my father, but he died over twenty years ago. My mother couldn't bring herself to throw any of his stuff away." His expression grew stern. "I figure someone must have broken in."

"Devon," Grant said sharply, as he nodded coolly at me. "I need to speak with Belinda in private. Please give my apologies to anyone I miss."

"Okay, Grant." Devon watched as the two of them walked away, an odd expression on his face. How I wish I could have overheard their conversation, but unless I could turn myself into a fly on the wall, it seemed that I was out of luck.

People had gathered behind me in the line, waiting to talk to Devon, so I quickly said goodbye and went to find Heather. My friend was sitting in the back row of chairs, her gaze sweeping back and forth across the room. She looked relieved to see me approaching, but at the last second, I spotted Jason and veered in his direction. He was standing near the window, studying an easel with Monica's pictures displayed on it.

"Hello, nice to see you again, Jason."

He looked up. "Well, if it isn't the lovely Leila. Still poking around asking questions?"

"My, you don't beat around the bush."

A small smile played at the corners of his mouth. "Correct. That is not my style."

"I met Belinda Fuller," I offered, "and ordered a hair clip from her."

Jason snorted back a laugh. "That's Belinda for you. Business first, mourning later. She is quite talented though. I'm sure you'll be very pleased with her work."

"Belinda told me that she and Monica have been best friends for years."

He nodded. "Indeed, they have always been close... until recently, that is. Monica treats her like a servant sometimes, but Belinda takes it with a grain of salt. Anyone who associated with Monica learned to do that."

Heather joined us. "Hello, Jason. What are you guys talking about?"

"I was asking Jason about Belinda, the woman who left the room with Grant. When you mentioned yesterday that Grant had a girlfriend—" I lowered my voice. "It's not—I mean—"

He gave a low chuckle under his breath. "No, I doubt it. Belinda and Grant have never been overly fond of each other."

"What happened between Belinda and Monica? Belinda acted like they were still the closest of friends," I asked.

Jason rolled his eyes. "Who knows. Something caused a rift between their perfect friendship, but Monica never said a word about it to me."

"Really?" I mused. "So, you have no idea what it might be?"

He looked amused. "Contrary to popular belief, I don't know *everything*. Belinda hasn't been in the store with any new pieces for a few weeks now. When I asked Monica why, all she would say was she didn't want to ever discuss *that* woman again."

"Sounds pretty serious," Heather remarked.

Jason bowed to us. "Please excuse me, ladies. I must speak with a customer who's just arrived."

Heather and I watched with interest as Grant came back into the room. He took his place in the receiving line as if nothing had happened. A few seconds later, Belinda reappeared and sat down in the second row of chairs. Her eyes were swollen and red-rimmed.

"They must have been having an affair," Heather murmured. "Think about it. That would be the perfect motive to get rid of Monica. We only have to decide who did it— Grant or Belinda."

"I think you're jumping the gun a bit." Grant was talking to a pretty blond woman in the receiving line. She looked to be in her twenties, and the short black dress she wore clung to her voluptuous figure. She kissed Grant on the cheek, and as she moved away, I noticed Grant checking out her figure.

"That's so gross," Heather said. "And at his wife's wake. I mean, really? This is terrible to say, but the more I see of my uncle, the more I dislike him. Why my father still grovels to him is beyond me."

"That woman is at least thirty years younger than he is," I observed. "I'm getting the feeling that your uncle Grant likes them at any age."

Heather shot a disgusted look in his direction. "I still think there might be something between him and Belinda, no matter what Jason says. Let's suppose Monica knew that Grant was having an affair with her friend. Did Monica fire her? Could Grant or Belinda have killed her as payback?"

"It would also explain the note in Monica's purse that I found," I said thoughtfully. "And true, they've got a motive. But you're forgetting one thing."

"What's that?" Heather asked.

"Everyone we've spoken to has a reason to want Monica dead," I said. "And I'm guessing there's more that we don't even know about yet."

CHAPTER ELEVEN

I HATED TO DESERT HEATHER in her hour of need, but I needed to leave soon or else I'd be late to meet Mark. We went into the ladies' room together where I fussed with my hair. Heather leaned against the sink, watching me.

"Are you nervous?" she asked.

I shrugged. "There's nothing to be nervous about."

"Hmm." She shot me a dubious look. "I want a full report when you get home."

"What are you, my mother now?"

Heather laughed out loud. "I bet she waits up for you."

I added a coat of lip gloss to my mouth. "I told her not to. We had an argument before I left the farm."

"Of course you did," Heather said breezily. "But tell her that she's got to wait at least a month before she settles on a wedding date. I'd like to have mine first."

"Real cute." I put my lip gloss back in my purse and

looked up to see Heather's big blue eyes filled with tears. Devastated, I placed an arm around her shoulders. "Oh, honey, don't cry! Everything's going to be all right."

"I wish I could believe that," she said sadly. "Oh, Lei, I don't know what to do. I told Tyler earlier that we're probably going to have to postpone the wedding and then downscale it when the time comes. We had a big fight because he's got relatives coming all the way from Europe and his parents want to know why mine won't stand up to Grant. They don't know about the loan." Her lower lip quivered. "Everything is such a mess right now."

"I'm so sorry you're going through this," I said, "but don't lose hope. The police might find out who killed Monica before then."

"I'm not counting on it." Heather's voice was strangled. "We only have until next Monday. We can't wait until the day before the wedding to notify everyone. That's why—"

A toilet flushed and we both jumped, unaware that someone else had been in the bathroom. A second later, the blond woman I'd seen Grant chatting with earlier appeared. She smiled and nodded at us, and we moved aside so she could wash her hands in the sink. She was prettier up close, with ivory skin and blue eyes, but the black dress she wore seemed more fitting for a cocktail party than a wake. It was tight and short, showing off her figure to its best advantage. When she lifted her arm to grab a paper towel, my attention was drawn to the diamond bracelet around her wrist. Diamonds and emeralds decorated the lovely gold band, and it triggered a recent memory in my brain. I'd seen the same bracelet on Monica's wrist at Heather's bridal shower.

Monica's bracelet. Who was this girl, then? It had to be Lexy, Devon's girlfriend. Monica wasn't even cold yet, and her son had already given away her jewelry?

"Sorry, I couldn't help overhearing." Her smile seemed genuine, but her voice was squeaky and high-pitched, reminiscent of nails on a chalkboard. "Aren't you the one who had the shower where Monica was found murdered?"

Heather winced visibly as she nodded. "That's right. My name's Heather."

"Oh!" The woman's face turned red. "Sorry, that came out wrong. I'm her daughter-in-law, Lexy. That is, I hoped to be her daughter-in-law someday." She giggled.

Jason had been right about her. Lexy seemed to be missing a few brain cells. "Hi, I'm Leila. I met Monica at Heather's shower on Sunday," I said, trying to save Heather from further explanation. "I'm sure she was very fond of you."

"We're sorry for your loss," Heather put in.

"Thanks," Lexy said. "Sorry that your wedding's going to be ruined."

Heather's face turned a ghostly white, but she said nothing.

"I think it's awful that Grant's being such a big stinker about your wedding. You shouldn't have to cancel." Lexy swiveled her head back in the direction of the mirror and ran her fingers through her blond locks. "But look on the bright side. At least you know you're getting married *sometime.* Devon and I have been dating for over five years, and there're days that I wonder if he's ever going to ask me."

"That's a shame." I tried to sound sympathetic.

Alexis watched me from the mirror. "What did you say your name was?"

"Leila. Leila Khoury."

"Oh, you're the one who found Monica!" Lexy said in awe, as if I was some sort of celebrity. "When you talked to her, did she mention me?"

I thought this was rather a strange thing for her to ask. "No, not to me. But we only talked for a couple of minutes." Monica's remark of how people were only nice to her because she had money came back to me at that moment.

"Shoot." Lexy made a face. "She never really liked me."

"Why would you say that?" Heather asked.

Lexy shrugged. "I think she thought that Devon could do better. But then, one day—poof! It was like someone waved a magic wand, ya' know? She started talking to me and acting all nice and stuff. So, I figured it was better not to ask any questions and enjoy it while it lasted. I mean, she wasn't my ideal mother-in-law, but I could have done a lot worse."

Sure, she could have. A mother-in-law who owned a ritzy jewelry store was not to be taken for granted. I nodded at the bracelet. "That's gorgeous. Did you get it at Treasure Chest?"

"Oh." Lexy wiggled her arm proudly. "Yeah, it was a gift from Devon. He gave it to me yesterday, in fact. But I wish I had an engagement ring instead. Men. He's so afraid of commitment."

"Any idea why?" Heather asked.

Lexy applied a coat of mascara to her lashes. "Darned if I know. Things were really good between us the first couple of years we dated. Now, it's like I only see him once a week if I'm lucky. He never has time for me. When I told Monica about it last month, she got all upset and started yelling at him. I'm so glad she took my side because she always acted like I was some kind of dumb blond." She giggled. "Life is really weird sometimes, huh?"

Apparently, so was the Butterfield family. "You're right about that."

"Well." Lexy put the mascara tube back in her purse. "I'd better get back out there to support Devon. It was nice meeting you both."

"Bye," Heather called after her. We waited the appropriate few seconds and left the restroom together. Heather walked me to the back door of the funeral home. "Doesn't it strike you as funny that Monica wanted Lexy to marry Devon?" she asked. "From what Dad told me, it sounded like she thought no one was good enough for his highness."

"It does seem strange," I admitted. "Who knows, maybe Monica decided to adopt my mother's policy. Get your kid married off, no matter what it takes. Who cares if they love the person or not. What's love got to do with it, anyway?"

Heather snorted back a laugh. "Okay, Tina Turner. Enough with the sarcasm." She gave my arm a squeeze. "Thanks for coming. And I think it's pretty awesome of you to have dinner with Mark when, in my opinion, he doesn't deserve two minutes of your precious time." She winked. "Remember, I expect a full report when you get home."

"Yes, Mom."

Medium Rare was a casual family-style restaurant about ten minutes from my house. Fortunately, traffic was light on the way back from New York, so I was only a few minutes late. When I entered the waiting area, there were at least three other groups ahead of me. I asked for the Salem table, and the host walked me over to where Mark was sitting. He'd always had impeccable manners and jumped up to hold the chair out for me.

"Thank you. Sorry I'm late."

His eyes lit up as he studied me. "No problem. You look beautiful."

"Thanks." He looked nice as well, but I wasn't going to say so. Unlike Noah, Mark had always been fully aware of how good-looking he was. In fact, it wasn't until I started dating Noah that I realized how large of an ego Mark had.

No, I had to stop this. It wasn't fair to Noah that I was comparing him with someone he'd never even met. In his defense, he was winning the race hands down.

"Would you like a glass of wine?" Mark asked when our server appeared.

"No, thanks. Iced tea will be fine."

When the server departed, Mark reached across the table to take my hand in his. "Leila, I wanted you to know that these past few years, I've never stopped thinking about you. If I could go back in time and fix things—"

"But you can't," I finished. "We've been over with for a long time."

Mark had the good grace to look embarrassed. "My mother said that you've been running the farm since Victor's death. He'd be so proud of you, Leila."

The server returned with our drinks, and I waited until he was out of earshot. "Thank you. I hope so."

Mark cocked his head to the side and studied me. "So, tell me. What's the story with you and Ned?"

I took a sip of iced tea to purposely delay my response. Mark always had a bad memory when it suited him. "His name is Noah."

His eyes didn't waver from my face. "Is it serious?"

Thankfully, the server returned with a basket of warm rolls and to take our order. When he had left again, I tactfully switched topics. "Are *you* seeing anyone?"

Mark shook his head. "I've only had one girlfriend in the past five years. And the relationship was nowhere near as serious as ours. What does that tell you?"

I shrugged. What was the purpose of this conversation? "What do you want from me, Mark? Tell me the truth."

He brought my hand to his lips before I could stop him. "Okay, I lied. I don't want to just be friends. I want us to get back together. To start over where we left off. Or, I mean, before that last day, because things ended so badly between us. I still love you, Leila."

I said nothing.

Mark paused. "I think you still love me. Things with Nick can't be that serious."

Good grief. "Noah." My voice was sharp this time. "His name is *Noah*."

Then, as I said his name, I spotted him. Noah was sitting at a table located across the room and against the window. He was not alone. Seated across from him in the booth was a beautiful little girl with curly blond hair and big blue eyes. I'd seen pictures of Ashley, her mother, and Emma was the spitting image of her.

Noah smiled at his daughter, who was in the process of finishing off an ice cream sundae. She lifted the spoon and Noah pretended that he was going to try and steal a bite. She giggled and quickly put it into her mouth. A server approached them and handed Noah the bill. He immediately opened his wallet while still talking to his daughter.

Panic swept over me like a tidal wave. Why, oh why hadn't I told Noah that Mark was the *friend* I was meeting? He and Emma would be getting up to leave soon, and there was no way that they wouldn't see us. As my father used to say, the syrup was about to hit the fan.

"What's wrong?" Mark asked.

I opened my mouth to reply as Noah's eyes shifted away from Emma and toward me. The grin on his face immediately disappeared. I tried to smile but failed miserably.

Our dinners arrived and Mark immediately dug into his steak. "Is something wrong with your lobster?" he asked.

"No." My elbow flew out as I turned back toward Mark, and my empty glass fell to the floor. Thankfully, the glass didn't break, but it made enough of a commotion that everyone nearby turned to look at us, including Emma. She started to squeal and jumped out of her seat before Noah could stop her.

"Leila!" she shouted and flung herself into my lap. "I didn't know you were coming."

And I sure as heck didn't know that you would be here as well. "Hi, Emma." I gave her a big hug.

Pleased, Emma looked at me, her bright blue eyes sparkling into mine. "Guess what? We went to see a Charlie Brown play today. It was lots of fun! And Daddy came too because he said that you didn't need him to work at the farm."

Having no choice, Noah joined us. He dug his hands deep into the pockets of his jeans and nodded toward Mark before addressing me. "Hello, Leila. This is a surprise."

Boy, was it ever. "Hi, Noah."

Mark's eyes shifted back and forth between us, and his mouth turned up at the corners. Emma seemed to notice him for the first time. "Are you Leila's friend?"

He laughed out loud. "I sure hope so."

Heat rose through my face. "Uh, Mark Salem, this is Noah Rivers. Noah works at the farm with me."

An odd expression that I hadn't seen before came over Noah's face, and I wanted to smack myself in the head. I was so flustered that I didn't even know what I was saying. "Noah is my boyfriend." The words came out too late, like an afterthought. At that moment, I realized what caused his odd expression. Noah had been hurt by what I'd said.

There was a long, awkward pause before Noah extended his hand toward Mark. "Nice to meet you. I've heard a lot about you."

Mark let out a chuckle. "I've been hearing a few things about you as well."

Emma put her arms around my neck. "Can you come over tonight? Please?"

"Not tonight," Noah said as he lifted Emma off my lap. "You've had a long day, and we've got to get you home and off to bed. Besides, Leila's busy with her friend."

It almost sounded as if he was mocking me, and if so, I didn't blame him. I hadn't told Noah about the dinner with Mark because it would have opened a new can of worms that I hadn't been ready to face. As it turned out, I'd only made things worse. Did Noah think that I'd gone behind his back? If pressed, I'd have to admit that I had.

I placed a kiss on Emma's satin-like cheek. "Maybe I'll see you tomorrow night too."

Noah cleared his throat. "Actually, Emma has a soccer game tomorrow night."

"Can't Leila come and watch me play?" Emma asked.

Noah didn't say anything, but I could take a hint. It was my turn to feel hurt and confused, and I didn't care for it much. I decided to make things easy for him. "Some other night, honey. Besides, I have to help Heather with wedding stuff."

"Okay, the next day then." Emma threw her little arms around my neck and hugged me, tugging at my heart as well. I glanced up at her father, who shifted from one foot to the other, looking uncomfortable with the entire situation.

"Enjoy your dinner," he said and nodded at Mark. I watched as the two of them left the restaurant hand in hand, Emma skipping happily at Noah's side.

A small smile tugged at the corners of Mark's mouth. "That must have been quite a surprise—for you both. I guess this is my lucky night. Maybe things aren't as serious as I thought they were."

My stomach twisted at his words, and I feared he might be right. Maybe Noah thought I was seeing Mark on the side. As soon as I could get away, I'd text him and apologize.

Mark finished off his wine and reached for my hand again. "As I was saying, I want us to get back together, Leila. I got cold feet last time, but it won't happen again."

Gently, I removed my hand from his. "You seem to have a bad memory for certain details." I tried to keep my tone neutral. "It was more than cold feet. I told you something that changed the way you felt about me forever. Please don't treat me like I'm stupid, Mark."

He looked shocked by my words. "I have too much respect for you to do that. Come on. Let's not dwell on the past anymore. The only thing important is that we still love each other. I'm going to be thirty in November. It's time for me to settle down with a wife and—"

Mark stopped suddenly, but his words hurt as if he'd driven a stake through my heart. He rambled on, trying to explain himself. "What I mean is, I realized how stupid I was and how much I hurt you. I still want to marry you. We could have a great life together."

I dipped a piece of lobster into melted butter and forked

it into my mouth. At least the dinner was delicious, so the entire evening hadn't been a waste. Almost. "It won't work, Mark. It's too late for us."

He smiled at me with eyes that radiated warmth like the sun. Eyes that had once been so easy for me to lose myself in, but not anymore. "You're forgetting something," he said softly. "I'm a lawyer, and I love a challenge. And you, my darling Leila, have always been a challenge."

CHAPTER TWELVE

DESPITE MY PROTESTS, MARK WALKED me to my car after dinner. He tried to kiss me good night, but I turned my face away at the last minute so the kiss fell upon my cheek. To my surprise, he laughed out loud.

"Leila, we were once engaged," he said smoothly. "I think I deserve more than a kiss on the cheek."

The words made my insides boil. *Deserved?* Why did he think that he deserved anything? I was just as annoyed with myself as I was with Mark. Before tonight, I had never realized how arrogant and egotistical my ex was. Heather had been right. Maybe at the young and immature age of twenty, it had been too difficult for me to see past his good looks and charm to discover his true colors.

The time had come for me to set the record straight. "No, Mark, I don't think that you do." There was a catch in my voice, but I continued. "I loved you once. Very much.

But we're not together anymore. I tried to tell you that I have a boyfriend. And even if I didn't"—I blew out a breath—"I still wouldn't want to get back together."

Mark's jaw dropped. "Come on, Leila. You don't mean that."

"Yes, I do." I was a firm believer in fate and that things happened for a reason. When Mark had broken up with me, I'd thought I'd never be happy again. Although the experience had been both painful and embarrassing, it made me a stronger person. I realized now I never would have been happy with the life Mark wanted us to have. Unlike me, Mark had been born in Lebanon and raised with different values. He wanted his wife to run the home, raise children, and make dinner. It's what his mother had done, his grandmothers, and probably any other woman in his life. And there was nothing wrong with that, if the woman wanted that too. More power to her. But I, in fact, had always wanted something more.

Despite what my mother told me, I knew that Mark would have hated me running Sappy Endings and may have urged me to sell the farm. I was finally happy with my life and had no intention of letting Mark or any other man take that away from me.

He was not about to be dissuaded. "Leila, my parents are having a party for me at their house this weekend. They'd love to see you. And it would give us another chance to talk. Would you come—as a friend only?" he added quickly.

"I don't think it's a good idea."

"Please?" Mark whispered. "It will be my last chance to see you for a while. I'm going back to New York City this weekend. My mother wants Selma to come too. And Simon is welcome if he can make it."

"Mom didn't mention the party to me," I said in surprise.

He looked faintly embarrassed. "My mother might be waiting to ask Selma about it. They're getting together this week for some kind of knitting club at her house. But I do know Mom wants her there. It would be great to see Simon too."

"He's been really busy at the newspaper lately, but I'll let him know." My younger brother had always gotten along well with Mark, but once confided to me that he thought my ex was too shallow. As long as I was happy, he'd said, that was all that mattered.

"Let me know what you decide, okay?" Mark moved closer, his eyes dropping back to my lips. I took a step away so as not to encourage him.

"Sure," I lied. As far as I was concerned, there was nothing to think about, but I wanted to be done with this evening. I reached for the car door, but Mark moved swiftly past me to open it. I hastily got behind the wheel, hoping he wouldn't try to kiss me again. "Good night, Mark."

He stood there watching me drive away, and I was reminded again of that day five years earlier when I had watched him zoom away in his new convertible after telling me that he'd wanted to break our engagement. Tears had been running down my face. He'd simply said good night, got into his car, and never looked back.

Karma was an interesting thing.

Mercifully, by some stroke of luck, my mother was asleep when I arrived home. Toast greeted me at the front door and immediately followed me upstairs. It was almost ten o'clock, and I could barely keep my eyes open. I got into bed and Toast stretched out at the bottom, watching me intently with large green-jeweled eyes as I dialed Noah's number. The call went straight to his voicemail. My fingers flew over the keyboard.

Hi, are you still up? Can we talk?

I waited a few minutes, but there was no response. Noah had once told me that he had difficulty sleeping since his wife's death. He might be ignoring me on purpose, and I couldn't blame him. I'd handled things so badly. With a sigh of weariness, I placed the phone back on my night-stand and turned out the light. Tomorrow was a new day, and a new opportunity. We would get everything straightened out then. Satisfied, I closed my eyes and drifted off into a much-needed slumber.

Noah had a tour scheduled for first thing the next morning, so I didn't have a chance to speak with him before it began. I stayed in my office, trying to get caught up on bills while also arranging a shipment of syrup to England. I left the office briefly at noon to chat with the gardener I'd hired for the summer. I wanted to put in more flower beds around the sugar shack and main building. The main building also needed a paint job, and I was busy getting estimates on that as well. These were all things that Noah could do, but he was only one person. There were far more important jobs I needed him for, such as the tours, checking and repairing sap lines, and making candles.

As I walked back to the main building, I decided an all-day festival might be a fun event in the fall to drum up some extra business with the holidays around the corner. We could host a waffle breakfast and rent space to local vendors for the day. A pie-baking contest might be fun as well. I couldn't wait to ask Noah his opinion about it. But the next thing on my agenda was coffee, so I headed into the Sappy Hour Café.

My mother had been busy baking muffins and short-bread cookies all morning. In addition to the breakfast sandwiches, there were a different variety of goodies available each day that she wrote up on a chalkboard. She liked to change things up. Mom had left the house while I was still in the shower, so we still hadn't gotten a chance to speak about my dinner date. Like a lion, she pounced on me when I went behind the counter.

"You got in late last night. Things must have gone very well." She beamed. "Tell me all about it."

Good grief. My face warmed. "There's nothing to tell, Mom. We went out to dinner, and that's all."

Thankfully, before she could grill me any further, a couple approached the counter and requested maple lattes. My mother made them in the espresso machine, served hot or cold. She used coffee, nutmeg, maple syrup, and whipped cream, and they always tasted delicious.

I quickly grabbed a muffin still warm from the oven and a cup of coffee. I was determined to get back to work in my office, but Mom was having none of it. She held up a finger. "Wait a second, Leila," she said as the couple paid for their lattes and sat down at a nearby table.

Oh no. Thinking fast, I held up my phone. "Sorry, Mom. I need to take this." I hurried out of the café, down the walkway, and over to my office. As soon as I sat down behind the desk, my phone buzzed for real, startling me. I glanced at the screen. *Heather.*

"What's going on?" she asked. "You sound like you're out of breath."

"I just lied to my mother."

She chuckled. "Uh oh. It must have had something to do with Mark or Noah."

"Why do you say that?"

Heather snorted. "Because I know you. Want to talk about it?"

"Not at the moment." I wrapped my hands around the mug. "How did the funeral go this morning?"

"Awful," she lamented. "Mom and I just got home. Grant broke down at the cemetery and flung himself on Monica's casket. Then Belinda started to carry on, and they both ended up hugging each other and crying. It was— awkward. Very awkward."

Her statement was not lost on me. "Do you still think they're having an affair?"

"It's exactly what I'm thinking," she murmured. "They

acted awful chummy, and Devon was clearly ticked off at them."

If Belinda and Grant were having an affair, that would have made things so convenient. It would also explain the motive for Monica's murder. I chewed my muffin thoughtfully. Jason had mentioned that Grant was having an affair. Monica recently had an argument with Belinda, and it may have been about the same topic. Everything lined up, so why did I still have doubts?

"You're so quiet," Heather observed. "Come on, what happened last night? You need to get it off your chest, and I know you don't want to tell your mother."

I checked my email as we talked. "You won't believe it. He wants to get back together."

"I knew it!" Heather shrieked so loudly my eardrum almost shattered. "What did you say?"

"You're kidding, right? You know what I told him."

Heather cleared her throat. "Yes. You told him that you were happy with Noah, and that he could take a flying leap."

"And it was all going perfectly—until I spotted Noah at the next table."

There was a stunned silence on the other end. "Come again?"

"You heard me right." I sighed. "Noah was having dinner with Emma in the same restaurant."

Heather gasped. "I don't believe this. It could only happen to you. So, what did you guys say to each other?"

I massaged the bridge of my nose between my thumb

and forefinger. "Not much. That's what we said. I really screwed things up. Why didn't I tell him about the dinner with Mark? Now, it looks like I was deliberately trying to hide it from him. Noah wasn't pleased."

"Noah's not a high schooler. He's a mature guy. Way more mature than your ex," Heather added. "You need to sit him down and explain everything. He'll understand."

I swiveled around in my chair and stared out the window. The sky was gray and gloomy, similar to my current mood. "We were talking about getting together tonight, but all of a sudden, Noah's busy. I haven't even had a chance to speak to him today. I wouldn't be surprised if he tries to avoid me."

"That's just your imagination going wild," Heather said softly. "So what if he was a little jealous? It might light a fire under him."

"You know that's not my style," I protested. "I want him to know that there's nothing between me and Mark."

Heather sighed into the phone. "Then tell him. It will be fine. Don't worry so much." She was silent for a few seconds. "So, if you're free tonight, I was wondering if I could ask a little favor."

"I think you're out of favors this week," I teased.

"True," she agreed, "but I'm going to ask anyway. My parents are planning a small get-together on Sunday at their home to honor Monica."

"Whose idea was this? Grant's?"

Heather sniffed. "Of course. Who else? Uncle Grant even offered to lend them some photos of Monica to use for the display." She paused. "And guess who offered to go and pick them up at his house?"

I gave a loud snort. "Gee, that's a tough one. You'll have to give me a hint."

"Will you go with me?" she pleaded.

"You know I will, but I have to ask…why did your parents agree to this? Because of the money they owe Monica and Grant for the wedding?"

"Yes." Heather's voice was so faint I barely heard her.

"Hasn't Grant put them through enough already? I'm sorry his wife is dead, but their marriage was already on the rocks. I know this sounds terrible, but it seems like everyone is bending over backward to honor a woman no one could stomach."

Heather was silent for a few seconds. "No, it's not terrible, it's the truth. My parents are only doing it because of the money, and they don't feel they have a choice. Uncle Grant said to dad at the funeral that no one showed any sympathy for his beloved wife. He said it was appalling, and that Monica deserved better. As soon as the ceremony was over, people started leaving. Many of them didn't even go to the grave site. Mom wasn't feeling well, so she and I didn't go to the luncheon afterward. Dad just called from there and told her only about fifteen people attended."

How depressing. "Wow, I hope I get a better turnout when my time comes."

"Don't talk like that, Leila." There was a note of disapproval in Heather's voice. "Nothing's going to happen to you for at least another eighty years. I won't let it. Anyway, if you can make the gathering on Sunday, that would be great. We could talk to everyone again, and maybe pick up a clue to Monica's death or—oh, I don't know." She sighed. "I'm out of ideas."

"Is Grant still living at the house? Wouldn't it be off-limits because of the damage from the fire?"

"Only Monica's study was damaged," Heather explained. "He goes over for short periods of time, but he's not sleeping there. I guess it smells pretty bad."

While she was talking, I confirmed an online reservation for a tour of the farm. "Maybe he won't open the door for us. He's not exactly the sociable type."

"He never has been," Heather admitted. "But heck, I'm family. Uncle Grant will let me in. Besides, he knows that I'm coming."

"Yes, but he doesn't know *I'm* coming though. And your uncle doesn't like me."

"It will be interesting, then," Heather mused. "But if Noah decides he wants to get together, no worries. I can go by myself."

As if on cue, there was a tap on my door and Noah stuck his head in. I almost dropped the phone in surprise. "I doubt that's going to happen, but if anything changes, I'll let you know. What time?"

"Is five thirty too early? And can you drive? Maybe we can stop and grab something to eat on the way," Heather suggested.

"I've got a better idea. I'll pick you up and we'll run back to my house. My mother made tabbouleh last night."

"Oh. My. God," Heather groaned. "You know that's my favorite. But aren't you afraid of the third degree?"

"She's stopping to see a friend after work, so we're good. See you soon." I clicked off and stared up expectantly at Noah.

His expression was guarded. "Plans for tonight?" he asked.

"With Heather," I said quickly. Did he think I was going out with Mark again? I needed to explain things to him.

Noah said nothing as he dropped into the chair by my desk. He was dressed in a pair of worn coveralls and a gray T-shirt that stretched tight over his muscular torso. I'd never thought it was possible for a man to look sexy in coveralls, but Noah would even look great in a paper bag.

"What's up?" I tried to sound casual, but my heart was thumping so loudly in my chest that I worried he could hear it.

He cocked his head to the side and studied me. "There's something I've wanted to talk to you about for quite a while now."

There was an awkward pause. I knew Noah would have questions about my dinner with Mark last night. Somehow, I had to convince him that the man no longer meant anything to me. "Sure, go ahead."

Noah drummed his fingers against the side of the chair while I waited breathlessly for him to continue. He was a patient man and always took his time. When I couldn't stand the suspense any longer and had opened my mouth to confess everything, he spoke up.

"I think we're going to have to raise the price of syrup."

"Excuse me?" I must not have heard him right.

Noah crossed his left foot over his right knee. "The cost of everything has gone up this year," he said. "Inflation is killing everyone right now. Supplies, glass bottles, tubing—you name it. If you want to continue to turn a profit here, that's what we'll have to do."

The subject was not one I'd been expecting, so it took me several seconds to respond. As Noah waited for my answer, I debated about broaching a different topic. I had to tell him how much he and Emma meant to me and that the past six months we'd spent getting to know each other had been nothing short of wonderful. Instead, I simply blurted out, "Yes, I've been meaning to talk to you about that too."

His forehead wrinkled. "You have?"

"Yes, it's been on my list of things to do." At the bottom of my list, but he didn't need to know that. "The last time my father raised syrup prices was four years ago." I was always researching Dad's files. "I hate to do it, but like you said, it's necessary. How much of an increase were you thinking?"

Noah didn't hesitate. "Fifty cents for the bottles and a dollar for the jugs."

"That does seem a little high," I admitted.

He shrugged. "It's your farm, Leila, and ultimately your decision."

There was a subtle note of irritation in his tone, but his face gave away nothing. I couldn't stand playing games any longer. The proverbial elephant in the room needed to be dealt with. "It's not what you think," I finally blurted out.

Noah drew his finely arched brows together. "Are we still talking about the syrup?"

"No." I clutched the sides of my chair. "I'm talking about my dinner with Mark last night."

"Leila, you're free to have dinner with whoever you want. You don't owe me any explanation," he said flatly.

"I think that I do." I exhaled sharply. "There's nothing between Mark and me anymore. He's only in town for this week and asked if we could talk. For me, it was just a good-bye dinner. Nothing more. I hope you believe me."

"Of course, I believe you." Noah hesitated for a moment. "But as long as we're setting the record straight, there's something you should know as well."

I waited, daring not to breathe.

"Leila, I care about you a great deal," Noah went on. "I realize we haven't talked about anything long-term yet, but when you mentioned diamonds the other day—"

"That had nothing to do with us," I interrupted hastily.

He smiled in understanding. "I know, but it got me thinking that you might be expecting a ring from me at some point, so I wanted to explain."

An awkward silence enveloped the room. My heart sank into the pit of my stomach, imagining the worst while I waited for him to go on.

He blew out a breath and bowed his head slightly. "I'm not sure that I'm over Ashley's death yet. Maybe I never will be."

"It's okay," I said gently. "I understand."

"I want us to continue seeing each other," Noah said, "but at the same time I have to be honest and consider your needs. So, if you want to break up with me, I wouldn't blame you." His voice turned low and husky with emotion. "I'd hate it but wouldn't blame you."

Noah never ceased to amaze me. I had been so certain he would be upset about my dinner with Mark, but instead, he was worried about me and my expectations. It was a relief to hear that we were still in a good place in our relationship, but a small part of me felt a little crushed too. Ashley's memory was tougher to contend with than I'd originally thought.

"I have no intention of breaking up with you. I'm happy with the way things are." At least I had been, until Mark arrived in town. All the talk about weddings hadn't helped either.

Relief spread across his face. "So, we're okay, then?"

"We're better than okay." I still wanted to know if there was chance of a future for us but couldn't bring myself to ask. Not now.

He leaned across the desk and kissed me lightly on the lips. "By the way, I didn't lie to you."

"About what?" I asked in confusion.

"Emma really does have a game tonight," he said. "It's parents' night at her school." There was a pregnant pause. "You're welcome to join us."

Talk about your awkward moments. A few weeks ago, when I'd been reading Emma a story at bedtime and Noah had been on the phone to his mother, she'd asked if I was going to be her new mommy someday. I'd been so startled that I'd dropped the book but managed to change the subject. What if she'd mentioned it to Noah?

"There's nothing I'd like more," I said honestly, "but I did promise Heather I'd take a drive to New York with her. We're still on for Friday, right? I could bring dinner." Too late, I'd stuck my foot in my mouth. I was no cook, so this meant either picking up takeout or asking my mother to put together something for us.

Noah's deep-set blue eyes lit up with pleasure. "I'd love that. It's a date." He kissed me again and rose to his feet. "I've got to get back to the sugar shack. There's another shipment of syrup to mail out before our price increase goes into effect."

"Sounds good. I'll contact the printer about updated flyers with new prices."

Noah reached for the doorknob and stopped. "Leila, I want to thank you for understanding."

"Understanding what?"

He smiled. "That Emma has to come first in my life."

"Of course. I already knew that and wouldn't expect anything less of you." I loved the fact that he was such a wonderful father.

Noah looked at me with a genuine expression of gratitude. "Thanks. I know it must be difficult for you to understand, especially since you don't have any kids of your own. Someday you'll realize what I mean though."

He shut the door quietly behind him. A stabbing pain pierced my heart as his words replayed themselves over and over in my head.

Someday you'll realize what I mean.

CHAPTER THIRTEEN

AFTER I PICKED UP HEATHER, we stopped back at my house for food. The delicious smell of my mother's tabbouleh salad—parsley, tomatoes, mint, and onion, mixed together with a lemon dressing—greeted us. Heather and I quickly descended upon the bowl and gobbled the salad up, then made sandwiches to take with us made out of *kibbi* and pita bread.

"I don't understand how you could ever leave here," Heather remarked as we drove off. "Your mother is such a good cook."

"Remember who we're talking about okay? You've never had to live with her."

"She only wants to see you happy," Heather said. "Maybe she goes about it the wrong way at times, but you have to know that she loves you."

"Yes, but it's beyond frustrating." I munched on a pine

nut from the *kibbi* as I stopped for a traffic light. "She knows that I'm dating Noah. She likes him and Emma, but now that Mark has turned up, it's like Noah doesn't exist anymore."

Heather rolled her eyes. "What can I say? Mothers always have that one favorite boyfriend they can't seem to get out of their system. My mom didn't even want me to date Tyler at first, remember? She thought that all doctors were too conceited."

"And that couldn't be further from the truth with him," I said.

Heather wiped her mouth with a napkin. "If anything, my family is way more arrogant than his, thanks to Uncle Grant. And now my parents are going to be in debt forever to him because they don't want to start any further trouble."

The WELCOME TO NEW YORK sign greeted us while an idea popped into my head. "Okay, let's try to think positively. Maybe we're going about this the wrong way. What we really need to find out, besides the motive, is who was in Vermont the day Monica was killed. It's almost an hour drive. No one has an airtight alibi. The country club must have surveillance cameras on the outside of the building."

"My mother asked Uncle Grant about that at the wake," Heather said. "Apparently, Monica's car was out of range. If she'd been parked next to the building instead of across the street, the cameras probably would have caught something."

"I'm not referring to when she was killed. I mean that

anyone with a motive to kill Monica who lived out her way had enough time to make the journey from New York to Vermont and back. I wish I'd looked at her phone messages that day. Monica might have texted her killer during the shower or happened to mention where she was."

"You didn't know at the time that she was about to be murdered—or already had been," Heather added. "Whoever killed her must have known something about the layout of the club or at least was familiar with her car."

I took a left-hand turn when we got to Grant's road. "That's a good theory, but having a license plate that reads *Diamond1* doesn't exactly make you inconspicuous."

"Bummer," Heather frowned. "I didn't even think about that."

We pulled up next to Grant's white Cadillac in the driveway. Before we even reached the porch, an outside light flicked on. Grant appeared in the doorway, wearing a maroon smoking jacket. His face broke into a grin that seemed forced when he saw Heather.

"Here's my favorite niece. Thank you for coming to get the photos of your aunt." Grant caught sight of me, and the grin faded. "Well, well. It's my brave little rescuer. How nice of you to accompany Heather. It's wonderful to see you again."

If Grant could play this game, so could I. "It's lovely to see you too. Heather said the damage to the house was minimal. I'm so glad to hear that."

"Yes, yes. It's unfortunate that Monica's study was damaged, but the room can be redone." He ushered us inside.

The family room looked neat and orderly, but there was an acrid and smoky smell to the entire house, and my eyes started to tear.

Grant looked faintly embarrassed. "Sorry for the smell. I can't spend too much time in here either. Gives me a nasty headache. As a matter of fact, I'm headed out for an appointment as soon as you two leave. Now, why don't you make yourselves comfortable while I run upstairs and grab those pictures? They're in Monica's bedroom."

As soon as he was out of earshot, Heather whispered, "It's like he did a complete turnaround. What's up with that?"

"He probably thinks we're suspicious of him." And I definitely was. The antique rolltop desk in the corner of the room caught my attention, and I wandered over to it. A laptop sat on the surface, and I glanced at the screen. Grant had been viewing Dun and Bradstreet's site. Grant's coffee mug was nearby, but it smelled more like brandy than caffeine. Next to the mug sat Grant's phone. I picked it up, but it was passcode protected.

Heather came to stand next to me. "What happened to the good old days when no one locked their phones?" She sighed.

As if on cue, Grant's screen lit up with a message. I can't wait to see you tonight. What time will you be here?

The sender's name was Hot Stuff. They followed it up with another message that consisted of heart emojis and the symbol for fire. Yikes. I dropped the phone back down on the desk as if it were a hot potato. "Isn't he a little too old for this kind of behavior?"

"Gross," Heather agreed, sounding like a teenager herself. "The message must be from the woman he's having an affair with."

"I'm dying to know who it is. What if we waited around outside and followed him to his destination?"

Heather licked her lips in nervous anticipation. "We can try. But what if he sees us?"

"We'll just have to stay back far enough." I gestured for Heather to move toward the doorway. "Keep an eye out and let me know if Grant comes down the stairs."

Heather's eyes gleamed with excitement, and she hurried to take her position. I opened the middle drawer of the desk, hoping to find a love note or anything that would give us a clue as to who the mystery woman was. I pulled open the side drawer and found a birthday card. On the cover of it was a huge heart with the message, *For the man who makes me smile*. Pay dirt.

I glanced over at Heather, who was still watching the stairs for a sign of Grant. I opened the card, hoping to discover the real name of Hot Stuff, but there was no such luck. The card was signed, *Love always, Monica*. Well, shoot. So much for that.

I was about to close the card when I took another look at the handwriting. A strange feeling of familiarity niggled at my brain. On a hunch, I pulled my phone out of my purse and took a picture of Monica's message. At that moment, Heather began to sneeze violently. I stared over at her. Her eyes went wide with alarm, and I could hear the heavy tread of Grant's gait on the stairs, drawing closer with each step.

I quickly shoved the card back into the drawer and moved away from the desk as Grant lumbered into the room, carrying a paper bag in his hand. He looked from Heather to me, and a peculiar expression came over his face. He shoved the paper bag into Heather's hands and then brushed past me, crossing the room in angry deliberate strides. When he reached his desk, he picked up the phone, but fortunately the screen had gone dark. The look he gave me turned my blood to ice.

"Thanks for dropping by, ladies." The comment was directed at both of us, but the cold stare had been meant for me. "I don't want to take up any more of your time, so let me show you out."

If that wasn't a subtle hint to leave, I didn't know what was. With no other choice, we followed Grant to the front door, which he wasted no time in opening. Heather reached out and gave him a hug. The gesture seemed to startle him.

"If there's anything else we can do, please let us know, Uncle Grant." Heather's peaches and cream complexion turned a deep crimson.

"Ah—yes. Drive safely, now," he said in a flustered tone.

We stepped onto the porch, and the door slammed shut behind us. We turned and walked down the driveway together.

"Wow, he couldn't wait to get rid of us," Heather mused as we got into my car.

I started the engine. "Well, he's got plans with his girlfriend. Hot Stuff won't wait all night, you know."

As I backed out of the driveway, Heather motioned to

an area at the bottom of the dead-end street. The surrounding area was dimly lit. "If you park there and turn off your lights, he won't see us when he leaves."

"Good idea." I drove down the street, turned around, and pulled up next to the curb after shutting off my lights. As we waited in the dark, I drew out my phone and showed Heather the picture I'd taken of the birthday card.

She was unimpressed. "It's Monica's signature. So?"

"Take a closer look at it." I pulled up the photo I'd taken the other day of the Post-it Note in Monica's purse. "Ah-ha. I knew it."

"What's going on?" Heather leaned closer over my shoulder to stare at the photo and gasped. "Oh man. I don't believe it."

The handwriting on the Post-it Note and birthday card were a perfect match.

"What does this mean?" Heather asked in confusion. "That Monica wrote the blackmail note?"

"It looks like it." I stuffed the phone back into my purse. "All along we thought that Monica was being blackmailed, only *she* was the one doing the blackmailing."

"That doesn't make any sense," Heather protested. "Monica had money to burn. Even without the jewelry store, she was a wealthy woman. She's always had money. Why would she blackmail someone for cash?"

"Maybe she wasn't blackmailing them for money," I said thoughtfully. "You saw what the Post-it Note said, right? *End it now or I tell him everything.* That doesn't mean Monica was asking for money. She wanted the affair ended."

Heather snapped her fingers. "It must be the woman who's having an affair with Grant."

"But what would Monica be telling Grant that he doesn't already know?"

"I still believe Grant and Belinda are having an affair," Heather said stubbornly.

I thought about how the two of them had interacted at the wake the other day, and Heather's reference to their behavior at Monica's funeral. "If only we knew for sure."

Heather grabbed my arm and pointed at the house. "Here's our chance. Look! That's his car backing out of the driveway."

I wasted no time putting my car in drive and taking off after the Cadillac. Grant's vanity plate, *DIAMOND2*, was easy to keep in sight as we made our way out of the subdivision. Grant took a right turn onto the main road, then went straight for about a mile. Another car jumped between us, but I considered it a good thing as I kept my eyes glued on the white Cadillac.

Heather crouched down in the seat. "Do you think he saw us?" she whispered.

I had to laugh. "Well, I know he can't hear us, so there's no need for you to whisper. Come on, sit up. Keep your eyes on his car in case I lose it. If Grant spots me, he knows you're along for the ride."

She groaned. "You and your puns."

The car between us turned off suddenly, and I eased up on the gas pedal. Grant glanced in his rearview mirror several times, but I wasn't sure if he could see us. The Cadillac picked up speed, and I was forced to increase mine as well. I glanced at the speedometer. We were going seventy in a fifty mile an hour zone. I didn't know this area at all but glimpsed a sign that the Thruway was approaching. Where the heck was Grant headed? I prayed that we wouldn't encounter the police on our journey. In irritation, I tapped the gas pedal again.

"Leila, slow down." Heather gripped the doorjamb.

"If I do, I might lose him," I said grimly.

An intersection with a traffic light was approaching. At the last possible second, Grant made a left-hand turn without bothering to signal. It was too late for me to hit my directional, so I followed him on two wheels, my tires squealing, as a tractor trailer approached us from the opposite direction. Horrified, I sucked in my breath as Heather let out a loud, terrified scream.

CHAPTER FOURTEEN

I GRABBED THE STEERING WHEEL tightly, jerking it to the left, and missed the tractor trailer by mere inches. Sweat trickled down the small of my back. "That was too close," I muttered.

Heather uncovered her eyes and squinted through the front windshield into the darkness. "There he is!" she pointed. "You're gaining on him!"

Grant was about a block ahead of us. He took a left, as another car shot out into the road from a nearby grocery store parking lot. I slammed the brakes and leaned on the horn, and the driver rewarded me by flipping his middle finger out the window.

By the time I headed down the street where Grant had last been seen, his car was long gone. I continued on for a while, checking all around us, but there was no sign of the Cadillac anywhere.

"Oh God," Heather muttered. "I bet Uncle Grant was headed for the Thruway, but he knew we were following him. He tried to cover his tracks."

"That would be my guess too." I backtracked and pulled my car into the grocery store lot. Once we parked, I brought up Google Maps on my phone.

Heather put a hand to her mouth. "Oh no. If he knows we were following him, I'll never hear the end of it. He'll tell my father. What can I give as an excuse? Who are you calling?"

"No one. I need to figure out how to get us back to Vermont because I have no idea where we are right now." A moment later, my directions popped up and a pleasant female voice told me to head east on Route 7.

As I pulled out, Heather leaned back in the seat and sighed. "It's no use, Lei. We're never going to find the person who killed Monica. I'm going to have to call all the guests and tell them the wedding is canceled."

"You still have over a week before the big day," I reminded her.

"No, I don't," she said sadly. "My parents want to start calling people this weekend. It's only fair. Some of my relatives are traveling across the country to be here, and a few are flying out on Monday."

I stopped for a traffic light and glanced over at my friend. The streetlights reflected off her face and a tear rolled down her cheek. I reached over and squeezed her hand. "Honey, don't cry. Everything's going to be all right."

She shook her head. "This wouldn't have happened if I hadn't been such a bridezilla."

Heather had dreamed of this day for so long. All she wanted was to marry the man she loved and have everyone rejoice along with her. It seemed horribly unfair that she wouldn't get the opportunity.

About halfway through the journey, I started glancing in my rearview mirror and spotted a dark sedan behind me. Since it was only a two-lane highway, I had to remind myself to stop jumping to conclusions and said nothing to Heather, who dozed in the passenger seat. Poor thing. The stress was wearing her out.

Traffic was light, and I made it to Sugar Ridge in only fifty minutes. The sedan followed us into town, but when I made a left-hand turn onto Heather's street, I glanced behind me in the mirror and saw that the car had disappeared. Relieved, I blew out a breath. My mind was working overtime these days, and I needed to learn to relax.

"Hey, sleepyhead," I called to Heather. "You're home."

Heather sat up in the seat, yawning and rubbing her eyes. She blinked several times as her eyes tried to adjust to the darkness around us. "Oh wow. I didn't mean to wipe out on you. I haven't been able to sleep the last couple of nights. Guess it all finally caught up to me."

"No worries," I said. "I know what that's like."

She peered out the window with a forlorn expression at her new home. Knowing Heather as well as I did, I could easily guess what she was thinking. She and Tyler had closed on the house last week and planned to settle in as soon as they got back from their honeymoon in Aruba.

Heather had been moving things in during her spare time and planned to spend the night here.

Heather whirled her head around and cast pleading eyes upon me. "Will you come inside for a little while? Ty's working at the hospital tonight, and I—" She broke off. "I'm feeling a little lonely right now. Isn't that silly?"

"It's not silly at all." Heather was clearly depressed, and I wanted to help snap her out of her funk.

"How about a cup of tea?" she suggested as we got out of the car.

"Sounds good, but it will have to be a quick one. This maple syrup lady has to get up early." I grabbed my purse and slammed the door before following her up the steps.

The house was adorable. A beige-colored ranch, it had red shutters, a white picket fence, and looked like the perfect place to start a family. There were three bedrooms, one and a half baths, and a full basement. Heather had planned to convert the primary bedroom into her own personal hairdresser shop as soon as she could get all the required permits and equipment. She wanted nothing more than to be able to cut hair out of her own home and be a stay-at-home mom to at least three children.

We went into the small blue and white kitchen, and I watched as Heather put the kettle on. Although they weren't fully moved in yet, the Formica countertops were covered in mugs and glasses still in their wrapping, a stack of RSVP cards for the wedding, her laptop, and a few unopened gifts. While she fixed our tea, I peeked into the combination living and dining room. The only furniture so far was a blue sofa, matching armchair, and coffee table. A stack of moving boxes rested against one wall, while the coffee table was covered with unwrapped gifts, many of them that I recognized from the shower. There were two rows of boxes stacked against another wall that hadn't even been opened yet. I surmised those were wedding gifts that had arrived by mail.

Heather joined me on the couch and handed me a mug of tea. I nodded at the presents on the table. "How many place settings did you receive?"

She rolled her eyes in dramatic fashion. "Sixteen, so far. My mother made me register for twenty, in case I ever wanted to have a dinner party."

I snorted. "Has she met you?"

Heather sipped her tea. "I know, right? The only way I'm ever having a dinner party is if I can hire your mom to cook it."

"That won't be necessary." I wrapped my hands around the mug. "She adores you and would do it for free. But seriously, what are you going to do with all this stuff? I thought most people sent money these days as gifts."

Heather leaned back against the cushions and closed her eyes. "That would be nice, but I could never come right out and ask for it. It's so tacky. I'm grateful for whatever people can afford to give us. Besides, I want them there to celebrate, not for their gifts."

I made room for my mug on the coffee table and set it down. "And that's one of the reasons I adore you. You could never be a bridezilla. Far from it."

She cocked her head to the side and studied me. "Right back at you, love. If memory serves, you were about as far from one as possible. Your mother and I practically had to drag you to the dressmaker to find a gown."

"Oh please. I think you're exaggerating."

"Yeah, right," Heather laughed. "I seem to remember someone saying, 'Why can't I just wear a simple dress?'"

The remark made me smile. I was glad to finally be able to laugh about my canceled nuptials because at the time, I was certain I'd never get over my broken heart. "Hey, you know me. The less frills, the better."

"That's the truth." Heather gestured at the boxes. "And this is what happens when over two hundred people accept your invitation, then you have to tell them it's postponed and will be only a small family affair so they are no longer invited. So. Much. Work."

"Don't lose hope," I urged. "There's still a few days."

Heather looked around at all the packages, and a sorrowful expression came over her face. "I'm not even going to bother to open the wedding gifts that arrived this week. It'll be easier to send back them back if they're not opened. And less expensive."

"We're going to find out who killed Monica, so you can go ahead with the wedding as planned. I don't want to hear any more about canceling it."

Heather chewed her bottom lip. "But we don't have any concrete leads. I don't even know what to do next. We've talked to everyone who might be a suspect. Sure, they all have motives, but we don't have any proof of who killed Monica."

I took a long sip from the raspberry tea and considered what she'd said. "I think Sunday's memorial will be another good excuse for us to talk to those who were closest to her. Maybe we could even case Grant's house again, but this time use your car or maybe even Tyler's so it's less conspicuous. He knows what mine looks like."

She nodded. "I'm booked solid with appointments all day tomorrow and Friday. Even Saturday is jam-packed. Since I'd planned to be off for two and a half weeks for the wedding and honeymoon, I overbooked to get everyone in who needs an appointment."

"We'll figure out something. I could always drive out to Grant's house after work."

"Please don't worry about it, Lei. You're busy at the farm all day, and you need some time to yourself. It's not right of me to keep asking for help."

"That's what friends are for," I said. "Besides, this time of the year at the farm isn't as busy. We'll be finished with boiling all the sap this week."

"Let's talk about something else," Heather suggested. "I feel like I've been monopolizing every conversation for the past six months with my wedding. How did Noah seem at work today? And has Mark been in touch since last night?" She gave me an impish grin. "Just think. My best friend has two gorgeous guys drooling at her feet."

"Not quite." I cupped my hands around the mug, savoring its warmth. "I don't expect to hear from Mark again. I told him that things had been over between us for a long time."

She barked out a laugh. "Like that would stop him. Mark always got exactly what he wanted, and I'm guessing not much has changed. He did get you to go to dinner with him."

"It was a goodbye dinner," I argued. "Mark only wants me back because he can't have me. He's always been like that."

Heather's face softened. "Are you sure that you're really over him?"

"There's a part of me that will always love him," I admitted. "But there's no way I could ever trust him. He broke my heart, and I'm not going to let anyone ever do that to me again."

Heather's eyes misted over. "You deserve the best. For the record, I think that you and Noah make a great couple. Now, what happened today? Did you guys talk?"

"Yes, we're okay." I placed my empty mug back on the table. "He didn't act that upset about last night. I really thought he was going to be angry."

Heather raised her mug in the air. "Cheers to dating a man instead of a boy. Remember the time that Mark saw you out with Simon's friend Kevin and thought there was something going on between the two of you?"

"It's a little hard for me to forget," I admitted, "especially since Mark broke Kevin's nose."

"Yeah, that was pretty bad." She hesitated for a minute, then dug her bare toes into the crocheted rug that my mother had given her for a shower gift. "Lei, I never told you this, but I was kind of happy when Mark broke your engagement."

"You were?" I stared at her in amazement. "Why?"

She swallowed nervously. "Okay, to clarify, I wasn't happy with the way he went about it, because that was horrible. But yeah, I was happy that you weren't going marry him. The truth is, I never liked him very much, because I thought he was pompous and stuck on himself. I always thought that you could do better."

I stared at her in disbelief. "So, you waited five years to tell me this? Why now?"

Heather smiled hesitantly. "Because you were so in love with him, and I wanted what you wanted. My opinion didn't matter. He treated you well—or at least I thought he did until that last day when he broke it off. Since you're over him, I figured there was no harm in telling you the truth."

"Well, I'm glad you finally told me, even though it took you a little while," I joked. "Maybe you could tell my mother your true feelings about Mark, and she'll stop trying to get us back together, because she's certainly not listening to me."

"If only it were that simple with your mom." Heather watched me thoughtfully. "Is there something else bothering you?"

"You *are* good." I rose to my feet and slung my purse over my shoulder. "I almost told Noah the real reason why Mark broke up with me."

She sucked in a sharp breath. "Oh wow. What stopped you?"

"It wasn't the right time." I stared at Heather and Tyler's framed engagement photo on the wall. "Noah was talking about Emma and how I would make a great mother someday."

Heather stood and squeezed my hand. "Oh, Lei. I'm so sorry. You need to tell him the truth. And honestly? I think you should have a talk with your mother about what really happened with your breakup. Don't keep trying to protect Mark. He doesn't deserve it."

I placed my arms around her shoulders and gave her a tight hug. "When did you get so smart?"

"Planning a wedding," she said dryly.

We walked to the front door together, but Heather pulled me back before I could open it. "Wait a second. I've got to get in the habit of leaving the light on. You can never be too careful these days." She flicked a switch on the wall and a bright flash flooded the porch and driveway. "There, much better. Thanks for coming with me tonight."

"No problem. It was kind of fun to play detective and go on a car chase." I decided I had to go to Detective Barnes with my theory about Monica's Post-it Note. He might not take my claim seriously, but it was worth a shot. "I'll call you in the morning, and we can plan our next strategy."

"Drive safe," she called as I ran down the steps. I reached out for the door handle and discovered that I'd left it unlocked. When the door opened and the dome light came on, I emitted a loud shriek.

While I'd been in Heather's house, someone had decided to slash my front car seats to pieces. The inside of my vehicle was decorated with bits of foam everywhere.

"What's wrong?" Heather called out and didn't wait for

my answer. She ran down the front steps in her bare feet and peered over my shoulder. "Oh my God."

"It looks like I've had a visitor," I said shakily. What was even worse than the ruined upholstery was the index card pinned to my dashboard with a knife. The knife's handle looked eerily similar to the one that had been in Monica's back. Five words printed in capital letters with a black marker were enough to turn my veins to ice.

BACK OFF, OR YOU'RE NEXT.

CHAPTER FIFTEEN

"LET ME GET THIS STRAIGHT." Detective Barnes leaned forward in his chair. "Your car wasn't broken into. You forgot to lock the doors, correct?"

I glanced at the time on my phone. Ten o'clock. I could barely keep my eyes open. Heather and I had spent the past forty minutes sitting in her living room, answering questions. To my surprise, Detective Barnes had been the one to arrive when we'd reported the incident.

"That's right." I sent off a quick text to my mother, letting her know I was okay. Mom was probably still at the Salems', but if she was home by now, my absence would cause concern.

Detective Barnes glanced at his notes. "You said that you didn't see anyone lurking around the house. Any idea how long your car was parked in the driveway?"

"About twenty minutes," Heather chimed in. "I

remember looking at the car's clock when we got back from New York, and the time said eight forty-five p.m. When Leila got up to leave, it was nine oh five."

"And you two were in New York earlier tonight." Detective Barnes appeared even more interested. "Did you happen to see anything suspicious or notice anyone following you?"

The comment made me think of the dark sedan that had been behind me. "I can't be certain, but there was a car behind us the entire way home. When I turned onto Heather's street, I looked in the mirror and saw that it was gone."

"You didn't tell me anything about that," Heather said in dismay.

"That's because you were asleep," I reminded her. "It didn't seem important at the time."

Heather seemed to have forgotten that the detective was there. "How long was the car following us? It couldn't have been on our tail when we left Grant's house because we stopped at the gas station to turn around. I know I would have seen it then."

The urge to reach over and pinch Heather was great, but the detective would be sure to see. At least she hadn't revealed how we'd tailed Grant from his house in hopes of discovering who his mystery lady was. That information wouldn't have exactly endeared us to the detective.

As I'd suspected, he immediately latched on to Heather's comment. "You were at Mr. Butterfield's house tonight? *Again?*"

"Yes, but we were there because I had to pick up some photographs of Monica," Heather explained. "My parents are having a special memorial celebration for her on Sunday and asked if they could borrow some pictures for the day."

"I see." Suspicion was etched into his tone. "And the note and knife were found in your car, Miss Khoury? Any idea why someone would be threatening *you*?"

Heather and I exchanged a glance before I responded. "Not really." I hadn't wanted to tell Detective Barnes that we'd been asking questions about Monica's murder. He wouldn't be pleased by our involvement, but at the same time, I did want to pick his brain about the Post-it Note.

He looked intrigued by my response. "Is there something else that you ladies would like to say?"

I swallowed hard. "I've been checking around with some of Mrs. Butterfield's family and friends about her death."

"It's not her fault, Detective," Heather said quickly. "I asked Leila to help me. If the person who killed my aunt isn't found soon, the wedding will have to be postponed, and my parents will lose a great deal of money."

Detective Barnes's jaw tightened. "Ladies, I promise you that the Sugar Ridge Police Department is taking Mrs. Butterfield's death very seriously. Contrary to what you might believe, I think we can locate the killer without your help. What happened tonight is a very serious situation. Someone may be targeting you because of how you've managed to involve yourself in the murder."

"We understand that." My response was polite, but at the same time, a little voice inside my head wanted to shout that I hadn't gotten involved in this situation all by my own choice. I had been the one to find Monica's body. Didn't he remember that?

Heather was not as easily silenced. "Leila solved a murder last year," she bragged. "Her father was killed at Sappy Endings."

"What *is* Sappy Endings?" Detective Barnes drew his eyebrows together. "A Hallmark movie title?"

"My father's maple syrup farm," I explained. "It came with the name when my father bought the place."

Heather stuck her lip out. "The farm has been in her family for many years. Anyhow, the person who killed Leila's father tried to make it look like a robbery gone wrong. She uncovered the real killer and also found out who—"

Heat burned my cheeks. "Uh, I don't think the Detective wants to hear any more about the incident, Heather." And I wasn't in any hurry to relive it either.

Detective Barnes studied me like I was a bug under a microscope. "How interesting. So, you're a detective now, Miss Khoury?"

"No, I'm not." I was slightly offended by his tone and the assumption that I was looking to make a career out of sleuthing. "I already have a job, detective, as manager and owner of the farm. Like Mrs. Butterfield's death, my father's was not random. He was murdered." My voice caught. "And there's no way that I was going to leave it up to someone else to find his killer."

"Don't downplay it, Leila," Heather insisted. "You

deserve all of the credit. The police were nowhere near finding the killer."

She wasn't exactly endearing me to the man. "Like I said, I'm not a detective, but I do want to see my friend happy, Detective Barnes. She's been planning this wedding for two years. Over two hundred people are scheduled to attend. It would be devastating if she had to cancel."

"Why does she have to cancel?" He looked confused.

"Because my family doesn't feel it's right to go ahead with the wedding before Monica—excuse me—Aunt Monica's killer is found," Heather explained. "My uncle Grant is making a big stink about it, and my father doesn't want to start World War III. Mom and Dad feel this is the best solution for everyone. Leila and I only want to help. Have there been any leads, Detective?"

Detective Barnes's features softened as he stared into Heather's wistful and beautiful face. She always had that type of effect on men. If I didn't love my friend so much, I might have hated her for it.

"Unfortunately, no. I'm truly sorry, Miss Turcot." Detective Barnes cleared his throat. "But we are doing everything that we can. Miss Khoury, I'm familiar with your father's murder. Although I had nothing to do with the investigation, I remembered hearing about it at the time and the effect it had on the entire town. Sounds like everyone was fond of Victor Khoury. I'm very sorry for your loss."

"Thank you." His words nearly brought me to tears. After six months, I thought that I'd managed to cope with my father's death well, but a sudden mention of his name in passing always brought a lump to my throat. I suspected that I would feel this way for the rest of my life.

Detective Barnes rose to his feet and tucked the iPad under his arm. "Thanks for your cooperation, ladies. If there's nothing else, I'll be on my way."

It was now or never. "Detective Barnes, I was wondering if you'd learned the identity of the person who wrote the note."

He gave me a blank stare. "What note are you referring to?"

"The Post-it Note I saw in Monica—Mrs. Butterfield's purse at the bridal shower. It was shortly before I found her body."

A muscle ticked in the detective's jaw. "I'm afraid that's privileged information, Miss Khoury."

"Maybe, but I'm pretty sure I know who wrote it."

His eyes widened in interest. "And who might that be?"

"Monica, and I think that I know why." I was hoping that Detective Barnes might give me something to work with here, but no such luck. He waited patiently for me to continue. "She was blackmailing someone. It wasn't the other way around."

Detective Barnes removed the iPad from under his arm and typed something into it. "Interesting. How did you know that it was her handwriting?"

"When we were at Grant's house, he showed us a birthday card that Monica had given him." Okay, maybe I was fudging the truth a bit, but I couldn't tell him that I'd practically ransacked the Butterfields' desk to find the card.

"It was mixed in with the pictures he gave me," Heather added quickly.

His gaze shifted from me to Heather. I had to hand it to my friend. No one would have ever dreamed from Heather's innocent-looking face that she was capable of such a lie.

"The signatures matched," I went on to explain. "I remembered because the Post-it Note had such distinctive handwriting."

Detective Barnes swiveled his head back in my direction. "You must have one heck of a memory, Miss Khoury. But it happens that you are correct. We called in a handwriting expert, and they confirmed that Mrs. Butterfield did indeed write the note you found the other day."

"Any idea who she wrote it to?" I asked.

He shook his head. "Unfortunately, no. I did mention the note to her husband, and he suggested I take a closer look at Treasure Chest's store manager."

"Jason?" Heather asked in surprise.

The detective stared at her keenly. "You know him?"

"We met him at the shop the other day," I volunteered. "Heather was looking for some bridesmaid gifts."

She shot me a confused look. "Oh! Right. I get the family discount."

Detective Barnes almost smiled, and I suspected he knew what we were up to. "Let's keep this conversation between us, okay, ladies? Mr. Butterfield told me that Mr. Ambrose has wanted to purchase the business for a long time."

"Jason told us all about it," I said.

The detective drummed his fingers against his iPad. "Did you also know that when Mrs. Butterfield refused to sell, he threatened her?"

"He did?" Heather gasped.

"Detective Barnes, I don't mean any disrespect," I said, "but that's difficult for me to believe. Jason volunteered a great deal of information to us, and it wasn't like we were putting a gun to his head." I shivered at my choice of words. "Okay, bad expression."

"He simply isn't the type to kill someone," Heather protested.

I snapped my fingers. "Wait a second. Jason couldn't have committed the murder. He told us that he always works on Sundays. There's no way he could have made the trip to Sugar Ridge to kill Monica."

"That's right," Heather spoke up. "He works alone at Treasure Chest on Sundays."

"Wrong," Detective Barnes corrected. "Treasure Chest was closed that Sunday. The entire shopping mall had a power outage. Jason arrived at eleven o'clock that morning to open, but he closed the doors early, under Monica's specific instructions."

"What time was that?" I asked.

He checked his notes. "Monica sent him a text with her wishes at one fifteen that afternoon."

A chill crept up my spine. Heather's shower hadn't ended until about four thirty, and Monica had been one of the last people to leave. Jason could have easily made the trip from Treasure Chest to Sugar Ridge in under one hour. There would have been plenty of time for him to travel to Vermont, lie in wait for Monica in the back of her car, commit the murder, then drive home.

"There were several other people who weren't fond of Monica," I pressed, hoping that Detective Barnes would continue to take us into his confidence. "Jason told us that Grant has had numerous affairs. Monica and her son were having problems, and she had issues with her best friend, Belinda Fuller, as well."

"Belinda designs jewelry for Treasure Chest," Heather remarked.

Detective Barnes glanced up from his iPad. "My, you ladies certainly found out a lot when you went shopping for bridal gifts."

His tone dripped with sarcasm, causing my face to warm. It was obvious that Detective Barnes knew what we were up to, but at least he wasn't acting as if our opinions were inconsequential.

He continued. "I happen to believe that Monica was holding something over the killer's head. The question is what."

"I think it had something to do with Grant's affair," Heather put in. "She was threatening to expose it, by the sound of her note. But to who?"

"Perhaps the mystery woman was involved with someone else too," I suggested, "and she didn't want them to find out about her affair with Grant."

Detective Barnes looked impressed. "That's a good

theory, Miss Khoury, and probably better than what Nancy Drew herself could have come up with. Jason was happy to inform me that Grant's had several affairs. He's certain that Monica knew about them too. We've been watching Grant and will continue to do so until we find his wife's killer." His eyes gleamed, and a smile formed at the corners of his mouth. "Ladies, thanks for the help, but I'd appreciate it if you would leave the investigation to me from now on."

There was nothing left to say to that. We walked with him to the door, and he shook hands with both of us. "I'm sorry about your car, Miss Khoury," Detective Barnes said regretfully. "I'm not sure that vandalism is covered by any vehicle insurance companies."

He wasn't telling me anything that I didn't already know. I'd gone through something similar when checking into my father's death. I'd had four brand new tires slashed last year as a warning. Killers seemed to enjoy taking their frustrations out on me and my vehicle. The tires had cost me a hefty sum, and now I'd have to turn my leased vehicle in with torn-up seats, unless I had them fixed first. Either way, it was going to cost me a pretty penny.

Heather must have read my thoughts. "Isn't there anything you can do to catch the person who did this to Leila's car? It's going to be awfully expensive for her to get that fixed."

Detective Barnes looked sympathetic. "I'm afraid not. I've filled out a report, but we don't have much to go on, with the exception of the threat and the knife. Honestly, I wouldn't expect much."

A light bulb clicked on in my head. "The knife that was in my car looked very similar to the one—uh, in Monica's car."

The detective looked impressed. "Yes, I noticed that too. My coworkers and I believe they may be part of the same set."

"Is there some way to trace them?" I asked eagerly.

"We're already working on tracing the first knife. The second one from your car tonight will definitely help us to narrow the search." Detective Barnes's cop mask was in place, and he said nothing further. Heather opened the screen door for him, and he smiled graciously at her. When he turned to me, the smile instantly faded.

"Please don't do anything foolish, Miss Khoury," he said. "You both strike me as smart and competent women, but threats such as these often catch people off guard. Don't take any chances, and try to avoid going anywhere alone. It shouldn't be long before we catch the person who killed Mrs. Butterfield, but try to be careful until that happens."

"Thank you for coming out," Heather said sadly.

He nodded. "Best of luck with your wedding. If I can be of further service, please feel free to contact me at any time."

We watched as Detective Barnes got into his vehicle and drove away. Heather closed the door and slumped against it. "Oh, Lei. I never meant to put you in any danger. And we aren't even any closer to finding the person who killed Monica."

"Maybe we are." I pulled out my phone and showed her

the picture I'd taken of the knife pinned to my dashboard. "Take a look at this."

Heather shrank away from the picture in horror. "Holy cow, Lei. Why did you take a picture? It's not a souvenir!"

"Look at the handle," I advised. "What do you see?"

She studied the picture and shrugged. "I don't know. It looks like some kind of chef's knife. There's nothing really special about it."

"The stone embedded in the handle could set it apart," I said. "Remember when we were at Treasure Chest the other day? Jason said that he knew all about knives."

"Oh yeah," Heather nodded. "He once worked for a distributor."

My fingers flew over my phone. "Jason gave me his business card the other day. I'm going to send this picture over to him and see if he has any thoughts. Maybe it's a rare set." His knowledge of knives gave me a tiny glimmer of hope that he'd help us narrow down what source the knife could have come from. I thought back to what Detective Barnes said. Was there a chance Jason could have killed Monica? Sure, it was possible. Treasure Chest had been closed that day, and he did have a motive. Jason bore a good deal of resentment toward his boss since she'd never fully intended to sell him the store. But what good would it have done for him to kill her? That didn't change the outcome. I had to trust someone, and he was my best option right now. "The police will most likely track down the knife, especially if there's a serial number on it," I observed. "Maybe we could do the same."

Heather shrugged. "Hey, it's worth a shot."

There was no time like the present. "Let's see if we can find anything on your laptop."

Heather led the way back to her kitchen while I finished typing out my text to Jason. She typed in her password and handed me the mouse, then opened the fridge door and gave a mournful sigh. "It's times like this I wish I knew how to cook." She shut the door and picked up a bag of Doritos on the counter. "Do you want something? I always eat when I'm nervous. Maybe I should take your mom up on her offer of cooking lessons."

"No, I'm good." I had no desire to learn how to cook but gave Heather points for trying. Since she was about to get married, she was consumed with guilt that Tyler would have to live on the hospital's cafeteria food.

I squinted down at the handle. There was some writing on it, but the figures were too fuzzy to make out. I tried googling different variations of numbers and letters for a while but came up with nothing.

Finally, I closed the browser and sighed. "This is getting us nowhere."

"Another dead end," Heather said.

"Let's pray Jason can come up with something, because I'm all out of ideas."

The kitchen clock informed me the time was ten thirty, and my bed was calling me. "Sorry, Heather, but I've got to run."

"Sure, I understand." She walked me to the front door. "Lei, did you ever wish you could go back in time?"

I wasn't sure what she was getting at. "Of course. I think everyone has at some point in their life. Why?"

"There's a lot of things I'd go back and do differently in my life if I could. One of them would have been to find a way to stop you from leaving Sugar Ridge after your breakup with Mark." Heather smiled sadly. "I was so lonely for you these past few years."

"That makes two of us," I said, "but at least you had Tyler."

"True," Heather admitted. "As much as I love him, though, it's not the same thing. You're my best friend and the sister I never had. I feel like you know me better than anyone." She twisted her hands together. "And if something happened to you because I insisted on involving you in—oh, I don't know! A crazy scheme to find a killer? I'd never forgive myself."

Her words touched me deeply, and I reached out and pulled her into a hug. "Stop worrying. Nothing's going to happen to me." It was a promise I fully intended to keep.

CHAPTER SIXTEEN

NOAH SHOOK HIS HEAD IN disbelief. "This is starting to become a habit with you, and I can't say that I'm a fan."

"What is?" I pretended not to know what he was talking about. We were in the sugar shack, watching the sap boil. It reminded me of the times I'd spent with my father, doing the same thing. Reverse osmosis pumped the sap under high pressure through a very dense membrane to concentrate it. The concentrated sap was then gravity fed into our six-thousand-gallon evaporator. The fragrant steam released during the process warmed the room and helped to disguise the guilty blush currently creeping into my cheeks.

Noah's deep-set blue eyes examined my face thoughtfully. "Leila, I hate the fact you always seem to be in danger. Now, I understood when you needed to look into your father's murder, but this is different."

"I promised Heather I'd help her. This isn't just about her having her moment in the sun, Noah. There's nothing I wouldn't do for her."

He said nothing as he moved the stainless-steel drums into their correct positions. Once the finished syrup was drawn off the end of the evaporator pan, it would be sealed, still hot, in the barrels for storage. Afterward, the syrup was poured into bottles and jugs and shipped to our customers. This was the last of boiling, for the weather had grown warm, despite the surprise snowstorm a couple of weeks ago. There would be no more collection of sap until late next winter.

"You're a good friend to her," Noah said finally.

"She would do the same for me."

He nodded. "I admire your loyalty, but that doesn't mean I won't worry about you."

"You're worried about me?" My voice cracked slightly as I posed the question. What I really wanted to ask him was if my mother was correct to assume he never wanted to get married again. Noah had already told me he didn't know if he'd be able to get over Ashley's death, and doubts had started to crowd my brain.

"Of course I am." He drew his eyebrows together. "Leila, is there something else you need to get off your chest?"

I blew out a long breath. "Where do you see us headed?" God, I hoped I didn't sound desperate. At least I'd finally said out loud what had been torturing me internally for weeks.

Noah stared down at the bottles of amber syrup he was

packaging. I checked the shipment off on my sheet and stood ready with the label I'd printed earlier in my office. He was silent for a long time as he fiddled with the bottles. The room was growing warm. Finally, without looking at me, he said, "I told you that I care about you a great deal."

I stood there, waiting for the other shoe to drop. "But…"

Noah wrapped packing tape around the box and took the label from my outstretched hand. He applied it and then faced me. "No *buts*. I like being with you. You're beautiful, smart, and kind. You've worked hard these past six months, and I'm proud of what you've done on the farm. Plus, Emma adores you. That's really important to me."

My heart melted into a giant puddle when I thought of the little girl. "I adore her too. Remember that night a couple of weeks ago when I came over with subs? I had the best time making chocolate chip cookies and reading her a bedtime story."

I caught him staring at my lips and wondered if he was thinking about what had happened after Emma had gone to sleep. We'd sat by the fire in his living room for a long time, talking about Emma, our lives, and the farm. Noah then walked me out to my car where we'd shared a long, passionate kiss. Things were so perfect that night, and I'd been secure in the knowledge we cared deeply for each other.

Since then, I'd become incredibly busy with preparations for Heather's upcoming shower, a last-minute dress fitting, the farm, and other pressing matters. After Mark's return to town, I'd also been filled with self-doubt. "I know

I've been busy, but it feels like something else has changed since that night. I told you there's nothing between Mark and me anymore."

"And I believe you." Noah placed several jugs of our dark robust brand of syrup into another postal box and surrounded each one with foam wedges. "But it got me to thinking—what right would I have to interfere if you did want to be with him again?"

As usual, I immediately thought the worst. "Are you saying you want us to break up?"

Noah walked over and put his hands on my shoulders. "No, I never said that. I want you to continue to be a part of my life and Emma's. I've always tried to be honest with you. I told you how difficult it's been for me to put Ashley and her death behind me, but now I get the feeling you're keeping something from me. Actually, I've thought that for a while."

I exhaled sharply. He was more perceptive than I'd given him credit for. There was no other choice—I had to tell him the truth. There was no way I would make the same mistake again—the mistake that had caused my breakup with Mark.

Noah rubbed his hands up and down my arm, turning newly formed goose bumps into a pleasant sensation that managed to distract me from the topic at hand. All of a sudden, I heard myself babbling a response. "I didn't tell you everything about my dinner with Mark the other night. He asked me if we could get back together."

A vein bulged in Noah's neck. "What did you tell him?"

"The truth. That I was over him and seeing you now. And that I'm very happy." I reached for his hand. Fortunately, he didn't pull away.

A frown crossed his handsome face. "Yeah, I was afraid he might try that. I have to confess, I *was* jealous when I saw you with him. You guys have a lot of history together. And I can't compete with it."

"It wasn't all good history," I reminded him. "By the way, you're not in competition with Mark."

He scowled. "I hate the fact that he hurt you. What I really wanted to do was break the guy's neck, not shake his hand."

The comment made me laugh. "You sure had me fooled. You were as sweet as maple syrup to him."

Noah kissed the tip of my nose. "I've learned patience the hard way, believe me. But I was starting to wonder if you were considering your options."

"Why would I do that?" I asked in disbelief.

"Because I haven't promised you anything long-term," he said. "To be honest, I don't know when that day will come. I guess a part of me feels like I'm being disloyal to Ashley, but at the same time, it's not fair to you."

I knew he spoke the truth. Noah and Emma had their lives turned upside down when Ashley died. The accident had occurred right before Christmas, which always made my heart break, especially for Emma. In search of a new start, Noah had left New York with his daughter and settled in Sugar Ridge.

While I had suspected he might not be ready to take our relationship to the next level, it still hurt to hear him say so. "I understand."

"No, you don't. And somedays, I don't either. The past year and a half has been a rollercoaster for Em and me. All I'm asking is for you to be patient a little longer." His voice was barely above a whisper, and there was no mistaking the look of anguish in his eyes. "I don't want to lose you, Leila, and what we have."

Relief settled over me as I squeezed his hand. "You're not going to lose me. We have lots of time."

He kissed me softly on the lips. "Has anyone ever told you how wonderful you are?"

"All the time," I teased.

Noah put his arms around my waist. "How about we go out for a real date on Friday? Dinner and a movie, while Emma is with my mom. Or anything else you'd like. You're the boss."

"Hmm." I reached up and ran my fingers through his hair. "I remember a time when you would have disagreed with me about that."

He chuckled. "No, ma'am. You'll always be the boss. But I do admit that when you first showed up at the farm, I figured you had no interest in running the place and would gladly sell it to the highest bidder."

"Then you quickly realized your mistake."

"I did," he agreed. "But you were ready to string me up from the nearest maple tree."

"Impossible." I laughed. "Sappy Endings would be lost without you. And so would I. I love having you and Emma in my life."

Noah reached up a hand and cupped my cheek with his

palm. "Thanks for being you. And I'm grateful that you love Emma. You're so good with her."

"Well, I was a teacher," I reminded him.

"Sure, but it's more than that. You have a natural way with kids. It's obvious how much you love them." He kissed me again. "Guess I'd better take off for the post office before it closes."

I helped Noah carry the boxes out to his car and watched as he drove away. My heart ached for Noah and Emma and all they'd been through, but I also cursed myself for not telling him the real reason for my breakup with Mark. He needed to be told, and this had been the perfect opportunity. When Noah said he didn't want to lose me, everything else had gone right out of my head. Why did life have to be so darn complicated all of the time?

My phone buzzed and Jason's number appeared on the screen. "Hello?"

"Miss Khoury? It's Jason Ambrose from Treasure Chest. You sent me a text last night. I'm terribly sorry that I haven't had a chance to respond sooner."

"That's okay. Thanks for getting back to me." I'd almost given up on him. "Do you remember when I was in the store the other day with Heather, and we were looking at the antique knives? You said you knew some details about their history."

Jason sniffed loudly. "I know a great deal about knives, madam. Then again, I know a great deal about most things."

His comment made me smile. "Did you have a chance

to look at the picture I sent you? It was a knife I found in my car last night."

"Yes, I did. What was the meaning of it? Did you receive some type of threat?" he asked.

I walked back into the sugar house and quickly tossed the remnants from the packaging into the garbage. "Looks like someone doesn't want me asking questions about Monica's death."

Jason gave a loud gasp on the other end. "Oh my. This is exciting! Well, not for you, of course. But it means you are on the trail of a killer. When you were in here asking questions the other day, I honestly didn't think you'd get very far."

"Thanks for the vote of confidence," I joked, "but I still don't know for sure who did it. The knife in my car was from the same set that killed Monica. At least, I think so. Heather and I tried to do some research online last night, but we ran into a dead end."

Jason snickered. "Of course you did. That's where I come in. The set is manufactured by a company named Denmark. They've made millions of this brand, and for a time, they were even sold on QVC."

"Great," I muttered. "So, looking for the owner of this set is like looking for a needle in a haystack."

"Let me finish," Jason went on. "What most people don't realize from the serial numbers is that this particular set started out as a limited one. If you look carefully at the first letter on the knife, it's not an *I* like most people think, but an *L*. That tells me the set is genuine, and the ruby on the handle is real. This also narrows it down quite a bit and makes the set quite costly. Not your run-of-the-mill kind."

"Seriously?" I clutched the phone tightly between my hands. "I never would have guessed it was rare. Is there any way you can find out who it belonged to?"

Jason paused for a moment. "Let me do a little more research, but I'm about ninety-nine point nine percent certain I can find out. Only—"

"What?"

"I feel like I've seen this knife before. Not in person, but maybe a photo of it somewhere."

My heart gave a sudden jolt. "Where?"

"I can't be certain," he admitted, "but Monica may have had a set—or a knife like this. I may be wrong, although that rarely happens. Let me think on it for a little while. I'm sure it will come to me. My mind is like a steel trap."

Jason was his usual confident self, but I worried he might not remember soon enough. We were running out of time. "I appreciate your help."

"By the way, your watch is ready," Jason said. "If you want to stop by tonight, maybe we could talk about the knife further? I have a cappuccino machine in the back. We can have a real confab."

I glanced at the clock on the wall. 4:45 p.m. "What time do you close tonight? Seven?"

"Tonight is six o'clock," he answered. "But I know you live in Vermont, so I can wait for you. Don't break the speed limit trying to get here on time."

I chuckled at the thought. Too bad Jason didn't know about my car chase with Grant the other evening. "Sounds like a great plan. I have to close up my farm, but I should be able to get there before six. See you then."

After I had disconnected, I walked into the gift shop to empty the cash register. Out of the corner of my eye I could see my mother wiping down the counters and tables in the café. Once I'd removed the money and shut off the lights in the store, Mom came out from behind the counter, wiping her hands on a towel. "Where's Noah?" she asked.

I put the *Closed* sign on the front door. "He went to the post office and is going home from there. I need to run an errand, so I'll be out for a few hours."

My mother's eyes gleamed with sudden hope. "Does that mean you're going to see Mark? We could drive over to their house together. Our crotchet club starts at six thirty, so we have plenty of time."

"Mom." I spoke in a gentle but firm voice. "You need to forget about Mark and me. It's never going to happen again."

"Don't say that!" Her eyes widened in shock. "Mark is perfect for you. Handsome, rich, and intelligent. How many Lebanese men do you think are around here? Not many."

I should have realized my mother would never stop hoping that I would marry someone from the same ethnic background. "None of that matters to me. I'm not in love with Mark anymore. And if I ever do get married, it will be to someone who doesn't object to my running the farm."

It definitely would have been another bone of contention between Mark and me.

"You could always hire someone to run the place," she said thoughtfully. "I'd help out too."

"You're doing too much as it is. I know you need a break." While she enjoyed baking and running the café, my mother had never been interested in making syrup, gathering sap, or candle making. She had no desire to tap trees in the middle of winter. My father had done all those things for years while she'd handled the baking and financial part of the farm.

She waved a hand dismissively. "I'm fine. You don't know what you're saying."

"I'm in love with Noah, not Mark."

Mom regarded me with suspicious eyes. "Does he love you?"

Heat rose in my face. "He hasn't said it, but I'm sure—"

She quickly cut in. "Don't get me wrong, Leila. Noah is a good man, and your father thought the world of him." Her eyes misted over, as they always did whenever she mentioned my dad. "But he was already married to the love of his life. Please think about this for a while. Maya called me earlier and said they were hoping to announce your engagement at a small party this weekend. On Saturday, because Mark leaves for New York City on Sunday."

"She said *what*?" I couldn't believe my ears. Did anyone ever listen to anything I said? "I told Mark at dinner the other night that it was over." He still thought he could wrap me around his little finger, and it made me furious. "I don't want to talk about this anymore."

My mother picked up her purse and shut the lights off in the café. "You're just like your father. Always avoiding the issue."

"Thank you for the compliment."

She opened the front door, glared at me for a second, and then slammed it behind her. With a sigh, I quickly set the alarm and locked up, but by the time I'd reached the porch, my mother had already driven away. I settled behind the wheel in my temporary seat constructed of chair cushions duct taped together and purchased from the local Walmart, and drove out of the lot.

In the past six months I'd been home, my mother and I made some wonderful progress in our usual stormy relationship. Sadly, that had all gone out the window. Her childlike behavior reminded me of the terrible arguments we'd had in the past, the worst occurring the day I'd told her and Dad my wedding was off.

Before I'd had a chance to explain to my mother what had happened that day, she'd leapt down my throat with accusations, wanting to know what *I'd* done wrong to make Mark walk away. I had been so hurt and angry by her reaction I had refused to say anything further and decided to get as far away from her and the rest of Sugar Ridge as soon as possible. Now, I wondered what would have happened if I hadn't been so impulsive that day. If I'd chosen to stay, I would have had more time with my family, especially my father.

This would haunt me for the rest of my life.

The solitude of a drive was exactly what I needed right now. Although fall was my favorite season in Vermont, spring was a close second. As I drove toward the border, the sun began to sink into wispy clouds. The surrounding scenery was beautiful, especially the Green Mountains, which were vibrant even at this time of year. Grass was beginning to grow, and buds from wildflowers starting to open. Lilacs, my favorite flower, were in abundance, but sadly they only lasted a couple of weeks.

Signs of new life were everywhere and filled me with aspirations. How I wished Heather could still have the wedding she'd always dreamed of. I hoped Noah and I could straighten things out in our relationship and continue to move forward. My father's presence was all around me, and I pictured him looking down and nodding approval. *You can do this, habibi.*

I tried to forget about the ugly episode with my mother earlier and concentrate on more pleasant things, but my train of thought was interrupted by my cell. I clicked the hands-free attachment on my steering wheel. "Hello?"

"Miss Khoury, it's Jason. I was wondering how much longer you might be."

My eyes flickered to the clock on my dashboard, which read 5:55 p.m. "It should be about ten or fifteen minutes. I'm sorry for the delay." I slowed the car to a snail's pace as a deer ran across the road. It was a known fact they traveled in pairs and were always more active during spring and summer months. Sure enough, another one appeared from out of nowhere and hurried across the road to join his friend.

"That's all right," Jason said. "I'm actually getting excited about playing Sherlock Holmes."

"You look more like a Hercule Poirot to me," I joked.

"Well, I can live with that." He chuckled merrily into the phone. "Anyhow, I think I may have figured out where the knife came from. Didn't I tell you earlier it would come to me?"

I stopped the car at a red light. "That's awesome. So, you know who owned that particular set?"

"I believe so," he replied. "If I remember correctly, it was a birthday gift that wasn't exactly welcome. Let me see. It must have been last year because—"

The sudden high-pitched sound of chimes filled the phone, and Jason muttered under his breath. "Oh, bollocks! I hate last-minute customers. Do hurry up and get here, okay? Drive safely."

He clicked off before I could respond, and I pounded the steering wheel in frustration. My curiosity had been piqued. If Jason knew who the set belonged to, then he must know who the killer was. We were finally getting close. A shiver of excitement crept down my spine.

Twenty minutes later, I pulled up in front of Treasure Chest. My arrival had been slowed considerably thanks to rush hour traffic. The parking spots in front of Treasure Chest were all vacant except for a black Aston Martin, which I figured must belong to Jason. I couldn't picture him driving a Honda or a Ford. When I'd first met the man, I thought he was snooty and pretentious, but Jason had quickly grown on me. He couldn't be the person who had killed Monica.

As I pushed open the glass doors and the chimes went off, a feeling of uneasiness washed over me. I had tried to convince myself of Jason's innocence, but what if he had been the one to vandalize my car? Maybe this was some type of setup. I'd experienced something similar last fall, when the person who had murdered my father was someone I had never expected. What if the same thing was happening all over again?

The showroom was deserted, and I assumed Jason was in the back room doing paperwork while enjoying a cappuccino. Or was it possible he was back there awaiting my arrival and brandishing a knife? *No. Stop thinking the worst about everyone.*

"Hello?" I called out. "Jason? It's Leila."

There was no answer.

My heart began to thump against the wall of my chest. A little voice inside of my head commanded me to run away while I had the chance. I stood by the front door, debating what to do next. On a sudden impulse, I pulled out my cell and dialed Jason's number. A second later, the sound of Beethoven's *Symphony No. 5* filled the room. My nerves began to tingle. If Jason's cell phone was nearby, then where was he?

I slowly walked across the room as the sound of the ringtone grew louder, then it stopped altogether. Holding my breath, I raised my finger to redial his number as I reached the main display case in the showroom. I leaned over the counter and peered down at the rug.

Jason was lying on his stomach, a knife buried halfway in his back. The weapon was undoubtedly from the same set we'd been talking about. A ruby stone on the handle shimmered from the light above, as if mocking me.

A terrifying scream filled the air. It took a few seconds before I realized that scream was coming from me.

CHAPTER SEVENTEEN

A HALF HOUR LATER, I watched helplessly as Jason's lifeless body was transported past me into a waiting van outside. Treasure Chest was a madhouse with EMTs, police officers, and a crowd of spectators outside trying to see what was going on. There was even a television news van parked in the lot. The sight sickened me. People were like vultures where death was concerned.

I stood by the front window of the store, trying to stay out of the way and get the image of Jason's lifeless body out of my head. How had this happened? I'd only spoken to him twenty minutes earlier and he'd sounded fine. Tears gathered in my eyes, blurring my vision as I thought of him. He hadn't deserved this fate.

"Ma'am?" A tall and wiry police officer approached me and gestured toward the back of the store. "I'm Officer Dunham. There's a kitchen out back. Let's talk in there, okay?"

I nodded and followed him to a small room directly across from the office. It consisted of only a table with two chairs, a microwave, and a dorm-sized refrigerator. With a pang, I noticed the cappuccino maker on the countertop. Across the hall, a man in rolled-up shirtsleeves was busy taking photographs of the office. Even from this distance, I could spot a broken porcelain cup and saucer lying on the floor and liquid that had spilled all over the desk. Jason must have been having his cappuccino when the killer attacked him with a knife.

This didn't make any sense. I'd been on the phone with Jason when the chimes sounded. He hadn't been killed at his desk. If he'd been attacked in the back room, Jason must have somehow dragged himself out to the showroom, where he'd collapsed behind the counter. The panic button was located there. Who had come into the store while he'd been talking to me? *I hate last-minute customers.*

Officer Dunham sat across from me and scribbled something on a small pad of paper. "So, from your call to 9-1-1, it appears the last time you spoke to Mr. Ambrose was at five fifty-five?"

I tried to focus on what he was saying, but it was difficult. "Um—I—"

"Take your time," he said gently. "I realize this must be a terrible shock."

"Yes." I exhaled sharply. "We talked for about five minutes."

Officer Dunham stared down at his notes. "Then, you arrived here at six fifteen and he was already dead?"

"It was only twenty minutes," I choked out. "Jason didn't deserve to have this to happen to him. He was a nice man and devoted to the store."

"Miss Khoury?"

I looked up in surprise. Detective Barnes was standing in the doorway. He nodded cordially to Officer Dunham, who immediately rose from his seat.

Detective Barnes held out his hand. "Detective Ryan Barnes from the Sugar Ridge, Vermont Police Department. Do you mind if I ask Leila some questions? We're old friends."

His remark deserved a snort, but I wasn't feeling up to it.

Officer Dunham shook his head. "Not at all, Detective. I'll go check and see how Forensics is making out." He smiled at me and left the room.

Detective Barnes sat in the officer's deserted chair as my cell rang. I glanced down at the screen. *Noah.* My call had gone unanswered fifteen minutes earlier, and I hadn't bothered to leave a message. "Is it okay if I take this?"

He nodded. "Sure, go right ahead."

I had hoped he might give me some privacy, but instead, he busied himself studying something on his phone. Having no other choice, I hit *Accept Call.* "Hi."

"Is everything okay?" Noah asked. "You didn't leave a message."

I glanced up at Detective Barnes, who was trying hard to pretend he wasn't listening. "Not really," I stammered. "I—um—I'm in New York. At Treasure Chest."

"What are you doing there?" Noah wanted to know. "More detective work?"

"Kind of," I faltered.

"Things can't be that bad," he said.

"Worse," I whispered. "Jason's dead."

"What?" Noah's voice thundered through the phone. "The jewelry store guy?"

Tears formed in my eyes. "Yes. I was on my way over to talk to him—er, I mean, to pick up my watch." Shoot. I hadn't wanted the detective to know about our secret rendezvous to discuss the knife. Detective Barnes remained intently focused on his phone screen, but it was obvious he'd heard every word. After all, it was his job to overhear things he wasn't supposed to.

Noah cursed under his breath. "What happened to him?"

I hiccuped back a sob. "Someone stabbed him. The same way they killed Heather's aunt Monica."

"Oh wow," he said breathlessly. "That's awful. Are you okay?"

"Not really." I accepted a tissue from Detective Barnes. "I'm being questioned by the police right now. I—I just wanted to hear your voice."

"Where are you? The store? Listen, I just put Emma in the bathtub. Her soccer game started late, and we only got home ten minutes ago. Let me see if I can find a babysitter, and I'll come right out."

"No." It was comforting he wanted to be here for me, but I had no intention of remaining any longer than was necessary. All I wanted was to go home. "We'll be wrapping up soon." What an optimist I was.

Noah was silent for a few seconds. "I hate to think of you going through this all alone."

"Don't worry about me. Besides, Heather's already on her way. She insisted on coming when I called. She canceled her last client."

"Are you sure?" His voice was husky and low, making me long for the safety and security of his arms. "Do you want to stop over at the house when you get back to Vermont?"

I tried to laugh but failed miserably. "I don't think I'd be much fun tonight."

"That doesn't matter," he said. "I'd like to be there for you, Leila. For God's sake, this is the second dead body you've found in less than a week. Things like this just don't happen—well, at least not to anyone else I know."

I was starting to feel like the world's biggest jinx. "We'll get together Friday night. Nothing will stop us." Besides, I had something important to tell him, and the sooner the better, before I lost my nerve again.

"It's a date then," Noah said softly. "Will you please do me a favor and call me as soon as you get home?"

"Yes, I promise."

I clicked off and stared across at Detective Barnes, who looked up from his phone at the same moment. "How are you doing, Miss Khoury?"

There was no point in lying to him. "I've been better." I decided to ask a question of my own. "Isn't this area out of your jurisdiction?"

Detective Barnes shifted in his seat and smiled. "Yes, it is, but I received a call from a member of the local force.

He knew I was investigating Mrs. Butterfield's death and this was her store. I wasn't far from the border when he called, so I decided to come and see what was going on for myself."

"Do you know if Devon or Grant have been notified?"

"I've heard Devon is on his way here," Detective Barnes remarked, "but it's doubtful they told him what happened over the phone."

Now I understood the real reason Detective Barnes had rushed over. He wanted to gauge Devon's reaction for himself. In the meantime, I decided to relay some information to him as well, hoping he might decide to take me into his confidence. It was a long shot, but worth a try.

"Grant is having an affair, you know."

"Is he?" Detective Barnes folded his arms across his chest. "You seem very interested in the Butterfield family these days, Miss Khoury. I thought I asked you to leave the investigation to me and my coworkers."

There was a slight edge to his voice, which I hadn't noticed before. I decided to come clean with him. "Like I told you, I'm only trying to help my friend. Heather's wedding is about to be ruined if we can't find the person who killed Monica. And now Jason is dead, and I'm convinced the murders have to be related."

Detective Barnes typed something on his iPad. "Why do you think this?"

Was this some sort of a test? The detective had to know it was the same person. "The knife is from the same set that killed Monica. Plus, Jason was killed in the same manner.

And it's also the same kind of knife that was used to slash the seats in my car. The police department must realize they're related."

He looked up at me and cocked one eyebrow. "Well, well. Are you gunning for my job, Miss Khoury?"

There was a note of sarcasm in his tone, but I pretended not to notice. "Not at all. Like you, I only want to know who did this."

Detective Barnes scratched his head. "The deaths do appear to be related, but what would the motive be? Any ideas?"

I swallowed hard. "I believe Jason knew the killer's identity. We were talking about the knife used to kill Monica and where it might have come from."

The detective looked unimpressed. "From what I've been told, it was a pretty ordinary knife. That also means it's more difficult to trace where this particular set may have come from, but we'll find out eventually."

"Jason once worked for a knife distributor. He said the ruby from the knife found in my car was real, and that's what set it apart. I sent him a picture of it and asked him to take a look. He said the knife looked familiar and called me while I was on my way here tonight—to pick up my watch." I added that part so he wouldn't think I'd been coming out here to play detective. "He remembered where he'd seen the knife before."

Detective Barnes leaned forward in his seat eagerly. "Where?"

"He didn't get a chance to tell me." Tears smarted in my

eyes. "The door chimes rang while we were talking, so he had to hang up. It was a last-minute customer. But he did think that he had seen a photo of the knife somewhere. Maybe he found one and it's on his desk."

"The entire area has already been checked." Detective Barnes motioned across the hallway to the empty office. "His phone was found on the floor next to his spilled cup of coffee. We checked it out but found nothing of interest. And his last call was to you."

I dabbed at my eyes with the tissue. "Did the person break into the store?"

"Not likely." Detective Barnes's mouth stretched into a thin, hard line. "There was no sign of forced entry, so the assailant probably came through the front door like everyone else."

"What about surveillance cameras?" I asked. "All jewelry stores have them. Wouldn't they have picked up the person?"

"The footage is being examined as we speak," Detective Barnes explained. "Hopefully it will tell us something, but don't get your hopes up. The person who killed Mr. Ambrose might have been masked, and it could take quite a while to identify them. There isn't a camera in the office, so if the killer entered from the rear of the building and never went into the showroom, there's less of a chance we can identify them."

I was convinced it was someone who had either worked at Treasure Chest or knew the layout of the store. Everyone that Heather and I considered had some kind of connection to the place. "If they entered through the back door, they must have had a key. Maybe it wasn't the same person who came into the store while I was talking to Jason."

"Possibly." Detective Barnes checked his notes. "The last sale for the day was recorded at five thirty."

I threw the tissue into the trash and straightened up in my seat. "What if the person came in through the back door while Jason was in the showroom talking to a customer? Maybe they spotted the picture on his desk and killed him because they knew he could identify them?"

"You've certainly thought this through, Miss Khoury," Detective Barnes said. "There's some merit to what you're suggesting. Tell me, do you really think that Grant could have done this?"

I shrugged. "I'm not positive, but Jason didn't seem to think Grant and Devon were above suspicion. He's worked here for years and knew all of their dirty little secrets."

Detective Barnes typed something into his iPad again. "I see."

Someone coughed from the doorway. It was Officer Dunham, who stared at us uncomfortably. "Excuse me, Detective Barnes. There's a Miss Turcot outside. She says she's here to take Miss Khoury home. Can I send her back?"

Detective Barnes's face brightened. "Yes, that's fine." He rose to his feet. "I've got your cell number, Miss Khoury, so I'll call you if I have further questions. For now, I suggest you leave this to the police and—"

"Leila!" Heather rushed into the room and threw her arms around me. "Oh my God. Are you okay?"

I nodded as she released me. Heather seemed to notice Detective Barnes for the first time. "Hello again, Detective."

"Nice to see you, Miss Turcot." His eyes grew soft and warm as they focused on her, and I was starting to suspect he had a secret crush on Heather. "Thanks for coming to support your friend."

I glanced at the time on my phone. "Wow. It's only been forty-five minutes since I called. Did you fly here?"

She cast a shameful look in Detective Barnes's direction. "I probably broke a couple of speed limits along the way, but I was so worried about you. Oh, Lei, this is awful! Jason was such a nice man. This has to be related to Monica's death."

"That's my guess too," I said grimly. "I think Jason knew who the knife set belonged to and—"

I didn't get a chance to finish my sentence. A loud male voice boomed from the showroom. "I want to see the Detective in charge this minute!"

Heather and I glanced at each other in amazement. The voice belonged to Devon Butterfield. A second later he tore into the room, followed by Officer Dunham and Lexy.

Officer Dunham grabbed Devon by the arm. "I told you to wait outside until Detective Barnes was finished talking to the young lady."

Devon shook him off. "This is my store, and no one is going to tell me what I can do." He looked surprised to see me and Heather. "What in God's name are you two doing here?"

Detective Barnes held up a hand. "It's all right, Officer. He can stay. Hello, Mr. Butterfield. I'm very sorry to hear about your employee's death. Miss Khoury was just telling me how she found him."

Devon pointed at finger at me. "Are you some kind of magnet for death?"

I was certainly starting to feel like one.

"What were you even doing here?" Devon wanted to know.

"Take it easy, Devon," Heather spoke up. "Leila came to pick up a watch."

"She lives in Vermont. There must be other jewelers in Hicksville she could have gone to," he spat out.

Lexy clung to his arm protectively and gave me a long, menacing stare. "That's the one I told you about, honey. She and her friend were asking me all kinds of questions at your mom's wake the other night."

Heather's nostrils flared. "We haven't done anything wrong."

Devon gave a low snicker. "For two people who live in Vermont, you spend an awful lot of time around here. You just happened to be at our house the night it caught fire, and my stepfather said that you were snooping around in mom's house when you came to pick up the pictures. All of the trouble started at your stupid bridal shower."

I found it interesting how Devon's attitude had changed suddenly. At Monica's wake, he had been unfailingly polite and went out of his way to thank me for trying to save the house. What had changed since then? Was he afraid Jason had shared information about the killer's identity with me before he died?

Lexy pointed a bony finger at Heather. "Yeah, that's right. Monica might still be alive if it wasn't for you!"

"Okay, let's try to stay calm," Detective Barnes said. "Mr. Butterfield, I'd like to ask you some questions." He turned to me and Heather. "Miss Khoury, you're free to go. I'll call you if I need anything further."

The problem was that since Devon and his girlfriend had arrived, I didn't want to leave. I wanted to ask my own questions and find out if one of them was responsible for Jason's death.

"What about me?" Lexy whined.

"Ma'am, if you would be so kind as to wait outside," Detective Barnes said pleasantly. "We'll only be a few minutes."

Lexy reached for Devon's arm again, but he shook her off. "Do as the detective says, Lexy."

Her lower lip quivered as if he had mortally wounded her. With no other choice, Lexy swiveled on her heel and flounced out of the room.

Officer Dunham spoke up. "Sorry, Detective. My boss is in the showroom and would like to have a word with you."

Detective Barnes sighed in frustration. "Don't go anywhere, Mr. Butterfield. I'll be with you in a second."

Heather and I hung back as Detective Barnes left the room. I took the opportunity to address Devon. "Why didn't your father come with you?"

"He's not my father. He's my stepfather," Devon said angrily. "Besides, it's none of your business."

"Are you afraid he might have been the one to kill your mother and Jason?" I knew I was playing with fire but no longer cared. Jason's death had affected me deeply, more so than Monica's.

"You don't know what you're talking about," he fumed. "My stepfather is a good man. He loved my mother more than anything else in this world."

I had my doubts about that. "If he loved your mother, then why was he having an affair?"

"Get out," Devon said between clenched teeth.

There was no turning back now. "Doesn't Belinda have a key to the store as well? If she was having an affair with your stepfather, maybe she's the one who killed Jason."

Devon's eyes had become dark endless cesspools of rage. He clenched his jaw and started to advance on me.

Heather grabbed hold of my arm and tried to drag me away. "Um, maybe it's time we left, Lei," she said in a feeble voice.

"That's a good idea," Devon whispered. "Get out of my store. And don't ever come back unless you want to be the next victim."

CHAPTER EIGHTEEN

"I DON'T BELIEVE THIS," HEATHER said as we hurried out of the store. "Devon's got to be the one, I'm sure of it."

"We don't know for certain," I argued.

"Are you kidding? Did you see his face? I thought he was going to hurt you."

A police officer was standing by the entrance of Treasure Chest, talking on his phone. The television van was still in the lot, but the number of people watching had dwindled, probably once Jason's body had been taken away.

"He's definitely hiding something." My body was still numb, but I wasn't sure if it was from finding Jason's body or the threat Devon had directed at me. Maybe a little of both.

"What if Devon knows who did it, and he's trying to protect them?" Heather put a hand to her mouth. "Maybe someone like his stepfather. Oh, God. My uncle might be a murderer."

"Sorry, but I'm not buying it," I said. "I know Devon and his mom were having problems, but I can't see him sticking up for Grant if he knew the man had killed his mother. Devon's got a role in this, but I'm not sure what it is yet."

Heather's car was parked next to mine. "Are you sure that you feel up to driving?" she asked. "We could leave your car here and pick it up tomorrow."

"No, I'm all right." I was still trying to get the ghastly image of Jason's dead body out of my head. Maybe if I listened to a podcast on the way home, it would help.

"Hey!" a woman yelled rudely. We turned to see Lexy walking rapidly toward us. I took a minute to take in her outfit. She was dressed in tight-fitting jeans, a cropped red shirt, and high heels of the exact same color.

Lexy paused to catch her breath. "I want you to stop bothering Devon." She spoke in her usual squeaky voice that always made me want to put my hands over my ears. "He's got enough to deal with right now."

Heather and I exchanged a glance. "Don't you want to know who killed his mother?" I asked. "It must be causing him—and you—a lot of grief."

As I'd hoped, Lexy took the bait. She folded her arms across her well-endowed chest. "You don't know the half of it. I just want my ring. Is that so wrong? And for the record, there's plenty of rings in the showroom, if you catch my drift."

It was nice to know Lexy wasn't self-absorbed. "Who do you think might have killed Monica?"

Puzzled, she stared at me. "How the heck would I know?"

"What about Grant?" I pressed. "Do you think it's possible he could attack his own wife?"

Heather nudged me in the ribs, worried I had gone too far. My hope was that Lexy might unintentionally reveal some information about Devon or Grant's relationship with Monica. She wasn't the brightest gem in the jewelry case.

Lexy glanced toward the store, as if worried Devon could somehow hear her. "I guess it's possible. Grant and Monica fought all the time."

Heather took a step closer to her. "Jason told us that my uncle was having an affair. Do you have any idea of who it was with?"

To our surprise, Lexy began to laugh hysterically. "Are you kidding? Who'd want to fool around with that old goat for free? He has to pay for his companions."

Heather's eyes widened in shock. "You mean he—"

"Yep," Lexy giggled. "He's a one-night-stand kind of guy. No strings attached. Monica must have known about it. Devon once told me his parents had separate bedrooms for the last few years."

This was way too much information for me. I had to wonder why Monica and Grant had gotten married in the first place. Maybe all he'd wanted was to get his hands on her fortune. "What did Grant do for a living before they got married?"

Heather spoke up. "He worked as a salesman. I guess he met Monica at some kind of trade show."

Lexy snorted. "Devon said Grant made himself out to be this big important businessman when he first met Monica. He really laid on the charm, and it wasn't until after they were married that she finally realized he was a nobody."

"Real nice," Heather murmured.

Lexy tapped her finger against the side of her head. "Devon never liked him from the start. He had a sick sense about him."

I managed to hide my smile. "I think you mean *a sixth sense*."

She looked at me, confused. "Yeah, that's what I said."

A red corvette pulled up next to my car. We all watched as Belinda alighted from the passenger side. She looked surprised when she saw the three of us. Recognition dawned on her face when she spotted me. "Leila, right?"

"Hi, Belinda," I greeted her. "Have you met my friend, Heather?"

Belinda smiled and extended her left hand for Heather to shake. Her right hand was wrapped around a square wooden box. "Not formally, but I saw you at Monica's wake and funeral. You're the bride-to-be, aren't you? Or at least you were, until Grant butted his nose in." She gestured toward the man who remained sitting in the Corvette. "This is my husband, Howard Fuller."

The driver's window was partially down, and Howard waved politely to Heather, Lexy, and me. He looked to be in his sixties, with a bald head and thick horn-rimmed glasses. He made no attempt to get out of the car. Instead, he unfolded a newspaper and immediately hid his face behind it.

"Sorry." Belinda shook her head. "Howie's a bit anti-social. Are you here to buy jewelry? Devon asked me to design some new pieces and drop them off at the store."

"I thought you weren't designing any new jewelry for Treasure Chest?" I asked.

Belinda's mouth was taut. "Yes, well, that was Monica's wish. But now that Devon said he'll be the new owner, things have changed. He likes my work and wants to see more of it." She raised an eyebrow at Lexy. "It's Lexy, right?"

Lexy nodded. "Yeah, hi. I've seen you at Monica's before."

Belinda wrinkled her nose, as if she found the woman offensive. She swiveled her head and seemed to notice the police cars for the first time. Her face paled. "What's going on? Was the store robbed? Jason said I could drop off the combs even if he'd already left for the evening."

"Oh, don't worry. Jason's not waiting around for you," Lexy said. "He's dead."

Belinda's hands flew to her mouth, and she dropped the box. It hit the ground with a heavy thud. Several jeweled combs flew out and littered the blacktop. Heather and I stooped down to help her retrieve them.

"Oh my God. What happened to him?" Belinda asked.

"He was stabbed," Heather said quietly.

"When did you last talk to him?" I asked. "You had a key to the store, right?"

Belinda placed the top back on the box. "I've had one

for a long time," she said shakily. "Monica gave it to me years ago. I—I can't believe someone would want to hurt Jason. He was such a nice man."

"We couldn't believe it either," I said.

"It looks like he was attacked with a knife similar to the one that killed Monica," Heather volunteered.

I had a sudden urge to nudge her in the ribs, but everyone would have seen. Although I hadn't wanted to reveal the information, it seemed to make no difference to Belinda.

"What time did you speak to Jason?" I asked.

Belinda stared at me as if I was an alien. Her face turned the color of paste. "Sorry—I—it was about four o'clock. I don't understand. Who is doing this and why?"

"I wish we knew," I said.

"Is Devon here?" Belinda asked Lexy.

Lexy nodded and popped a piece of bubble gum into her mouth. "Yeah, he's inside talking to the police guy."

Belinda glanced over in Howie's direction, but he was still absorbed in his newspaper. "I can leave these on the front counter. I don't want to disturb Devon right now. He can pay me whenever he gets a chance. It—it's really no big deal."

"I'll take you in." Lexy popped a large pink bubble on her face, removed the gum, then promptly stuck it back in her mouth. "I want to know what's going on, anyway."

"Thank you," Belinda said and smiled weakly at me. "Leila, I haven't forgotten about your comb. If I'd known you would be here—"

"Please, don't worry about it," I said. "There are more

important things to deal with right now. There's plenty of time."

Belinda nodded. "All right then. Maybe I'll see you ladies on Sunday at the memorial." She started to follow Lexy, who was already strutting across the pavement in her high heels.

Heather exhaled sharply as she unlocked her car. "If Belinda's making you a comb for my wedding, she shouldn't worry. At this rate, she's going to have all the time in the world she needs."

It was nine o'clock when I arrived home. Mom had texted me earlier that her washer and dryer had been delivered in the garage, but the handyman she used wasn't available until tomorrow to install them. I was surprised to see her car in the driveway as I'd thought for certain she'd still be at the Salems. Time to brace myself for an oncoming lecture. With a resigned sigh, I entered the house and switched on the light, expecting to see her sitting in the kitchen, brooding. Fortunately, the room was empty.

A meow sounded from behind me. Toast sauntered into the kitchen, blinking sleep out of his eyes. I stooped down to pick him up and cuddled him against me.

"Did I wake you? Sorry, buddy. I need some sleep too." I climbed the stairs with him purring contentedly in my arms. A light shone underneath my mother's door. I set Toast down, tapped on the door, and called out good night, but she didn't answer. Mom had suffered from insomnia for years, and it had only gotten worse since my father's death. She often took sleeping pills to get much-needed rest. I opened her bedroom door and peered inside. She was sound asleep with a Sandra Brown novel open across her chest.

I closed her door noiselessly and breathed a sigh of relief. The last thing I wanted was to have another argument with my mother tonight. Ever since Mark had come to town, we seemed to be on a disastrous course. We would have to talk about this again. She needed to respect my wishes and my relationship with Noah.

After I had gone through my nightly routine, I settled into bed with Toast at my feet. This had been a horrible day and all I wanted was for it to end. Sleep couldn't come fast enough.

The next morning, I was up at six o'clock, determined to leave bright and early for work. I had payroll to take care of, and with the candy making, I'd gotten behind on some other duties as well.

My mother was in the shower when I slipped down the stairs forty-five minutes later. Toast hopped up on one of the kitchen chairs and watched me with luminous green eyes as I grabbed a piece of *manoush* from the bread basket. I adored the flatbread flavored with herbs best when it was warm and nuked a piece of it in the microwave. After a quick search in the fridge, I came up with a container of baba ghanoush Mom had made and spread the appetizer on the bread. I savored the taste of the roasted eggplant and seasonings as I scribbled a quick note, letting Mom know I had an early day planned and would see her at work.

Toast continued to watch me with what seemed like strong disapproval as I fastened the note to the front of the fridge with a Sappy Endings magnet. She'd be sure to see it there. I patted Toast on the head, and he meowed plaintively. "No judgment," I whispered. "I'm not chickening out. Honest. She'll make sure she gets her say later."

As I unlocked my car, I made a mental note to call the dealership this morning about getting my seats replaced. I had hoped to avoid it for a while since the repair would be costly, but the concoction I'd made from seat cushions was not as comfortable as I'd hoped.

When I reached the end of the street, I tried to slow down for an upcoming stop sign, but my car kept rolling forward. I slammed on the brake, but the pedal went all the way to the floor. With a shriek, I sailed through the stop sign. Fortunately, there was no one coming from the opposite direction.

The road began to slope downward as I approached another traffic light. It turned red as I sailed underneath, barely missing a Subaru from the opposite direction. The driver blew his horn and made an obscene gesture at me.

In desperation, I tapped the pedal again, but the car was gaining speed instead of stopping. My heart jumped into my throat. I couldn't understand what had gone wrong with my vehicle. The brakes had been working fine yesterday. I sucked in a sharp breath as the car began to zoom downhill.

"Please, please stop." I begged and pulled hard on the emergency brake, but nothing happened. Sweat beaded on my upper lip and fear gutted at my insides. I kept hitting the brake and praying for some type of miracle to occur. A deer bounded out from behind a tree and stood in the center of the road, watching and waiting as my car approached. I laid on the horn, hoping he would move, but no such luck. In an attempt to avoid hitting him, I swerved to the right. At the last possible second, he ran across the road before we collided. Unfortunately, the mailbox I'd veered toward instead did not scramble out of the way, and I plowed right through it, then skidded down into a ditch about three feet deep. I screamed at the top of my lungs as the car turned over onto its roof. A quick, searing pain shot through my head, and the entire world turned black.

CHAPTER NINETEEN

"LEILA, CAN YOU HEAR ME?"

The voice was male and sounded far away. My eyelids were heavy; it was a struggle to open them, but I finally managed. The light shining down into my face made me wince and felt as if it was cracking my head into two pieces.

"Everything is okay. You're going to be fine. The doctor said you were very lucky."

Noah was sitting next to me, holding my hand. I glanced around the room. I was in a hospital bed with an IV hooked up to my arm. Weakly, I tried to sit up as he adjusted the pillow behind my head and pushed the button to raise the top of the bed.

Noah looked as if he hadn't slept in days. His eyes were fixed worriedly on my face. "What time is it?" I asked.

"Three o'clock in the afternoon," he replied. "You've been in and out of consciousness for a few hours."

Then I remembered what had happened. "My brakes stopped working."

He nodded grimly. "Detective Barnes was here earlier. The police took your car to a local repair shop. It's definitely totaled. Someone cut your brake lines."

My mouth went dry. "You mean it was done deliberately?"

He narrowed his eyes. "First the note, and now this. Someone wants to kill you, Leila. This has to do with Monica's death, doesn't it?"

I leaned against the pillows, thinking of the message in the note. *Back off, or you're next.* The person hadn't been kidding around.

Noah covered my hand with his. "Your car flipped over in the air. You were out cold when the ambulance got there. The guy whose mailbox was hit saw the accident happen from his driveway and called 9-1-1. Your mother phoned me in a panic. I was so afraid you were—" He didn't finish the sentence.

I glanced around the semiprivate room again, but we were alone. The curtain was pulled back to reveal the other bed was unoccupied. "Where is she?"

"Selma went down to the cafeteria with your brother," Noah said. "Simon insisted that she have something to eat."

"And you've been here all day too?"

He nodded. "I wasn't going anywhere until you woke up. The worst part is over."

"What about Emma? She's home from school by now."

"My mom's already taken her for the weekend." Noah

brought my hand to his mouth. "So, you're not going to get rid of me that easily."

"Wait a second. The farm. There's no one there." I threw back the covers as if to get out of bed, but Noah stopped me.

"Whoa! Where the heck do you think you're going?" He brought the sheet back up over me and smoothed the hair back from my face. "We closed the farm for the day. There's no way we could function until we knew that you were going to be okay."

My body shook as I remembered those final moments before I blacked out. "I couldn't stop the car." I'd never felt so helpless before in my life.

"You were lucky," Noah went on, "to come out of it with only a concussion." There was an unmistakable flash of pain behind his baby blues. "Leila, there's no way—" He hesitated for a second. "I couldn't have survived that again."

A nurse interrupted us then. She came into the room and set a pitcher of ice water and plastic cups on my tray. Her name tag identified her as April. She smiled brightly at me. "I see that we're awake. The doctor will be in soon to check on you." April hummed a tune low in her throat as she checked the IV and took my temperature.

"Can I go home now?" I asked.

"That's the doctor's call, hon," April replied. "But I do believe he's planning for you to stay the night for observation. You hit that head of yours pretty hard." She pointed to a bright red button on the side of my bed. "Press it if you need me for anything. They'll be bringing your dinner in about an hour." She smiled at me and Noah, then left the room.

Noah was silent for several seconds. "There's something that I haven't been honest about with you, Leila."

My heart sank into the pit of my stomach as once again, I imagined the worst. No, I had to stop thinking such thoughts. Not every man was like Mark. "What is it?"

He fixed his troubled eyes on my face. "I've been worried about growing too close to you."

Oh God. Maybe my mother had been right after all. I braced myself for what was coming next.

Noah closed his hands around mine. "When we first started dating, I didn't know I was going to fall in love with you. I thought we were good friends taking things at a nice, slow pace and enjoying each other's company. But the other day when you mentioned shopping for diamonds—"

"I thought we already straightened that out. I'm not waiting around for you or any other man to pop the question."

He smiled. "Of course. But you were supposed to be married five years ago, so I wasn't sure what your expectations were."

"None," I said. "Contrary to what people may think, I don't need to get married or have children for a happy life."

"I'm sorry. That came out wrong." Noah paused. "I guess I was scared. Not of falling in love with you or getting married, but of losing someone I love. When I got the call from your mother this morning, it was like some sort of horrible déjà vu all over again."

A lump the size of a mountain formed in my throat, and I was unable to speak.

Noah continued. "She told me you'd been in an accident..." He swallowed hard before continuing. "I immediately thought the worst. Then, when I found out you were all right, I started thinking. I don't want to live my life worrying about what might happen every minute, because that's not really living. I want to enjoy every second I spend with the people I care about."

I blinked back tears. "I had no idea this was how you felt. I wish you had told me."

"You're right." He nodded solemnly. "I should have been more honest about my feelings. I promise never to keep any secrets from you again."

My stomach twisted at his words. It was time. I had no idea how Noah would react to what I was about to say, but I couldn't keep this from him any longer "I have to tell you something as well."

His face looked stricken. "Is it about Mark?"

"Not in the way you might think." I shifted in the bed, trying to find a more comfortable position, and perhaps stalling a bit as well. Noah leaned over to adjust the pillows for me again. The smell of his spicy aftershave wafted through the air, a temporary distraction, but I was determined to follow through.

Noah sat back down and waited for me to continue.

I exhaled a long, deep breath. "I can't have children."

His eyes widened in shock, and for a long agonizing moment, he was speechless. I waited with bated breath, afraid of what he might be thinking until he reached for my hand. "I'm sorry, Leila. That's why you seemed so upset the other day when I said you were going to be a great mother."

"Yes." I bit into my lower lip, determined not to break down. I'd learned to accept the hand I'd been dealt years ago, so there was no point in crying about it now. "I didn't tell Mark until after we became engaged. It was a big mistake on my part. He never handled it well, and things only got worse. All he ever talked about was having a big family, especially since he was an only child. I should have told him sooner, but—" This was the most difficult part for me to say. "I think I knew deep down once I told him the truth, he'd leave me."

Noah's handsome face grew stern. "Sorry, but that makes him a coward in my book. He didn't deserve you, Leila."

"That's sweet of you to say." I smiled up at him. "But I should have been honest with him from the start."

"Don't blame yourself." There was a question in his eyes, and I knew what it was, but also that Noah didn't dare to ask it. He was too much of a gentleman.

"I had to have an emergency hysterectomy when I was eighteen," I explained. "There wasn't any other option."

An expression of pity filled his face and made me cringe. "Please don't feel sorry for me. That's not why I told you. It happened a long time ago, and I've learned to live with it since then. I can still be a mother—someday—if I want to."

Noah smiled warmly. "Sure, you can. There's plenty

of kids out there who need good homes. Ashley and I talked about adoption. We always wanted a large family. She had a difficult pregnancy with Emma and wasn't sure she wanted to go through it again." He paused. "And you thought something like that would matter to me? Did you really think I'd behave like Mark?"

"No, I didn't think so, but I wasn't sure," I admitted. "We haven't been dating that long, and I—"

He leaned over to kiss me, and I never finished the sentence. When we broke apart, he tucked a curl behind my ear and stared down at me intently. "It wouldn't have mattered one bit to me, and I'm not saying that because I have Emma either." His voice was barely above a whisper. "When you love someone, all that matters is making them happy."

Someone coughed in the doorway. We both looked up to see my mother and Simon standing there. Simon was the first one to react. He strode across the room and kissed me on my cheek. "Man, you had us all worried, sis."

I reached for his hand. "Thanks for coming."

"Are you kidding?" he asked. "You're my only sister. Who would pester me if I didn't have you around?"

"It's nice to know I'm appreciated," I joked.

My mother watched me with a thoughtful expression. Her face was chalk white, and there were circles of weariness under her eyes. I gave her a warm smile. "I hope they let me come home, because I'm starving and not for this hospital food. I want *kibbi*."

Her eyes shone with happiness. "That is the best news

I've heard all day. Simon and I just saw your doctor in the hallway. He's on his way in here shortly. He wants you to stay the night, but that doesn't mean Simon can't run home and grab some dinner for you."

"Sounds like bribery to keep her here," Noah teased as he rose from the chair and handed it to my mother.

"It's for the best," my mother said stubbornly. "Leila needs her rest. I'll bring her home tomorrow."

I heaved a sigh. My mother always thought she knew what was best for me, including the man I should marry. This wasn't the time to get into it. From her weary expression, I knew that she'd been worried sick, so I decided to let it go. "Fine. I'll stay."

Mom gripped the back of the chair Noah had vacated and glanced over at him. "Would you and Simon mind if I had a moment alone with Leila?" she asked.

"Of course not," Noah said. "I think I'll go and get some of the wonderful cafeteria food Leila's been craving."

I was too tired to roll my eyes at his comment.

"Well, for my part, I guess I better go fetch that *kibbi* before my sister starts banging on the walls," Simon joked.

"I'll walk out with you," Noah offered. He leaned down to kiss me. "Be right back. Don't go away." He smiled at my mother and left the room with Simon.

My mother sat down in the chair and folded her hands in her lap. "Leila, I know you aren't happy with me right now, but there's a few things I need to say to you."

"Mom, I'm really not in the mood for a lecture," I said.

She ignored the comment. "First off, I was terrified

when I got the call you'd been in an accident. All I could think about was your father." Her voice quivered.

I reached for her hand. "It's okay. Nothing's going to happen to me."

"Why didn't you tell me you were looking into Monica's murder?" she asked.

Oh no. "Where did you hear that?"

"I called Heather earlier to tell her what happened. She started crying on the phone and said your accident was all her fault."

"It's not her fault," I protested. "She asked for my help. I didn't want her to have to cancel the wedding."

She gave me a sharp look of disapproval. "Maybe, but I wish you had told me what you were up to, and that your car had been vandalized. Anyway, I told Heather you were fine. She's on her way over to see you tonight and said she's bringing cheesecake."

"Cheesecake and *kibbi*? Maybe I should get concussions more often," I joked.

My mother frowned. "This isn't funny, Leila. You should have told me about your car getting vandalized."

"I didn't want you to worry." I reached for the paper cup on my tray and took a sip of water. "Yesterday wasn't a good time to bring it up. All we seem to do is argue lately."

She twisted her hands in her lap. "That was my fault. Anyway, I wanted to tell you how sorry I am about trying to get you and Mark together again. I shouldn't have tried to force you into a marriage you obviously don't want anymore."

I stared at her in amazement. Perhaps she was finally taking my relationship with Noah seriously. "What made you change your mind?"

Mom lowered her eyes to the floor. "When I went to Maya's house to crotchet last night, I wanted to talk to her about getting you and Mark back together."

Frustrated, I closed my eyes. I didn't want to hear any more. "What did you say to her?"

"Nothing," she admitted. "It was a pleasant evening at first. I enjoyed catching up with all my friends I haven't seen in a while. Mark came in while we were there and said hello, then went into the kitchen. Maya followed him. After a little while, I decided to go and get some more coffee and overheard them talking behind the door. Your name came up."

My eyes flew open. "And?"

Her face turned a deep crimson. "I didn't mean to eavesdrop, but of course I wanted to hear what they were saying about you. It appears Mark is inheriting a substantial amount of money from his grandfather when he turns thirty."

"I already know this," I said. "When he died eight years ago, Mark mentioned to me that his grandfather had put a trust fund away for him."

A muscle ticked in her jaw. "Yes, but maybe you didn't know that the only way Mark will inherit the money is if he's married by his thirtieth birthday."

I sucked in some air. It all made sense now.

My mother watched me anxiously, deep wrinkles

forming in her brow. I fumed in silence. What a jerk. How was it possible I had never seen my ex's true colors before? Had I really been that blind to him while we were dating?

"Mark was dating another woman for about three years," my mother continued. "I have no idea what happened, but when I saw Maya in the store last month, she said they had broken up. So, it sounds like you—"

"I was his last hope." Deep down, I'd wondered if Mark had some type of ulterior motive for wanting me back. The truth was more satisfying than hurtful, and it almost made me laugh. "That's so typical of him."

She took my hand in hers and stared at me with a guilty expression. "I was so angry when the two of you broke up. I had my heart set on you making such a good match. But I see now I was wrong to do this, and I'm sorry. You're my only daughter and I love you very much. It doesn't even matter why you broke up. I'm glad you never went through with the wedding."

"Mom." My throat was tight with tears. "The reason we broke up—"

"Like I said, it doesn't matter anymore," she interrupted. "Mark wasn't ready to get married. At least that's what Maya told me back then."

"Not quite. He broke up with me after I told him I couldn't have children."

She looked at me like I had two heads. "I can't believe he'd do such a thing," she gasped. "Why didn't you ever tell me that was why you had broken up?"

"Because it wasn't any of your business," I retorted.

"You immediately thought it was all my fault. You wanted to believe the worst back then, so I let you."

A tear ran down her cheek, and she squeezed my hand tighter. "Leila, I'm so sorry for the way I treated you. All I ever wanted was for you to be happy—as happy as your father and I were. Can you ever forgive me?"

"Of course. It's all in the past," I said. "I finally found a man who really cares about me. Mom, I'm not sure if Noah and I will ever get married, but if things don't work out, I'll be fine. I'm happy with him and the way things are right now. I just want to enjoy our time together, and whatever happens, happens."

"All right," she conceded. "But there is one thing I would like to know."

Oh, jeez. "What's that?"

She beamed at me proudly. It was a look she usually reserved for Simon. "I want to know when my daughter became so much smarter than me. Or maybe you always have been."

"Nope." I laughed. "I still have a lot to learn."

CHAPTER TWENTY

THE NEXT DAY WAS SATURDAY, and my mother brought me home from the hospital early in the morning. She was adamant I stay in the house for the entire day. I tried to convince her that I felt fine, but she wouldn't listen.

"The doctor said you're to rest today," she said firmly. "No arguments."

Once I'd been settled on the couch with the television remote, books, and about ten pillows, Mom reappeared with a breakfast tray. There was fresh fruit, pancakes, sausage patties, and *Ahweh*, which I'd been missing dearly, especially since the hospital's version of coffee was similar to mud.

My mother was all business and efficiency. She was dressed in her work attire, which consisted of jeans and our trademark Sappy Endings blue T-shirts, which bore a maple leaf in the center.

"Now, I'm only going to run by the farm for an hour or so," she told me. "I'll make up some breakfast sandwiches so that Noah can manage the café. At least there will be something for people to eat. Do you think you'll be okay without me? Shall I ask Heather to come over and keep you company?"

"Mom, I'm fine, and Heather's working. Please go ahead. Stay until two o'clock." That was the new closing time on Saturdays. I couldn't stand her hovering over me like a helicopter. "Noah will need you. Look at all the business we've lost the last two days."

She waved a hand in the air, as if swatting at a fly. "Things like that don't matter at a time like this. And I can't leave you alone for so long. What if you black out or something?"

"The doctor said I was all right. Besides, you're the only one who can make the breakfast sandwiches and other treats. I promise if I'm not feeling well, I'll call you."

My mother made a face, then bent down and kissed me on the forehead. "Well, make sure you do. And Simon said he'd call and check up on you as well. He had to go out of town on assignment this morning. I guess it's a pretty big story. Anyway, he won't be back till next week and left his car here for you to use until you get a new one."

"That was nice of him," I said gratefully.

She narrowed her eyes. "Don't get any ideas. You're not using it until Monday."

"But I'm fine," I objected. "The doctor said I could drive if I felt up to it."

"Please don't argue with me, Leila."

At ten thirty she finally departed, leaving Toast as my official babysitter. He sat next to me on the couch, staring longingly at the plate of food in front of me. I gave him a couple of pieces of sausage, and he gobbled them up gratefully, as if he hadn't eaten in weeks. Satisfied that the begging had not been in vain, Toast curled up in a ball at my feet and went to sleep, his deep purrs reverberating through the room.

My cell buzzed and I glanced at the screen. Heather. "What's up?"

"How are you feeling?" she wanted to know.

"Fine." I set my empty mug of coffee down on the tray and leaned back against the mountain of pillows. "My headache is gone. I wish everyone would stop making such a fuss and let me get back to work. Noah and my mother can't handle the farm all by themselves."

Heather let out a groan. "For cripes sake. Someone tried to kill you yesterday, but all you're worried about is if the farm can survive without you. Typical Leila."

Irritated, I flicked through the television channels while she talked. There was nothing interesting to watch. I finally settled on an episode of *Murder, She Wrote*. Maybe Jessica Fletcher could provide some useful hints about my current situation.

"Anyway," she went on. "I'm siding with your mother this time. No work for you until Monday, or maybe even Tuesday."

"Yeah, well, that's too bad because I'm going back on

Monday. Maybe I'll even stop over tomorrow after the memorial service and get some paperwork done."

Heather gasped into the phone. "Your mother will have a fit!"

"She'll get over it. By the way, we called a truce yesterday." I proceeded to tell her about our conversation and the reason for Mark's sudden interest in me again.

"I'm so glad you never married him," Heather admitted. "He wouldn't have made you happy, Lei. But I hate that he managed to hurt you again."

I squinted at the television. Jessica Fletcher was on the phone talking to the police. I hoped they took her claims more seriously than they did mine. "He didn't. I've put him behind me forever."

"I was wondering if you felt up to some company," Heather said. "I have a couple of more appointments today, but I'll be finished about one. My last two clients canceled. As much as I need the money, I'm kind of glad. I can't seem to concentrate on my work anymore."

Poor Heather. The days were dwindling down, and we were still no closer to finding Monica's killer. "That's totally understandable, with everything you've been going through. I'll be here all day. Where else would I go?"

"You'd better be," she warned, "or else I'll have to tell your mother. And you know what will happen then."

"She'd probably ground me." I disconnected the phone and tried to concentrate on the television. Jessica Fletcher provided no assistance with the murder I was trying to solve. With a sigh, I turned it off and dozed for a while. I awoke to the sound of my phone chiming. Noah texted to see how I was, and I'd missed a text from Simon asking the same. I responded to both that I was fine, and I was…except for the fact I was already going out of my mind with boredom.

I lay back and went over the details in my mind of everything that had happened since Monica's murder. Before yesterday's accident, I'd simply been trying to help Heather find her aunt's killer so her wedding could be saved. But the stakes had risen considerably since then. After Monica's death, Jason had been murdered, and now someone was after me as well. They must be worried I knew their identity, even though I still had no idea.

Despite everyone's warnings to leave it alone, there was no way I could do so. The killer wasn't going away, and they had me in their sights. I refused to give this person another chance to try and finish the job.

Heather knocked on the front door early in the afternoon. Toast and I had been lying on the couch, watching another episode of the *Murder, She Wrote* marathon while I finished a piece of baklava. After I let Heather in, Toast immediately started rubbing against her legs. She laughed and stooped down to pet him.

"How's our patient doing, Toast?" she asked as she scratched him behind his ears. "Has she been behaving herself?"

Toast emitted a squeaking sound and rolled over onto his back so Heather could give him a belly rub. She glanced at the television and snickered. "Are you hoping that Jessica will speak to you through the television?"

"Something like that." I bent down for my sneakers next to the couch and began to put them on.

Heather's eyebrows rose. "What do you think you're doing?"

I stood and headed toward the coat closet for my jean jacket. "I thought maybe we could go for a ride and visit your favorite uncle. Don't worry, I'll let you drive."

Her jaw almost hit the floor. "No way. You're staying right here. Your mother texted me and said you were not to go anywhere. If you go out, she's going to blame it all on me!"

"No, she won't," I said quietly. "My mother adores you. She'll blame *me*."

Heather shook her head. "Okay, you're giving me no choice here. I'm firing you."

I barked out a laugh. "Excuse me?"

She folded her arms across her chest. "We're not looking for Monica's killer any longer. All bets are off. No more playing Jessica Fletcher. I accept defeat. My parents have already accepted it, and we need to as well. This was far more dangerous than I realized."

"Heather, I can't stop now," I insisted.

She ignored me. "Tyler and I had a long talk yesterday. We're going to wait a couple of weeks and get married at the county courthouse. It'll just be the immediate family—and you, of course."

I knew how difficult this was for Heather, but to her credit, she sounded resigned to her fate. "Are you sure?"

She wiped her eyes and nodded. "Life happens. At least,

that's what my parents said, and sometimes there isn't a thing you can do about it. Tyler and I don't want to wait until we can afford a huge wedding again. So, we'll get married at the courthouse, and then have a nice dinner out afterward with family."

"What about your honeymoon?" I asked.

She was silent for a moment. "I can get my money back on the plane tickets. Tyler and I have decided to give the money to my parents. It's nowhere near what they've spent on the wedding, but it would make me feel a little better about everything. For now, Ty and I will drive down to the Cape and spend a long weekend there. It doesn't get crowded until June. Besides, I love going there any time of the year."

It seemed desperately unfair that Heather had to give up her dream wedding *and* honeymoon destination. "My mind is already made up. I'm going to see Grant, even if I have to drive myself."

"Are you crazy?" she shrieked. "What good will it do, anyway? We don't even know for sure that he killed Monica and Jason."

I picked up my purse. "There's no way I can let this go. Someone tried to kill me yesterday. If you don't want to come, I understand. He is part of your family."

Heather stood there with a panicked expression, unsure of what to do next. Toast watched us from his perch on the couch, his eyes moving back and forth between Heather and me, as if we needed some type of referee.

"I've been thinking about what Jason said on the phone

the other day." My voice started to shake. "He talked like he'd seen those knives before, or maybe a picture of them. Think about it. If he had seen a picture, who would the photo have belonged to? Who did he spend the most time with?"

"Oh my God." Heather's eyes grew round. "Monica?"

"It has to be." I placed my phone in my purse and turned off the television. "I think Monica owned that knife set, and Jason saw a picture of her with it somewhere. Have you looked through all the photos Grant gave your parents?"

Heather shrugged and shook her head. "There was no reason for me to. We picked the photos up from Uncle Grant before Jason was murdered and didn't know about the knife set. He might not even be home. And if he finds out we're on our way, he'll make sure not to be there."

"Well, it's a nice afternoon for a drive anyway." I gave her my most winning smile.

She let out a sigh and picked up her car keys. "All right, I'll drive. How the heck do I get myself into these messes?"

Once we were settled in Heather's SUV, she made me text my mother and tell her we had gone out for a drive. I didn't mention where we were headed because she would freak out for certain.

We made good time and reached Grant's house by two thirty. His Cadillac was parked in the driveway. As we alighted from the vehicle, a window blind moved, and a second later, Grant opened the front door. His eyes narrowed as we climbed the stairs.

"What do I owe this pleasure to?" He sounded anything but pleased.

"Hello, Uncle Grant." Heather spoke in her usual warm and cheery voice. "My parents sent me back for more photos. They don't have enough."

His nostrils flared. "You could have called first."

Heather's cheeks turned a bright pink. "I'm sorry. That was thoughtless."

"Even a photo album would be helpful," I broke in. "We could always remove the pictures for you and refasten them to the pages later."

Grant gritted his teeth together but stepped aside to allow us entrance. "I suppose you might as well come in," he said grudgingly. "I'll check again."

He climbed the stairs while Heather and I examined the foyer. There were a few real estate agent cards lying on a table along with the mail. I peeked into the family room. Several packing boxes were stacked against one wall.

I whispered to Heather. "Is he selling the house?"

Her mouth opened in astonishment. "Dad didn't say anything about it to me. Wow. Monica hasn't even been dead for a week. What's his rush?"

Grant hurried down the stairs with a photo album in his arms. He thrust it into Heather's hands. "This is all I could find. I'd like the photos returned as soon as possible. These are mostly pictures of Monica from her twenties."

"You don't have any others?" I asked. "No pictures of her within the last few years or so?"

He shook his head. "There was another photo album with more current pictures of Monica, but that was destroyed in the fire."

I craned my neck in the direction of the study. "How's the cleanup going?"

Grant followed my gaze. "Fine. I have a construction crew and painter coming in this week. Everything will be finished—er, it will all be as good as new in a few days." He opened the front door for us and waited expectantly. It was our not-so-subtle invitation to leave.

"I heard you were thinking about selling the house," Heather blurted out.

Grant regarded her coldly. "Where did you hear that?"

She shrugged. "I think Dad mentioned it."

Grant didn't bother to reply. He waited until we were out on the top step, and then slammed the door, missing my face by mere inches. We walked down the driveway back to Heather's vehicle. As I fastened my seat belt, I glanced toward the front bay window. The curtain moved slightly.

"What do you think?" Heather asked. "Was it worth the trip for a bunch of old photos that won't tell us anything? He's sure to call my father and complain about me."

I tapped the album on my lap. "Yeah, I think so. The trip was very helpful."

"How?" she asked in a bewildered tone.

"Because I think I know why someone started the fire in Monica's study. My guess is they remembered there was a photo of the knives in there."

Heather started the engine. "So what? Why would the killer care about Monica being photographed with the knives?"

"Oh, they would care," I said thoughtfully, "if they were in the picture as well."

CHAPTER TWENTY-ONE

THE MEMORIAL SERVICE ON SUNDAY consisted of less than thirty people who filled the Turcots' living room to capacity. Most of the attendees seemed content to stand around drinking wine and eating hors d'oeuvres. From the empty boxes in Olivia's kitchen, the snacks had been provided courtesy of the frozen food department at the Jolly Green Grocer. Like Heather and me, Olivia wasn't much of a cook.

The priest who had married Monica and Grant said a prayer and a few kind words about her. After everyone joined him in "Amen," the atmosphere became subdued and dull. Some people milled around, examining the photos of Monica on display, then made a quick exit. A few others gathered in the family room downstairs, out of immediate view of Grant, to watch an afternoon Red Sox and Yankees game.

"This all feels so phony," Heather muttered as she sipped her first glass of wine. "My mother didn't even like Monica, and Dad wasn't crazy about her either. It's just another situation where my father has to bend over backwards and indulge Uncle Grant's whims. He's only been doing this for his entire life."

I glanced across the room at the fireplace, where Heather's parents were standing. They were talking to a couple close to their own age. The strain was evident on Garrett's face, and Olivia looked as if she was ready to collapse.

"How long is this going to last?" I whispered.

Heather shrugged. "An hour or two at most. Mom may need me to go out and pick up some more wine soon. I think she should just tell everyone we ran out. Maybe then they'd leave sooner. It's pretty obvious no one really wants to be here."

She was right about that. Even Grant, who had insisted on the memorial, was standing next to Devon with a bored expression. He was texting on his phone, which I thought was in poor taste.

Devon stood with his back to the fireplace and a nearly empty glass of red wine in one hand while Lexy clung to the other. She was wearing a short black minidress, similar to the one she'd worn at Monica's wake, but this one had a plunging neckline and didn't leave much to the imagination. The jean jacket she wore over the dress looked oddly out of place. Devon released her hand; then she wrapped both arms around his waist.

"It's too bad we didn't find out anything from looking

through the photos," Heather observed. "We still have no idea who killed Monica and Jason."

"No, we don't." I watched as Belinda helped herself to a cheese puff and poured a glass of wine from the portable bar the Turcots had set up. "But I have a feeling that person will show up at your parents' today. We know we've met them at some point."

Heather shivered and gulped down the rest of her drink. "I'd better put another tray of cheese puffs out. Be right back."

She passed Belinda, and they exchanged a smile. Belinda caught me staring and made her way over to me. She clucked her tongue against the roof of her mouth in distaste. "Monica would have hated this."

"Hated what?" I asked in confusion.

Belinda swallowed the cheese puff and dabbed at her mouth daintily with a napkin. "This so-called memorial. Grant's only doing it to prove what a good stand-up guy he is. He's planning to put Monica's house up for sale next week. The louse can't wait to cash in on her death."

"Really?" I tried to feign surprise. "Monica didn't leave her house to Devon?"

"She added Grant's name to the deed when they got married," Belinda explained. "Devon isn't pleased that Grant's getting the house and her money, but he has no right to complain either. They both made out well. Better than they deserved."

I detected a note of bitterness in her tone. "What about you? Do you know if she left you anything?"

She looked surprised by my remark. "The will hasn't been read yet, and it needs to go through probate, so I honestly have no idea. But I seriously doubt it. If she did leave me anything, it certainly wouldn't be of enough significance to go through the trouble of knocking her off."

Her comment startled me. "That's not why I asked."

Belinda laughed. "No worries, honey. Everyone here knows you've been asking questions about Monica's murder. Grant told me that you've been out to his house three times this week. Frankly, he said he's a little sick of the sight of you."

This didn't exactly come as a surprise.

She stared across the room at Lexy, a sly smile on her lips. "I overheard Lexy say she believes you suspect her."

"Really?" At that moment, Lexy caught my eye and immediately looked away. "I don't know why she'd think so."

Belinda opened her purse and started rooting around inside it. "Well, the girl can barely think, so I wouldn't worry about it if I were you. Devon's wasting his time with that one." She cursed under her breath. "Shoot. I'm sorry. I forgot to bring your comb."

"No worries. Wow, you do work fast."

Belinda snagged a pig in a blanket from a nearby tray. "They're quite simple for me to do—if I have the time, that is. Anyway, I'd be glad to drop it off at your house or your farm. I'll be out this way again on Monday. Do you have a business card?"

I reached inside my purse and presented her with one. "Can I send you the money by PayPal?"

"Certainly, but you don't have to pay until delivery," Belinda assured me. "I always want to make sure my customers are satisfied with my work."

My cell buzzed from my purse. I glanced down at the screen. It wasn't a number I recognized. "Would you excuse me for a second?"

Belinda smiled pleasantly. "Of course. Nice talking to you." She reached for another pig in a blanket while I answered the call. "Hello."

"Hi, I'd like to speak to Leila Khoury, please," a breathless female voice inquired.

"This is Leila."

The woman cleared her throat on the other end. "Hi, Miss Khoury, you don't know me, but my name is Morgan Winston. I'm a friend of Ava Benson's. She gave me your number and said maybe you could help me out. I need some maple candy, like, yesterday."

Ava Benson had been my roommate in Florida. We'd lived together for over three years prior to my returning to Sugar Ridge last year. Like me, she'd been a teacher. "Of course. How is Ava, by the way? I keep meaning to call her."

"Oh, she's fine," Morgan replied. "Busy, with the end of the school year coming up. I need the candy for a girl-friend's bridal shower on Friday. Can you help me? I need two hundred pieces."

My jaw dropped. "*Two hundred pieces?*" I had made candy earlier in the week, but we didn't have anywhere near that much available. Noah had hosted a tour yesterday while I was home recovering and told me that one person had purchased thirty pieces.

"Sorry for the short notice," Morgan said. "My friend is originally from Vermont, and she just sprang this on me the other day. She said something about how she wished there would be favors at the bridal shower to remind her of home. Of course, she always has these brilliant ideas at the last minute. Anyway, I thought she'd be tickled pink if everyone at her shower got a piece of maple candy as a favor. Can y'all make them into heart shapes? I realize leaves are probably the norm up there, but—"

"Unfortunately, we don't have many available right now," I broke in. "I believe there's about fifty pieces or so left in my store. If you want to place an order for next week, we'd be happy to—"

Morgan interrupted, sounding distressed. "Is there any way y'all can get them ready by Tuesday? I'll pay extra."

"There's no need to pay extra," I said. "But the candy takes a few days to make. I'm not back at the farm until tomorrow so I couldn't have them ready until Wednesday at the earliest."

"Oh no," she lamented. "I did try to order from a couple of other places, but they couldn't guarantee arrival in time. I was so hoping that you could help me out. I'd also like to purchase twenty bottles of your maple syrup."

Holy molasses. "Twenty bottles?"

"My parents own an all-day breakfast café in Florida," Morgan explained. "And I'm sure they'd love to reorder when they run out"—she paused for effect—"if you could help me out."

I drew a pen and pad out of my bag. "Would you want it shipped?"

"No. I'm actually in New York this weekend, visiting family," she explained. "I'm driving back to Florida on Tuesday with a friend of mine. We'll be home on Thursday, just in time to get things ready for the shower. So, I'd need to have the syrup by Tuesday morning."

I wanted to say no, but this had turned into a large order, with the promise of more. I racked my brain, calculating the sale in my head. With the syrup, it would come to at least a thousand dollars. My father's face flashed before me. I could see him clearly, shaking his head, and pointing a finger at me. "We never, ever refuse a sale, *habibi*. Word of mouth goes a long way in our business."

I glanced at the clock on the wall. It was almost three. If I went to the farm now, I could boil syrup and fill the molds by dinnertime. I was having dinner with Noah and Emma, so if I hurried, I could make it in time. Tomorrow, when I went back to work, I would take the candy out of the molds first thing, and coat them again. They should be ready to go by Tuesday morning. "All right, that will be fine. You can pick the candy up after nine o'clock on Tuesday. Will that work?"

Morgan breathed a sigh of relief. "Yes, it sounds perfect. Thank you so much, Miss Khoury."

"Please call me Leila. Since this is a large order, I'll need a five-hundred-dollar deposit. You can pay by credit card, PayPal, or Venmo."

"No problem. Let me know when you're ready." Morgan

recited the numbers, expiration date, and three-digit code on the back of the card. As soon as I got to the farm, I'd plug the information into our credit card machine at the store. I jotted down her cell phone number, in case there were any problems with the card, but I didn't think there would be.

"Thank you so much," Morgan said gratefully. "I'll see you Tuesday morning."

After I clicked off, I noticed Belinda was helping herself to more hors d'oeuvres nearby. I glanced around the room for Heather but didn't see her, so I went into the den. It was deserted. I stopped for a moment to take another look at the photos on display. Heather and I had looked through the photo album Grant had given us last night, and the loose pictures from earlier in the week. The ones on this particular board I hadn't seen before and wasn't sure where they'd come from. Olivia had put the board together herself.

From Monica's appearance, the photos were only a few years old. The top photo showed her sitting at a kitchen table with Grant. The picture had shifted slightly, partially obscuring the one next to it. I moved it aside to find one of Belinda and Monica sitting together at a kitchen table, their arms around each other. There was a birthday cake in front of them, and an unwrapped gift surrounded by pink tissue paper. I squinted at the box, and my mouth went dry when I realized what was inside.

It was the same knife set that had killed both Monica and Jason.

Holy mother of God. An icicle formed between my shoulder blades as I separated the photos and quickly shoved the ones with Monica and Belinda into my purse. I kept telling myself it didn't prove anything. Had Belinda given Monica the knife set? This didn't mean she had killed her. Sure, she was a suspect, but what could her motive have been for killing Monica? Monica hadn't even left her anything in her will.

Did I dare to ask anyone here about the picture and the knife set? *No.* It was a giant red flag, waiting to be waved in the air. The best thing would be to call Detective Barnes. I pulled out my phone, located his number under contacts, and pressed *Send.* The phone rang twice, and the call went to his voicemail.

"Hi, Detective Barnes, this is Leila Khoury calling. I have a matter I'd like to discuss with you. In person would be best. I'll be at Sappy Endings until about six o'clock if you have a chance to stop by. Or please call me as soon as you can. Thanks."

"Oh! I'm sorry, Leila. I didn't know you were in here." Olivia was standing in the doorway. "Is everything okay, dear? You're not overdoing it, are you?"

I fished Simon's car keys out of my purse. "No, I'm fine, Mrs. Turcot. I just got an order for maple candy, so I need to head out to the farm. Do you know where Heather is?"

"I sent her to the store for more wine." She rolled her eyes at the ceiling. "We've gone through more than I thought."

From the way that everyone had been guzzling it down,

I wasn't surprised. I stepped forward and gave her a hug. "Don't worry. I have a feeling that everything is going to work out."

She smiled and patted my back. "Thank you, dear. I hope so. Please thank your mother for sending the tray of baklava over. It was the first to go. Is she working today?"

"Mom's at home doing some baking. She says it relaxes her."

Olivia shook her head. "I've never seen her idle. She needs to give herself a break every now and then."

"It's probably never going to happen," I remarked. "Would you please ask Heather to call me when she gets back? I need to talk to her about something."

"Certainly, dear." She gave me a little finger wave. "Drive safe and take it easy."

I took a shortcut and went out the side door of the Turcots' home, preferring not to interact with any of Monica's immediate family again. Maybe I was afraid the expression on my face would give me away, or someone might discover that I had the picture in my possession.

Simon's car was parked on the street, a few spaces down from the house. After I unlocked it and got inside, I dropped the keys onto the floor. When I'd located them and sat back up, I spotted movement behind the cypress trees on the opposite side of the Turcot home. Two people were involved in a passionate embrace. I rolled down the window and squinted in their direction, hoping for a better look. The man's build and reddish hair told me immediately he was Devon Butterfield. The woman was partially obscured from my line of vision by his frame, and all I could see was her full-length black trench coat. I knew it couldn't be Lexy because she'd been wearing a short dress and jean jacket. My heart gave a little jolt, and I slid down in my seat, hoping not to be noticed.

As I continued to watch them, the last piece of the puzzle fell into place. I wasn't positive but finally had an idea of who Monica and Jason's killer was. At the very least, it was a good enough theory to talk to Detective Barnes about. I needed to get out of here before they saw me. When I straightened up in the seat, I accidentally leaned on the horn. In a panic, I fired up the engine and zoomed down the street, silently praying they had not seen me.

CHAPTER TWENTY-TWO

WHEN I ARRIVED AT THE farm, I quickly unlocked the main building and shut off the alarm. I ran Morgan's credit card through the machine and recalled what I'd just witnessed. The more I thought about it, the more it all made sense. I pulled out my cell and called Detective Barnes again. I was forced to leave another message when he didn't pick up.

"Detective Barnes, this is Leila Khoury again. I'd like to talk to you about Monica Butterfield. I think I know who's responsible for her death. Please call me as soon as possible or come by my farm. I'll be here for another couple of hours." I clicked off and decided that if he didn't show up or call, I'd head for the police station soon. Would he take my claim seriously?

I locked up the building, then went out the back door and walked down the grassy path toward the sugar shack.

Within minutes, I had poured syrup into a large stainless-steel pot, inserted the candy thermometer, and turned the burner on underneath. I dug out the picture of Monica and Belinda with the knife set and laid it on Noah's desk. As I stared down at their smiling faces with their arms around each other, bile rose in the back of my throat. I thought about Monica's words the day of the bridal shower. *Learn to trust no one in this world.* Had she known then that her life was in danger?

While I checked on the syrup, I distracted myself by picturing my father in this same spot making candy. He was chatting with me as I played nearby. Dad always gave me the first piece of candy to sample when he'd finished making it. I wondered what he would have thought of Heather and me trying to find a killer. It brought a smile to my face. Dad undoubtedly would have wanted to be in on the action. He was always up for a challenge.

I stayed close to the stove, watching as the syrup came to a boil, and kept an ear out for the buzz of my phone. After a few minutes, the syrup was hot enough to be poured into the molds.

I glanced at my watch. Before I removed the pot from the stove, I remembered I had left the syrup pitchers on Noah's desk. As I reached for them, the door to the sugar shack squeaked. My first thought was that a customer mistakenly thought we were open. As I turned toward the door, a stinging pain pierced my neck. I stared into the smug face of Belinda. Unable to speak, I tried to grab her arm, but my entire body quickly went numb. Feeling utterly helpless and confused, I slumped to the floor, and everything went dark.

When I came to, I was lying on the hard wooden floor, next to Noah's desk. I tried to raise myself into a sitting position but was unable to move. Parts of my body were still numb, and I noticed my hands had been tied to one of the legs of the desk with some type of scarf. I glanced toward the stove and saw that the burner was still on. I'd never had a chance to switch it off. The syrup was slopping over the sides of the pot, causing a giant cloud of steam to rise in the air.

Belinda was standing a couple of feet away from me. She held a hypodermic needle in one hand and the photograph in the other. Her eyes narrowed to tiny slits as she made a *tsk-tsk* sound.

"I had a feeling you knew," she said. "That's why I started following you around. I warned you to back off, but you were too stupid to listen."

My phone began to buzz from the desk's surface. Belinda leaned over and studied the screen. "Oh. It's your friend Heather. Shall I tell her you can't come to the phone right now?" She chuckled, picked up the phone, and then dropped it on to the floor next to me. Before I could reach for it, she slammed her high-heeled boot into the screen. The definitive crunching sound seemed to satisfy her. "There, much better."

"You—you drugged me?" My words were slurred, as if my tongue was too large for my mouth.

"Don't worry, it's only a tranquilizer. It pays to have a husband who's a pharmacist. Howie's a real sweet guy, but he's too old and feeble these days. I need someone younger who can keep up with me."

When I had seen the picture of Belinda and Monica together with the knife set, I wondered if Belinda might have killed her friend, but I couldn't come up with a solid motive. A few minutes later, when I had laid eyes on Belinda and Devon kissing passionately outside the Turcot house, I knew Belinda had to be the one. All along Heather and I had thought Grant and Belinda might be having an affair, but we'd been wrong. So wrong. My blood quickly turned to ice.

"That's why Monica had a change of heart about Lexy," I managed to say. "She—she knew about your affair. And started threatening you to stay away from her son."

Belinda brought her hands together in a mock clap. "Very good. I'm impressed."

I tugged at the bindings around my wrists, but they wouldn't budge. It was difficult to talk, but I forced the words out. "Monica. She didn't like Lexy, but she'd rather have her as a daughter-in-law than you. You, the—the woman who was fooling around with her son." Belinda had stabbed her best friend in the back, and in more ways than one.

"You did a good job," Belinda admitted. She pressed the heel of her boot into my palm. "Can you feel that?"

"Yes," I whispered, wanting to die from the crippling pain.

She pretended to look sympathetic. "Oh, too bad. Anyway, Monica didn't need to worry. It was all just fun and games with Devon and me. It's not like we're planning to get married."

"You're not?"

Belinda laughed out loud. "Gracious, no. Devon's a fantastic lover, but he's not husband material. Howie's a good man and makes a great living as a pharmacist. His family comes from old money, like Monica's. I'd be stupid to give all that up. I hate to admit it, but I'm no spring chicken and have to think about my future. Devon and I meet a couple of times a week at a local hotel, and we'll keep doing so. You'll be out of the way soon, and no one else has any idea about us."

"Monica must have hated it," I said weakly.

Her smile deepened. "Oh, she did. That's why we started having fights and she refused to sell my jewelry anymore. She should have just left us alone. Devon's not a baby, he's a grown man, for cripes sake. Monica wasn't happy unless she was controlling everyone else's life. She started leaving me all kinds of stupid little notes when she found out. The last straw was when she ordered me to end the affair, or she was going to tell Howie. He would have left me high and dry, and I couldn't afford to take that chance."

The smell of burned syrup permeated the air. I began to worry a fire might start, but Belinda appeared not to notice or care about the potential hazard. There was no other choice but for me to try and stall her with the hope help would arrive soon. "You didn't have to kill Jason. What did he ever do to you?"

"I had no other choice." Belinda's nostrils flared. "I was on my way to pick up Howie from work that day but decided to stop at Treasure Chest first and drop off my combs. Jason was sitting at his desk in the office. He nearly jumped out of the chair when he saw me and spilled his drink all over the floor. That was when I noticed what he had on his desk. It was the picture of Monica and me and the knife set she gave me for my birthday last year."

"There were two copies of the photo," I said.

Belinda nodded in disgust. "I didn't realize there was more than one copy until I saw this a few minutes ago."

"She—" It was getting more difficult for me to articulate as time went on.

Belinda snorted. "Monica must have moved the picture from her study. That's where I saw it last year." She tore the picture into tiny pieces and dropped them on my head. "Who the heck gives their best friend a knife set, and such a common one, for their birthday? God, I never met anyone so cheap in my entire life! She even tried to tell me that it was a rare set she'd picked up on a trip overseas, and that the rubies were real."

"They *were* real," I whispered.

"Yeah, right," Belinda scoffed. "And to think that I made her a special jeweled comb for her birthday last year *and* gave her a Gucci wallet. The woman was worse than Scrooge. She had money to burn, for crying out loud!"

Sadly, Monica had learned the hard way that you couldn't take it with you.

"I liked Jason," Belinda went on. "Oh sure, he was bit of a prude, but hey, no one's perfect. When I saw the photo on his desk, I knew he'd figured it out. And I overheard you say on the phone that you were coming to Sappy Endings today, then saw you outside the Turcot house watching me and Devon. I figured we should have a little chat."

I struggled to keep my eyes focused. "What—what are you going to do?"

"What do you think? I've got to get rid of you like the others." She scanned the inside of the building. Her gaze came to rest on the evaporator, which was up a flight of stairs and resting on a platform. "Let's see. What's the quickest way to get rid of you and erase any sign I was ever here? I can't use another knife. That would be too obvious."

I held my breath as she crossed over to the stove, surveying the steam and syrup with interest. Instead of switching the burner off, she turned it up as high as it would go. Sweat started to pool in the middle of my back as I watched Belinda grab some packing material from Noah's desk. She stuck it in the burner's flame until the edge caught fire, then dropped the burning mess onto the wooden floor where it quickly started to spread.

"No! Don't do this!" I yelled.

Belinda's face had hardened as if carved out of stone. She opened the front door of the cabin and peered outside in both directions, then glanced back at me.

"No!" I shouted and struggled to free my wrists from the desk. "You can't leave me here like this!"

Belinda's eyes were cold and devoid of any feeling. "It's all your own fault," she said quietly. "If you'd minded your own business, this wouldn't be happening. Goodbye, Leila." She slammed the door behind her, the sound echoing in my ears with a definite finality.

"Help!" I began to scream. The fire continued to spread along the wall in my direction. I tried to drag the desk toward the door with me, but it wouldn't budge. Tears ran down my cheeks. I was going to die a horrible death and prayed that it would be over quickly.

Moments from my life passed before me. Sitting on my father's lap as a child while he made maple candy. Playing at the beach with Simon when we were teenagers. A sleepover at Heather's house and being in Noah's arms. "Someone help me, please!"

"Leila!" a familiar voice shouted. "Where are you?"

"I'm inside the shack!" I screamed. "Please help me— the fire is spreading!"

A second later, the door was thrown open and my mother raced inside. She didn't hesitate for one second, throwing her body on top of mine as she worked to free my wrists. Within seconds, she had helped me to my feet, but because my legs were still numb, I stumbled against her and fell back onto the floor.

"Hurry!" she screamed.

"Drugged—" I gasped. "She drugged me."

My mother was a fragile-looking woman, but she

grabbed my hands with infinite strength, dragging me across the room as if I were an empty paper sack. With one final tug, she yanked me out the door. We collapsed onto the grass a few feet away as sirens blared in the distance.

Mom grabbed my face between my hands and examined it. "Are you all right, my precious girl?"

Tears rolled down her cheeks. My mother rarely cried. In fact, she hadn't shed one tear at my father's funeral. For as long as I could remember, she'd always looked as delicate as a china doll, but she was built of sturdier material. They didn't come any tougher than Selma Khoury.

"I'm okay." I tried to catch my breath as she threw her arms around me, sobbing.

"I passed a car on my way here. A woman was driving. Is she the one who did this?"

A fire truck screeched to a halt on the sidewalk, and two firefighters jumped down and hurried over to us. "Are you both all right? Is there anyone inside?"

My mother shook her head. "The shack is empty."

"Police," I coughed. "We have to call the police. Detective Barnes needs to know that Belinda Fuller did this. She—she's the one who murdered Monica and Jason. And tried to kill me as well."

Mom put her arms around me and rested my head in her lap. She hadn't done this since I was a little girl as she read to Simon and me at night. "Heather was going to contact him," she said softly.

I stared up at her. "How did you know to come out here?"

She stroked my hair. "Heather called me when she

couldn't get a hold of you. Her mother said you were headed to the farm, and she got nervous about your being here all alone. I decided to come out because I wanted to get my baking pans anyway. The woman I passed along the way—"

"Belinda Fuller," I interrupted.

"She was going very fast, and it worried me. I thought something might be wrong. Then I saw the smoke coming from the sugar shack and called 9-1-1." My mother's quivered. "I was so worried you'd end up like your father."

I threw my arms around her neck, trying to blink back tears. "It's all right. Hopefully the police will catch her before she leaves town."

"Did she hurt you?" Mom examined my bruised palm in horror. "I swear to God that I'll hunt that woman down and—"

Her phone buzzed at that moment, and she never finished the sentence. She quickly fished it out of her coat pocket. "Hello? Yes, Detective Barnes. We're at the farm, and Leila's okay. That Belinda Fuller tried to kill her and—" She listened for a moment, letting out a ragged breath that sounded like she'd been holding it forever. "Oh, thank goodness. All right, I'm going to run her over to the emergency room to be checked out." She paused. "Yes, I will. Thank you."

She clicked off, and a smile formed at the corners of her mouth. "They caught her, my dear girl. The only place Belinda's going is to prison."

Two hours later, my mother and I were leaving the hospital when we spotted Detective Barnes in the parking lot. He was standing next to his car, talking on his cell. When he saw us approach, he quickly finished the call and strode over in our direction, moving as if he had all the time in the world.

"Hello Leila." He stretched his hand out to my mother. "Are you Mrs. Khoury?"

She nodded. "It's nice to meet you. Thank you for coming."

Detective Barnes turned back to me. "How are you feeling?"

"Better, now that I can finally feel my legs again," I joked.

Anger flashed through my mother's dark eyes. "That horrible woman drugged her and started the fire, Detective Barnes. She left my daughter there to die. I hope she rots in prison."

"Belinda Fuller killed two people," Detective Barnes remarked. "Don't worry, Mrs. Khoury. She won't be going anywhere for a very long time."

"Thank goodness," my mother said in relief.

Detective Barnes shifted from one foot to the other. "How bad is the damage to the sugar shack?"

"It's not a total loss," I said. "Someone driving by spotted the blaze and called 9-1-1 right before my mother got there. The evaporator is okay, and most of the syrup was salvaged. It could have been a lot worse."

My mother locked her arm through mine and smiled gratefully at me. "That is true. It definitely could have been much worse, my dear."

CHAPTER TWENTY-THREE

Six Days Later

"OKAY, THIS YOUR LAST CHANCE to make a run for it," I teased.

"Never. Are you kidding?" Heather's blue eyes shone with happiness. "I've been ready for this moment since I was twelve."

I stepped back to admire her. Heather looked more stunning than I could have imagined in the white tulle gown with a crystal-embroidered bodice and romantic lace sleeves. A sweetheart neckline accented the lovely pearl necklace her parents had given her for a wedding gift. She carried a simple bouquet of red and white roses, which had always been her favorite flower.

She reached out to hug me. "Lei, I can't thank you enough for everything. If it weren't for you, Tyler and I would have had to cancel our special day."

"Back atcha. If you hadn't called my mother last week, I wouldn't be here." It was hard to believe that fateful day had been almost a week ago. Belinda's husband, Howie, had already filed for divorce, and she'd confessed to both murders in hopes of a lighter sentence.

Heather dabbed at her eyes with a blue silk handkerchief. "I told myself I wasn't going to cry, and look at me. Jeez, I haven't even made it to the altar yet."

"Are the Butterfields here?" I asked.

She narrowed her eyes. "Nope. Grant called my father last night and told him he wasn't feeling well enough to attend. Can you believe it?"

"Maybe he was too embarrassed," I suggested. "What about Devon and Lexy?"

"They're not here either." Heather glanced at her reflection in the full-length cheval mirror. We were alone in a private room of the church, and time was ticking away. "I guess Devon decided that he didn't want to lose both women in his life, so he proposed to Lexy earlier this week. He even gave her a three-carat diamond. Do you know what she did?"

"She couldn't wait to accept?" I guessed.

Heather's smile was triumphant. "Wrong. My father said that she threw the ring back in Devon's face when she found out about his affair with Belinda. The woman has more intelligence than I gave her credit for."

"Good for her. She's better off without him."

Heather fussed with the tendrils that adorned the sides of her face. Her blond hair had been styled into a French twist and fastened in back with a pearl hair clip I had lent her. My parents had given it to me as a birthday present a few years ago.

As if she could read my mind, Heather brought a hand up to the back of her head. "Are you sure you don't want to wear it, Lei?"

"It looks perfect on you. Tradition dictates that the bride has to have something borrowed, right?" I stole a glance at my reflection in the mirror. "Besides, I feel like wearing my hair loose today. Noah said he likes it this way."

"Aha." Heather's eyes shone. "I thought that might have something to do with it."

A knock sounded on the door, and I walked over to open it. Heather's dad stood there in his black tuxedo, beaming with pride at his daughter. "You look beautiful, baby. Are you ready?"

"Yes, Dad." She kissed him on the cheek and hugged him tightly. I blinked back a tear as I watched, thinking of my own father at this beautiful moment.

Heather left the room on his arm while I trailed after them, shaking out her three-foot train ahead of me.

The music started, and the bridesmaids began their procession down the aisle. Heather stared straight ahead, a serene and peaceful look on her face. She watched as I took my place in front of her, then winked at me.

"Let's do this." She grinned.

Four hours later, I stood with a group of about forty single women at the foot of a winding mahogany staircase, waiting for Heather to throw her bouquet. Both the wedding and reception had gone off without a hitch, and everyone was having a wonderful time. I'd proudly taken a few moments to admire the little glass bottles of maple syrup from the farm that Heather and Tyler had decided on as wedding favors, decorated with red ribbons the same color as the bridesmaids' dresses. Their names and wedding date had been engraved on the front of them, the sight filling me with enormous pride.

Heather's face lit up the room when she appeared on the landing. She searched the crowd of women below her and nodded at me with a smile. She turned her back on us, then tossed the bouquet over her left shoulder. A few women screamed and giggled as the bouquet landed at my feet. I leaned down and picked it up while everyone around me started to cheer.

My gaze connected with Noah's from across the room. He was standing against the wall with a glass of champagne in his hand, watching me. He was dressed in a navy-colored suit that brought out the blue in his eyes. He looked elegant and handsome enough to grace the cover of *Esquire* magazine. I walked slowly toward him, basking in the glow of the moment.

Noah gestured at the bouquet in my hands. "Congratulations."

Heat flooded my face. "Oh, Heather set that all up. She played softball in college and has a great arm. Plus, I think she might have threatened the bridesmaids lives if they went near it."

Noah laughed as he set down his glass on a table. He extended his hand to me. "Well, pretty lady, how about that dance you've been promising me all evening?"

"I'd love to." The band was playing a waltz, and we joined several other couples on the dance floor. In all the time Noah and I had been dating, we'd never danced together before. I wasn't very good at it, but Noah was light on his feet and twirled me around the room in perfect time to the music.

I followed his lead, feeling lighter than air. "Where did you learn to dance so well?"

His eyes twinkled into mine. "Remember, Miss Khoury, that I am a Southern gentleman at heart. I've cut many rugs over the years."

I leaned my head on his shoulder, loving his strong arms around me. He interrupted the tender moment by asking, "What about Mark?"

Startled, I lifted my head. "What about him?"

"Has he gone back to New York City?" Noah wanted to know. "Or is he still planning on working in the Bennington office?"

I shrugged. "No idea. I think he left last week. It doesn't matter to me if he goes to Bennington or not. I don't plan on seeing him again."

He cocked his head to the side and studied me. "You mean he never even called after your dinner that night?"

"Nope." I smiled up at him. "There was no reason

for him to. I told Mark that it was over between us—correction. It had been over for five years." I could have gone on to tell Noah all about Mark's true motivation and what my mother had discovered, but I didn't want to waste any more breath talking about the man. He wasn't important to me anymore. My relationship with Mark seemed like another lifetime ago. I had everything I needed here in Sugar Ridge. It was a long list that included Noah, Emma, Heather, Simon, my mother, and of course, Sappy Endings.

Although I couldn't see my father, I had no doubt he was in this room tonight—and smiling down at us. My heart was full, and I thanked my lucky stars for all of life's blessings.

"There's something you need to understand about me, Mr. Rivers," I teased, as he held me close against him. "I'm one tough cookie. As my father used to say, God broke the maple candy molds when he made me."

He tipped his head back and laughed. "So, I guess that means you're a chip off the old block, huh?"

I stared across the room at my mother, who was dancing with Simon. As if on cue, she turned her head in my direction and exchanged a knowing smile with me. "I couldn't have said it any better myself."

RECIPES

MAPLE BUNDT CAKE WITH MAPLE CINNAMON GLAZE AND CANDIED PECANS

For cake:
- Vegetable shortening and granulated sugar, for pan
- ¾ cup unsalted butter, room temperature
- ½ cup packed dark brown sugar
- 2 cups all-purpose flour
- 1½ teaspoons baking powder
- ½ teaspoon baking soda
- ½ teaspoon salt
- ½ cup pure maple syrup
- ½ cup milk
- ¼ cup sour cream
- 2 eggs, room temperature
- 1 teaspoon vanilla

For glaze:
- 1 cup confectioners' sugar

- 4 to 5 tablespoons pure maple syrup
- ½ teaspoon vanilla
- ¼ teaspoon cinnamon
- Optional sugared pecans
- 1 tablespoon pure maple syrup
- 3 tablespoons dark brown sugar
- 2 tablespoons granulated sugar
- ¼ teaspoon cinnamon
- Pinch of salt
- 1 cup pecan halves
- Cinnamon sugar for sprinkling: 1 tablespoon granulated sugar mixed with ¼ teaspoon cinnamon

For the Cake

Heat oven to 350°F. Grease a 12-cup Bundt cake pan with vegetable shortening, and generously sprinkle granulated sugar to cover the surface. Set aside. In a large bowl, cream the butter and brown sugar with an electric mixer on high speed, about 2 minutes. In a medium bowl, whisk together the flour, baking powder, baking soda, and salt. In a separate bowl, whisk together the maple syrup, milk, sour cream, eggs, and vanilla. Alternating between the flour mixture and egg mixture, add to the butter mixture in three additions, mixing well after each addition. Pour the batter into the pan, spreading evenly with a spatula. Bake 35 to 40 minutes or until edges are golden and a wooden skewer inserted into the center comes out mostly clean. Cool 15 minutes in pan. Place a serving platter on top of the Bundt pan, and invert to transfer the cake to the platter. Cool completely, about 1 hour.

For the Glaze

In a small bowl, beat the glaze ingredients with a whisk until smooth. Add more powdered sugar or maple syrup if necessary for desired consistency. Drizzle the glaze over the cooled cake, letting it drip down the sides. If desired, top the glaze with sugared pecans. Let the glaze set at least 30 minutes before serving.

For the Sugared Pecans

In a saucepan, whisk together the maple syrup, 1 teaspoon water, brown sugar, granulated sugar, cinnamon, and salt. Heat over medium-low heat, stirring until the sugars dissolve. Add in the pecans, stirring until well-coated. Continue to cook over medium-low heat, stirring constantly, until the liquid completely evaporates. Cook another minute, stirring constantly. Immediately remove from the heat and spread the pecans in a single layer on a parchment-lined baking sheet. While the pecans are still hot, sprinkle with cinnamon sugar and toss to coat. Spread into a single layer and allow to cool completely. Use to garnish the glazed cake. Makes 6 to 8 servings.

MAAMOUL COOKIES

Author's Note: Maamoul is a traditional Middle Eastern cookie made with a wooden mold that can be found in specialty stores. Different molds are required depending on whether you use dates or nuts. If you are making the cookies without a mold, you can use both dates and nuts.

The cookies are similar in style to Italian wedding cookies. This recipe was the creation of my beloved aunt, who passed away many years ago, and I consider it a personal tribute to her memory.

- 1¼ cup sugar
- 8 sticks unsalted butter
- 5 cups all-purpose flour, plus extra for coating the mold
- 2 cups walnuts, finely chopped (or whole seedless dates can be used instead)
- 1 teaspoon rose water
- 1 jigger rye whiskey (approximately 1.5 ounces)
- 2 eggs, beaten
- Confectioners' sugar

To Make the Dough by Hand with a Mold

Beat 1 cup of sugar, butter, and eggs together. Add the flour a little bit at a time. Knead until the dough starts to fall off your hands. In a separate bowl, add the nuts, ¼ cup of sugar, rose water, and rye whiskey and mix well. Coat your mold with flour to prevent sticking. Add the dough, flatten it out in the mold, add a teaspoon of the nut mixture, and cover with more dough.

To Form the Dough by Hand without a Mold

Follow the same directions as above to make the dough. Remember to coat your hands with flour to prevent sticking. Take a dough ball about the size of a walnut, flatten it slightly, and lay in it the palm of one hand. Take a nut or date and lay it on top of the dough. Finally, take a smaller dough ball, about one inch in diameter, flatten it slightly, and place it on top of the nut or date filling. (Basically, the palm of your hand becomes the mold.) Gently press the edges of the dough on top into the dough on the bottom so the nut or date filling is completely covered. Shape the cookie into a slightly flattened circle. Use a fork to make a decorative cross pattern on the top.

To Bake the Cookies

Bake at 325°F for 20 to 25 minutes or until the cookies are lightly browned around the edges and light on top. Cool for 5 minutes before dusting lightly with confectioners' sugar. Makes about 5 or 6 dozen cookies.

MAPLE STRUDEL MUFFINS

For strudel:
- ¾ cup rolled oats
- 6 tablespoons cold unsalted butter, cut into small pieces
- 6 tablespoons sugar
- ½ teaspoon salt
- 6 tablespoons all-purpose flour
- 1 tablespoon pure maple syrup

For muffin batter:
- 2¼ cups all-purpose flour
- ½ cup rolled oats
- 2 teaspoons baking powder
- ½ teaspoon baking soda
- ½ teaspoon kosher salt
- 2 sticks unsalted butter, room temperature
- ¾ cup pure maple syrup, room temperature,
  plus additional for glazing, if desired
- ½ cup sugar
- 2 large eggs, room temperature

- 1 teaspoon pure vanilla extract
- 1 cup plain yogurt

For the Strudel

In a medium bowl, combine the oats, butter, sugar, salt, and flour, and work with hands until mixture is no longer dry and large clumps form. Add the maple syrup and mix to combine. Cover and refrigerate.

For the Muffin Batter

Preheat oven to 400°F with racks in upper and lower thirds. Line two standard 12-cup muffin tins with baking cups. In a medium bowl, whisk together the flour, oats, baking powder, baking soda, and salt. With an electric mixer on medium speed, in a separate bowl, beat the butter, maple syrup, and sugar until pale and fluffy, 3 to 5 minutes. Add the eggs one at a time, beating well after each addition; mix in the vanilla.

Reduce the mixer to low. Add the flour in three additions, alternating with two batches of yogurt; beat until combined. Transfer the batter evenly among 24 muffin cups (a scant ¼ cup per tin). Remove the strudel from the refrigerator and break up into small pieces. Scatter evenly over the top of the muffins. Bake, rotating once, until the tops spring back and a toothpick inserted into the middle comes out clean, 16 to 18 minutes. Let cool 5 minutes in the tin, then transfer to a wire rack to cool completely. Brush the muffins with more maple syrup while warm, if desired. Makes 24 muffins.

KIBBI

- 1 cup fine-grain bulgur
- 1 pound lamb shoulder, ground fine
- ¼ cup grated onion
- 1 teaspoon cumin seeds, toasted and ground,
  or 1 teaspoon ground cumin
- Pinch cayenne pepper
- Salt and pepper
- Ice water
- 3 tablespoons olive oil, plus more
  for oiling the baking dish
- 2 cups sliced onions, ¼ inch thick
- ½ cup pine nuts, lightly toasted
- Greek-style yogurt, for serving

Rinse the bulgur well, then cover with cold water and soak for 20 minutes. Drain well. Put the drained bulgur, lamb, grated onion, cumin, and cayenne in a large mixing bowl. Season with 2 teaspoons salt and ½ teaspoon pepper. Mix well with your hands to distribute the seasoning. With a wooden spoon, beat in about ½ cup ice water. The mixture should be smooth and soft.

Heat the olive oil in a cast-iron skillet over medium heat. Add the sliced onions and fry gently, stirring occasionally, until they soften, about 5 minutes. Season generously with salt and pepper. Raise the heat and add ¼ cup of the lamb mixture from above. Continue frying, allowing the meat to get crumbly and the onions to brown nicely, another 10 minutes or so. Stir in the pine nuts to taste. Let cool to room temperature.

Heat the oven to 350°F. Lightly oil a shallow 9 x 13–inch baking dish; then, with wet hands, press half the remaining lamb mixture evenly over the bottom of the pan. Spread half the onion–pine nut mixture over the meat. Add the rest of the meat to the pan, patting and pressing it to make a smooth top. If desired, score the top with a sharp paring knife to make a traditional diamond pattern at least ½ inch deep.

Bake uncovered for 35 to 45 minutes, until the top is golden. Spread with the remaining onion-pine nut mixture. Serve warm, at room temperature, or cool, with a dollop of yogurt. Makes 8 to 10 servings.

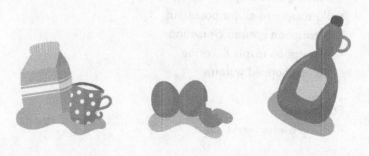

MAPLE AND BUTTER TWISTS

- 3¼ to 3½ cups all-purpose flour
- 3 tablespoons sugar
- 1½ teaspoons salt
- 1 package (¼ ounce) active dry yeast
- ¾ cup 2 percent milk
- ¼ cup butter
- 2 large eggs, room temperature

For filling:

- ⅓ cup packed brown sugar
- ¼ cup sugar
- 3 tablespoons butter, softened
- 3 tablespoons maple syrup
- 4½ teaspoons all-purpose flour
- ¾ teaspoon ground cinnamon
- ¾ teaspoon maple flavoring
- ⅓ cup chopped walnuts

For glaze:

- ½ cup confectioners' sugar

- ¼ teaspoon maple flavoring
- 2 to 3 teaspoons two percent milk

In a large bowl, combine 1½ cups flour, sugar, salt, and yeast. In a saucepan, heat the milk and butter to 120°F to 130°F. Add to the dry ingredients; beat just until moistened. Add the eggs; beat on medium for 2 minutes. Stir in enough remaining flour to form a firm dough. Turn onto a floured surface; knead until smooth and elastic, 5 to 7 minutes. Place in a greased bowl, turning once to grease the top. Cover and let rise in a warm place until doubled, about 70 minutes. Grease two 9-inch round baking pans. In a small bowl, combine the first seven filling ingredients; beat for 2 minutes. Punch the dough down; turn onto a lightly floured surface. Divide in half; roll each into a 16 x 8–inch rectangle. Spread the filling to within ½ inch of edges. Sprinkle with the nuts. Roll up jelly-roll style, starting with a long side. With a sharp knife, cut each roll in half lengthwise. Open the halves so the cut side is up; gently twist the ropes together. Transfer to the baking pans. Coil into a circle. Tuck the ends under and pinch to seal. Cover and let rise in a warm place until doubled, about 45 minutes.

Bake at 350°F for 25 to 30 minutes or until golden brown. Cool for 10 minutes; remove from the pans to wire racks. Combine the confectioners' sugar, maple flavoring, and enough milk to reach desired consistency and drizzle over the warm cakes. Makes 2 coffee cakes (16 slices each).

SALTED MAPLE PIE

- One 9-inch pie crust
- ½ cup plus 2 tablespoons unsalted butter
  (1¼ sticks), melted and cooled
- 1 cup dark robust maple syrup
- ¾ cup packed light brown sugar
- ¼ cup fine yellow cornmeal
- Heaping ¼ teaspoon kosher salt
- 3 large eggs, at room temperature
- 1 large egg yolk, at room temperature
- ¾ cup heavy cream, at room temperature
- 1¼ teaspoons pure vanilla extract
- 1 large egg, beaten
- Flaky sea salt, for sprinkling

To Prepare the Crust

On a lightly floured surface and using a lightly floured rolling pin, roll out a disk of dough into a circle about ¼-inch thick. Starting at one end, gently roll up the dough onto the rolling pin. Unfurl the dough over a 9-inch pie plate and press it in lightly, making sure it's lining the plate.

Trim so there's about ½-inch of excess dough hanging over the edge of the pie plate. (If the dough feels warm, refrigerate it for 15 minutes.) Tuck the excess dough under itself so it is flush with the edge of the pie plate; leave the pie like this for a straightedge finish, or crimp as desired. Freeze for at least 15 minutes. Heat your oven to 450°F with the rack on the lowest level.

Remove the pie crust from the freezer, tear off a square of aluminum foil that is slightly larger than the pie shell, and gently fit it into the frozen crust. Fill the crust with pie weights or dried beans (they should come all the way up to the crimps) and place the pie pan on a baking sheet. Transfer the baking sheet to the oven and bake for 25 to 27 minutes. Check for doneness by peeling up a piece of foil. The crimps should be light golden brown. Remove the baking sheet from the oven and transfer to a cooling rack. After 6 minutes, carefully remove the foil and beans. You are now ready to fill the pie. Reduce your oven to 350°F.

To Make the Filling

In a medium bowl, whisk the melted butter and maple syrup. Whisk in the brown sugar, cornmeal, and kosher salt. In another medium bowl, crack the 3 eggs and add the yolk. Add the cream and vanilla, and whisk until combined. Slowly pour the egg mixture into the maple mixture, and whisk just until combined.

To Finish the Pie

Place the blind-baked shell on a parchment-lined baking sheet. Brush the crimped edge with the beaten egg. Pour the maple filling into the pie shell until it reaches the bottom of the crimps.

Transfer the baking sheet with the pie on it to the oven and bake for 45 to 60 minutes, until the edges are puffed and the center jiggles only slightly when shaken. It will continue to set as it cools.

Remove the baking sheet from the oven and transfer the pie to a wire rack to cool for 4 to 6 hours. Once fully cooled and at room temperature, sprinkle generously with flaky sea salt. Store leftover pie, well wrapped in plastic wrap or under a pie dome, at room temperature for up to 3 days. Makes 8 to 10 servings.

Acknowledgments

A very special thanks to Jenna Baird and her family at Baird Farm in North Chittenden, Vermont. They are always willing to answer my questions about their awesome maple syrup farm, no matter how busy things get! Watch for a "Jenna" to make her appearance in book number three!

As always, thank you to my amazing agent, Nikki Terpilowksi, for being in my corner, and my editor Margaret Johnston, Findlay McCarthy, and the rest of the incredible Sourcebooks/Poisoned Pen staff. Kudos to retired police chief Terrance Buchanan for his assistance and amazing beta readers Constance Atwater and Kathy Kennedy, who always come through for me.

Thank you to Kim Davis for the use of her yummy maple Bundt cake recipe. Lastly, warm hugs and gratitude to my cousins Ellen Giannini and Betty Ann Stavola for sharing the family's Middle Eastern recipes with me, especially the one for Aunt Selma's maamoul cookies, and all the stories of our wonderful heritage.

About the Author

USA Today bestselling author Catherine Bruns lives in upstate New York with an all-male household that consists of her very patient husband, three sons, and several spoiled pets. Catherine has a BA in both English and performing arts, and she is a former newspaper reporter and press release writer. In her spare time, she loves to bake, read, and attend theater performances. She's published more than twenty-five mystery novels and has many more stories waiting to be told. Readers are invited to visit her website at catherinebruns.net.